KELLER

Judi,

 I've heard wonderful things about you. Keep your chin up.

 Tracy Winegar

KELLER

Tracy Winegar

Bonneville Books
Springville, Utah

The views expressed within this work are the sole responsibility of the author and do not necessarily reflect the position of Cedar Fort, Inc., or any other entity.

This is a work of fiction. The characters, names, incidents, places, and dialogue are products of the author's imagination, and are not to be construed as real.

ISBN 13: 978-1-59955-115-9

Published by Bonneville Books, an imprint of Cedar Fort, Inc., 2373 W. 700 S., Springville, UT 84663
Distributed by Cedar Fort, Inc., www.cedarfort.com

LIBRARY OF CONGRESS CATALOGING-IN-PUBLICATION DATA

Winegar, Tracy.
  Keeping Keller / Tracy Winegar.
    p. cm.
  ISBN 978-1-59955-115-9 (acid-free paper)
  1. Mentally ill children—Fiction. 2. Parent and child–Fiction. I.
Title.
  PS3623.I628K44 2008
  813'.6—dc22

                              2007052223

Cover design by Angela Olsen
Cover design © 2008 by Lyle Mortimer
Edited and typeset by Annaliese B. Cox

Printed in the United States of America

10 9 8 7 6 5 4 3 2 1

Printed on acid-free paper

Acknowledgments

My sincere thanks to my husband, Ben, for allowing me countless hours to engross myself in writing, for reading every scrap of paper I threw at him, for his insights and suggestions—especially his help on the book's ending—and most of all for believing in me. I am so grateful that he is my partner and my support system in raising our children. Without his help, I doubt that I could have finished such a huge undertaking.

I am also grateful to Wilma Belvill for allowing me to know and understand her personal story. She has raised a remarkable son, Steven, with courage and grace and bravery. I hope that I can be as resilient as she has been in the face of adversity.

I also need to give a big thanks to friends and family. To my brothers and sisters: Kelly, Kym, Jennifer, Adam, Jessica, Ashley, and Grant, who have read my words and given me feedback, help, support, and assistance as I have struggled to bring my vision to life. My husband's grandmother, Leola Prigmore, spent a great deal of time reading and editing my manuscript for grammatical errors so that I could submit it.

Last but not least, a big thanks to Richard Peterson for sharing his talent for editing. Without his suggestions, my book would never have been completed. It has been a wonderfully rich and eye-opening experience for me to see how many people were willing to give me their love and aid.

Preface

Could it have ended any differently, she wondered as she watched the flat green landscape, peeking out from beneath remnants of snow, pass by through the bus window on its way to Fort Wayne. The opposite direction of Muncie. Perhaps it was meant to be, just as Keller had been meant to be. No amount of speculation could change what had happened. Beverly was alone, frightened, unsure of what her future would be. It was incomprehensible to her how it all could have spiraled out of control so quickly. Everything had come crashing down so thoroughly and completely that there was very little left to salvage from the wreckage.

As she reflected upon her current conditions, it occurred to her that the chain of events that had set it all in motion began with such everyday familiarity that she simply had not seen it coming, could not have fathomed its approach. And now with all of the cards played out, she held the losing hand. Looking at it from every angle, there was no positive side to it. She would be the one to suffer.

one

A circle of gold gleamed on the bathroom countertop next to the sink, reflecting the lights from the fixture above the mirror. She picked it up and inspected it closely, making a mental note of every ding and dint it had acquired over their nine years. She tried it on each of her fingers, but it only slightly fit her thumb, still loose enough to fall off easily. It came to rest in the palm of her hand, where she contemplated what she should do with it. Only for a brief moment was she indecisive before she went to her purse, unclasping it and dropping the wedding band from her thumb and index finger into the change compartment. She didn't want it getting lost, she reasoned. And then she forgot about it in her efforts to prepare for her outing.

Often the walk to town did much to calm his nerves and make him more agreeable. It was roughly a mile, but it seemed to get all of his excess energy out. Today, however, was an exception. Keller continued to moan and shake his hands stiffly in front of himself, irritable and unreasonable. Beverly kept close to her son, steering him back to the side of the road when needed. "Stay with Mama, Kel," she cautioned. He slapped at her hand as she guided him, with an unyielding grasp upon his elbow, back to her side. It was customary for him to resist; it was his nature to defy authority. It was, however, still her job as a mother to protect him, even if it was from himself.

Their home was only eight blocks from the main downtown hub, but at times it seemed like an eternity walking with Keller. The sun was high in the sky and Beverly grew wet with perspiration. The trek was no more than a mile or so, but she felt unusually weak and tired. She wondered if they should turn back, debating whether that might bring on a tantrum that she could not control. If he threw himself to the ground, she was not strong enough to heave him back up.

She would have to let him wriggle about on the grass until he decided that he had had enough. He was always so determined to have his way and would most likely try to head toward town again once his fit was over anyhow. Best to finish the trip and at least make one stop on their designated schedule. It was Thursday, and Warren would be expecting them. He might worry if they didn't show.

Walnut Street was the central spine of downtown. It spread twelve blocks in either direction down that main strip, with the courthouse being the center of it all. Muncie was fortunate enough to have Sears and Roebuck, J. C. Penney, and Ball Stores for the convenience of the patrons looking for household items, shoes, and clothing. There were several furniture stores, and other high ticket items could also be purchased. Muncie was blessed as well with the newest rage: fast food. A McDonald's had just moved in. And for those who felt McDonald's was overpriced, a Mr. 15 was available. The menu sold all items for fifteen cents each, a penny pincher's delight.

Once the wider sidewalks began, the signal that they had nearly reached their destination, Keller began to count the squares, avoiding the cracks that ran through the pavement. This kept him occupied for a moment, until Walgreens came into view. Besides carrying the usual sundries and drugstore items, there was also an ice cream parlor nestled in the back. They served deli-style sandwiches along with the sweets that many people visited the store for, but Beverly had never attempted to purchase one. When Keller ate sandwiches, there was sure to be a frightful mess to follow. He separated the slices of bread from the lettuce and tomato, tore the deli meat into minute, shredded-up pieces, and then only ate the bread anyhow, leaving the crusts, like unwanted melon rinds, on his plate.

Keller raced for the door, abandoning Beverly. This was a typical occurrence, causing Beverly to feel that he was always one step ahead of her. She picked up her pace and followed him in. The boy had launched himself onto one of the swiveling bar stools and began to grab at the pies that were displayed behind the spotless glass domes. They were spotless no more, for Keller had left his little finger prints as a souvenir. Beverly pulled his hands away and shook her head. "No, Kel, you mustn't touch the pies. You know better. If you want a soda, you best act like a gentleman."

Mr. Ferrin smiled sympathetically at Beverly, who was wiping her brow with her gloved hand. "Good day to you, Mrs. Vance. It's a hot one, eh?"

"Yes, unseasonably so!" she agreed, smoothing her dress as she sat next to Keller. She liked Mr. Ferrin very much. With his dark hair, peppered with gray, and his thoughtful gaze, he was a kind man, eager to please.

"Well, it will be getting cold soon enough. Enjoy it while it lasts."

"I suppose you're right, Mr. Ferrin. I should count my blessings."

"What'll it be for you today?"

"You know what he wants," she said with an amused tone, gesturing with a nod of her head to the child sitting beside her. Keller leaned forward eagerly, unable to control the delight aroused in his little heart.

"Certainly, a Coca-Cola with vanilla syrup," he nodded with a broad smile upon his lips.

"I'll just have a soda water with chocolate syrup."

"Sounds good," Mr. Ferrin agreed, as he got down to business preparing their order.

Keller watched contentedly as the man put the glass up to the spigot and the dark, bubbly fluid filled the empty space, his face filled with a far-off grin. Mr. Ferrin turned to Keller. "You want to help today, Kel?"

Keller didn't reply, but he came around the bar and pushed down on the vanilla dispenser, smiling contentedly, as it shot out into his glass. When he was finished, he went back around the bar and sat down on the stool again. Mr. Ferrin slid the glass across to him and handed him a straw. Keller drank long and deep, then let out a loud belch.

"Keller, what do you say?" Beverly urged, with mock indignation. She didn't want Mr. Ferrin to think that she condoned such behavior.

Again he did not acknowledge his mother, but he replied dutifully, "S'cuse me."

"I so wish I could stop him from doing that. I think he does it on purpose, for he does it so often. I can't imagine that he would have a need to do it that much."

"Well, he's polite about it anyway," the man pacified. He began to hum along with the Fontane Sisters. Their song "Hearts of Stone" was turned down low on the radio.

Beverly waited patiently for her soda and then quietly sipped away when it was presented to her. Keller was done long before his mother, and he stood up expectantly, unwilling to wait for her to finish. His primary objective had been met; the Coke was gone, and that was the only thing that had held him here. His schedule beckoned, just as a sailor is called by the sea. Beverly took a few more hurried sips and then got up too. Keller was nearly out the door before she grabbed him and dragged him back in. "Now, Kel, we must pay Mr. Ferrin." She opened her purse and left some change on the countertop. "Say thank you to Mr. Ferrin."

"Say fank you, Mr. Ferrin."

"You're welcome, Kel. We'll see you next Thursday," he said as he took the change and glasses from his bar. Keller was gone before Mr. Ferrin could finish.

"Slow down, Kel. Slow down." Beverly was trotting after

him, grabbing at his arm, which he pulled forward and tucked close to his body in an attempt to evade her. She finally got ahold on his shirt sleeve and reeled him in. "We'll have to go home if you don't listen to Mama."

He was practically pulling her down the sidewalk when she wouldn't loosen up her grip, resembling a dog pulling his master. He had a mission, and she wasn't going to stop him. Approaching the corner, she regained control and made him stop to look both ways. There were no cars in sight so they crossed. Keller knew where he was going and headed straight for the bright green door. The glass read VANCE & SON in bold black lettering.

He crossed the threshold in a hurry, ready to breach the front desk. Miss Barbara Clark was caught off guard momentarily but regained her composure quickly, jumped from her chair, and rushed after Keller, who by now had opened the door to his father's office. Warren Vance looked slightly surprised when he saw his son running toward him with outstretched arms. "Daddy, Daddy!" the boy cried as he jumped on Warren's lap. Keller regarded the two women, hot on his heels, then hid his face in his father's shoulder, evidently seeking asylum.

The older gentleman, who sat opposite Warren's desk, appeared uneasy but waited patiently while Warren sorted through it. Miss Clark gasped, "I am sorry, Mr. Vance. I would not have let him in, but he made a dash for it." Her overall air was one of disapproval. Beverly sheepishly stood behind the secretary, swallowing hard.

"That's quite all right, Miss Clark. He has a mind of his own, this one," Warren said as he patted Keller's head. "It's difficult to dissuade him from what he wants."

"A thousand apologies, Mr. Trip," Miss Clark gushed, brows knit, as she petitioned Warren Vance's client. Her eyes flew up and connected with Warren's, giving him a flustered and intense stare, which he looked away from quickly.

"It was my fault. I should have had better hold of him," Beverly offered.

"Mr. Trip, this is my wife, Beverly. Beverly, this is Mr. Trip.

He's looking at that vacant building two blocks from here. He's thinking of opening up shop there," Warren explained. Mr. Trip stood from his chair and shook Beverly's hand, smiling warmly and exposing a row of teeth browned from tobacco.

"It's good to meet you, Mr. Trip. Are you thinking of settling here, then?"

"Not particularly. I've a son-in-law who would be running it for me. My wife and I would never think of leaving Indianapolis. But Muncie certainly is a lovely town."

"Well, then you mustn't eat at Rosie's across the street there, for if you do, you'd never dream of leaving here either," she quipped with a grin playing at her lips. Miss Clark still stood in the doorway with a pout. She did not approve of Warren Vance's wife or son, mostly because she felt that she should be his wife. In her mind, Warren could have married much better. He could have married her.

Miss Clark saw him as a social climber who had been stifled by his family, held back by a woman who was nothing special and a boy who was an embarrassment, at best an imbecile. There were many occasions when Warren could have made very lucrative deals that would have put him in the running with some of the top dogs, but he stubbornly kept to his small-time connections, wary of having to leave his wife overnight with their simpleton son.

"My curiosity is piqued. I'll have to drop in before I leave and see if it's as good as you say it is." He turned back to Warren, who was in the process of extricating himself from Keller's grasp. "And who is this strong young man?"

Warren managed to break free and stood, pushing Keller in front of him, until he was squarely before Mr. Trip. "This is Keller, my son." Warren bent down so that he was eye to eye with Keller. "Can you give Mr. Trip a handshake, Kel?" Keller refused to make eye contact but obediently put his hand out.

"Well, certainly he can," Mr. Trip said jovially. "How old are you, Keller?" Keller dropped the man's hand and wandered over to the desk, fiddling with the picture frames that were lined up neatly across the polished mahogany top.

"He's nearly six now," Warren answered.

"Why, he's as tall as my nine-year-old grandson. He's a big boy." Mr. Trip seemed impressed.

"Would you like me to take him out, Mr. Vance?" Miss Clark asked pointedly as she looked at Beverly. It was not so subtle a hint. Beverly understood perfectly well that Barbara Clark was sending an unspoken message. It was obvious that she was implying that the missus ought to remove the unruly boy.

"I'll take him," Beverly offered. She turned to Mr. Trip with a grateful smile. "I am truly sorry for the interruption, Mr. Trip, but it was very pleasant meeting you." She advanced toward Keller, who tried to coyly elude her by rounding the desk, keeping track of her out of the corner of his eyes. She followed and grabbed his reluctant hand. It took all the force she had to drag him from the room. He began to wail, "Help me, help me!"

As Beverly shut the door firmly behind her, she heard Warren explain, "We have lunch across the street on Thursdays. He never misses it. I hope that it wasn't too much of an inconvenience to be interrupted so." With her screaming child in tow, face burning, she passed Miss Clark, who was standing with hands on hips, obviously exasperated. They made it out the front door of the office before Keller went limp and threw himself down onto the sidewalk. He lay with his arms and legs extended, as if he were in the midst of making a snow angel.

"Keller, you get up this instant," she demanded. If she weren't in such a public place, she thought to herself, she would really let him have a few choice words. She had to choke back the scathing reproach that was forming in her brain.

"I want Daddy," he cried. "I want Daddy, pwease."

"Daddy will come soon. Do you want to go to Rosie's and wait for Daddy?" She was desperate now, her voice coated with sugar, trying to persuade him to get up from the pavement. Beverly was just a little thing, short and small framed. There was no possibility of physically picking him up from his sprawling position. "We can go to Rosie's and get some chicken. Would you like that?"

He stopped his insistent moaning. "Shicken?"

"Yes, chicken. Do you want some chicken?"

"DADDY!" he yelled as he tried to kick her. Beverly went around behind him and, with both hands under his arms, strained to get him up. Gavin Tyler saw the commotion as he made his way down the sidewalk and stopped to try to assist her.

"Hello, Mrs. Vance. Looks like Keller is in a state."

"He is, Mr. Tyler. His father can't join us for lunch right away and he is set upon it. I can't coax him from this spot." She again heaved, trying to get some leverage in order to get him up. Mr. Tyler watched for a moment. Gavin Tyler was a barber, and he knew the Vances from his years of service to them. It had fallen upon him to cut Warren's and Keller's hair, a job that he certainly did not relish. Keller loathed having his hair trimmed and caused quite a commotion each time he was brought in, once even going as far as grabbing the scissors by the blades from Tyler's hand, slicing his little fingers with their razor sharp edges in the process.

"Would you like some assistance?" He did not want to, but it seemed the courteous thing to do. She was, after all, a damsel in distress.

"I certainly hate to ask it, Mr. Tyler, but that would be very kind of you."

Gavin Tyler stooped and grabbed hold of Keller's arms, pulling until Keller was upright again. Once on his feet, Keller lunged at him with his mouth open, baring his teeth, as if he was about to bite the man. Gavin recoiled, growing annoyed. "Now, there's no cause for that, son," he admonished sternly. Gavin Tyler thought the boy needed a good spanking. The root of this kid's problems lay, quite simply, in bad parenting.

Beverly swatted his mouth, "No, Keller! No biting. That's not all right." Keller regarded the two of them with his eyebrows drawn together. Then without further notice, he took off in a run across the street and into Rosie's Diner. Beverly picked up the purse she had discarded in her attempt to move Keller and shot a hasty thank you over her shoulder as she chased the errant child, leaving Tyler to shake his head disapprovingly as she disappeared.

Keller was nearly done with his chicken when Warren showed. Her husband walked with a confidence that Beverly envied, with his broad shoulders drawn back and his solid form relaxed in an easy stride. He sank down heavily next to Beverly, who sat quietly eating her meal. "Did you order me anything?"

"Yes, the turkey Manhattan," she said with a halfhearted smile as she pushed the open-faced turkey sandwich with mashed potatoes and a side of gravy toward him.

"Thank you. What are you having, Kel?"

Keller did not answer. He took a gulp from his cup and then burped. "S'cuse me."

"Why must he always do that?" Beverly asked, barely disguising her impatience. She was nearly at her breaking point, and the polite formalities were beginning to fade.

Warren pulled his plate to him and spread a napkin across his lap. "Hope it's not too cold. I didn't think I would be that long." He took the fork and dove in.

"I'm sorry we made such a scene, Warren. I didn't know you were in a meeting."

"Mr. Trip didn't mind. It's of no concern," he replied casually.

"I thought Miss Clark was going to have a fit."

"Well, Mr. Trip is a very important client. We've had no interest at all in that vacant building. It's been empty for years now. If he's willing to lease it in a five-year contract, that would mean a pretty chunk of money." He buttered his toast vigorously. "My father would certainly be pleased," he said as he crunched the toast between his teeth.

"That's wonderful, darling. I do hope that Kel and I didn't spoil it for you."

"No. Indeed, Mr. Trip appeared quite pleased to meet the two of you."

"He seemed very kind. Still, I should not have come. Perhaps if you had phoned me. But it's Thursday and he knows it," she complained as she eyed Keller. "If I hadn't brought him, he probably would have run off to town on his own anyhow."

"I don't doubt it. When that boy gets something in his head, he won't let it go."

Keller pushed away the half eaten food that was before him. "I want cake pwease."

"You didn't finish your lunch, Kel," Beverly chided. "If you want cake you need to eat your chicken." She pushed the food back toward him.

"I want cake . . . pwease," he insisted.

"Oh, let him have it. After all, he only gets to come to town once a week, Mother."

Beverly was inwardly irritated at Warren's dismissal of her feelings but shrugged her shoulders and conceded. It would be easier to give him the cake than to have to peel him up off of the floor again. If they were at home she might have insisted, but being in public was a very different matter. She suspected that Keller understood this and used it to his advantage. As childlike as he was, he was also very smart. She watched him as he picked up the chocolate cake with his hand and tried to shove the whole thing into his mouth.

"Keller!" Beverly reproached.

Keller paused and put the cake down, picking up his fork to eat it properly. He knew very well what was expected of him. "There, now, that's Mama's good boy," she praised.

"He eats like his father," Warren chuckled.

"That's nothing to be proud of," she countered, allowing herself to laugh, despite her earlier annoyance with her husband. "I have something for you," she admitted cryptically.

"You do?" Warren seemed perplexed.

Beverly pulled her purse to her lap and opened it up, searching through it for a moment. "Here we are," she said, pulling his wedding band from the black interior of the handbag. "You forgot it at home," she explained, with a hint of an accusation in her voice, but still keeping it light and playful.

"I didn't realize I left it," he claimed as he slipped it back onto his finger.

"It was by the sink in the bathroom."

"I must have forgot to put it back on when I was finished shaving this morning."

"There it is, back on your hand where it belongs," she teased. "Whether or not you want to be, you're taken."

"I didn't realize that making as simple a mistake as inadvertently leaving my ring would put me on trial," he grumbled.

"Warren, I was only teasing you," she threw back defensively. "What's the matter with you?"

"Nothing," he maintained. "Absolutely nothing." And he went back to eating as casually as he could muster. The conversation had successfully been killed, however, and the remainder of their visit was spent in relative silence.

*　　*　　*

The Vance home was a modern rambler, the perfect size for their small family. Every detail had been lovingly planned and carefully thought out by Beverly. There was a deep jade green carpet throughout, except for the bathroom and kitchen. She had chosen a muted linoleum for those areas. Her living room was comfortable but stylish, with a couch that she had felt was both cozy and attractive. It was a stunning peacock blue with matching throw pillows. A practical choice as well, for the salesman had eagerly pointed out that the fabric was durable and easily kept clean.

She took great care and time with decorating, for she felt that it was a reflection upon her. Beverly and Warren had never seen eye to eye on such matters. He did not like investing in such trivialities. But even he had to admit that she had a gift for making their home warm and inviting. He liked the results as much as she did. A two-way shelving unit separated the dining area from the living room, which Beverly had filled with inexpensive but attractive pieces of pottery as well as photos and some of the first edition books that she had collected before her marriage to Warren.

Through the dining room an archway opening cut to the kitchen and laundry areas. It was an impressive kitchen with ample cabinet space, a large, farm-style sink, and a Thermador double-wall oven, a luxury for any housewife since the model had just come out that very year. When Beverly and Warren had chosen this house, she had felt that the kitchen had been the crowning jewel, everything that she had hoped for. While the dining area had a more traditional solid wood table and matching buffet, the kitchen showcased a sleek laminate-topped table, with cushioned bright cherry red vinyl seats. They were easy to wipe down and keep clean. Generally speaking, the trio rarely ate their meals in the dining room, preferring the casual atmosphere of the kitchen.

The home was an echo of Beverly's personality, and she felt most comfortable and safe here. After a long day she could truly relax and regroup. With Keller now in bed, Beverly began the official cleanup. She bent down and retrieved the blocks that were scattered across the floor. Her favorite part of the day. The only time that there was order and tranquility in their home. She would tidy the room and put away the things that Keller had left in his wake and then sit quietly with her reading or knitting while Warren reviewed the paper. He rarely had time to read it before he left for work, so he made it a ritual to do so at night, when he could review it at his leisure.

Keller never gave her trouble when it was time for bed. He welcomed bedtime. It was washing his face and brushing his teeth and combing his hair that he so grievously resisted. Once that was over with, he was a lamb. He could dress himself in his pajamas; his favorites were peppered with spaceships. Then he would dutifully clasp his hands for prayer before he climbed beneath his covers to nod off to sleep. Beverly always said the prayer, but she was always amused by his enthusiastic "A-men!"

With Keller safely in bed, Beverly plopped upon the sofa, letting out a sigh. "Anything of importance in the paper, darling?" she asked. He was always peeved when she interrupted his reading.

"I suppose not," he muttered. "Looks like the president is on the mend." He was referring to Eisenhower's recent heart attack.

"I think that Keller took the comics out of the paper today."

"That's all right."

"There was a picture of an elephant. You know how he is about elephants. He carries that postcard that your mother sent from Africa around with him everywhere he goes. But he very carefully ripped out this comic strip with the elephant in it, and now he is carrying around that as well." She was amused with her story and didn't notice that Warren was doing his best to ignore her. "Sometimes I wonder what's in his head."

"I don't think that we will ever really know that, Bev, but it sounds like he may be Republican."

"Very funny," she said, put out. "It would help if I could read to him or something, but he can't stand to sit and look at books. He seems so bored. It's like a punishment when I get a book out."

Warren rattled the paper loudly and gave her an annoyed look. "Do you mind, Bev? I'm trying to read the paper here."

"I'm sorry if I disturbed your evening wind-down, darling, but I hardly have anyone to talk to during the day. I get lonely. It would be nice if you wanted to talk to me too." She got up from the sofa and headed for the kitchen. His withdrawn demeanor of late was beginning to grate on her nerves.

Warren sighed deeply and went back to reading his paper. Inside he knew that he should pursue her, but he was just too tired to make himself move out of his comfortable overstuffed chair. It wasn't until he had finished reading the paper that he folded it neatly and went to find Beverly. She was sitting at the table eating cold roast from a glass dish. "What are you doing?"

"Eating leftovers from the icebox."

"Why?"

"I don't know. It sounded good."

She dropped her fork with a fickle toss and put the food back in the icebox. He walked up behind her and stroked her back affectionately. "You're acting awfully strange."

"Am I?"

"You seem very unsettled."

"I feel unsettled." She twisted herself so that she was firmly in his arms facing him. "Do you remember when we use to go dancing?"

He grinned. "That was a long time ago, Bev. A long time ago."

"Why don't we dance anymore?"

"No time, I suppose," he said, with a quick shrug as he ran his hand through his hair, a tiny smirk on his lips, worried that he was a part of an argument in the making.

"Didn't you enjoy it?" she pressed.

"Certainly I did. It was a clever excuse to hold you close. Your skin was so soft and your waist so slender. I liked to feel you next to me, against me."

She seemed shocked by his words. "Warren!"

"Nine years of marriage and you still feel you have to be modest in front of me?" He caressed her cheek and leaned in for a kiss. She returned his affections, feverishly delving into his kisses, looking for comfort, seeking solace. They were completely absorbed in one another when Beverly caught a glimpse of a figure in the doorway. She gasped and jumped from Warren's arms, startled by Keller, who stood quietly observing from his vantage point, a solitary figure with the look of an old man in his dark eyes. She knew that he did not understand what was transpiring, but she felt slightly guilty at this intrusion upon their personal moment.

"Keller, what are you doing? You frightened Mama," she told him. "You should be in bed." Warren was running his fingers through his hair in an attempt to gain control of himself. With a sympathetic purse of his lips, he patted Beverly on the shoulder. When he did that, it reminded her of a similar thing his father did.

"I'll put him back to bed. You go relax," he offered.

He took Keller securely by the arm and guided him out of the kitchen and down the hall. Keller was led back to his bed, and then Warren gently pulled the covers up to his chin. The boy ran his hand under his pillow, pulled out the comic strip he had ripped out of the paper, and held it up to his father. "Elephant," he mumbled, in a rare attempt at communicating.

"Why, it is an elephant, Kel. A big elephant."

Keller endeavored to imitate the sound of an elephant. "Go to the jungle?"

"No, no jungle. You need to stay in bed. You mustn't get up again. Mama and Daddy need to be alone sometimes." He smoothed Keller's hair. "You know, alone? Quality time? Won't you try to be kind to your old pop and go to sleep?" Keller again thrust the elephant at his father. "Kel, I want you to go to bed. It's time to sleep."

"Elephant."

Warren took the picture and studied it. "Elephant. A big elephant." He passed the picture back to Kel, who took it lovingly and smoothed it between his fingers. "Did you have a busy day in town? Did you go to Rosie's and have chicken?"

"Shicken?"

"Little boys who have busy days in town need to get some rest. You need to go to sleep now. Don't get up out of bed. All right?"

"Wuv you," Keller called out to his father as Warren turned off the light on his way out of the room. Warren made his way back to the living room to find Beverly draped out on the sofa, sound asleep. He sighed deeply as he approached her, his visions of a romantic evening dashed by her deep breathing and relaxed facial tone. "Bev," he whispered gently. "Come on, Bev, let's get you to bed." She allowed him to help her up and walk her to the bedroom.

two

Beverly yawned and stretched as she rolled onto her back, eyeing the clock on the bedside table. Most days Keller woke her up, tugging her from a deep sleep with sounds of clatter from another room. It had been a joke between her and Warren that they did not need an alarm clock. He was as constant as an alarm clock could ever be. She was mildly surprised that he had slept in. She got up and went into the bathroom to splash water onto her face, then headed for the kitchen. She was even more surprised to find Warren and Keller sitting at the table eating breakfast.

"What are the both of you up to?"

"Just having some breakfast," Warren replied.

"You should have woken me."

"I tried."

"Really? I'm sorry. I must have been very tired."

"That's all right. Kel and I found our way around. He wanted toast."

"That's funny; he won't eat it for me." She pressed herself against Warren's back and put her hands on his shoulders, giving him a brief back rub. "You must have the magic touch."

"You fell asleep before I could prove it," he joked.

"Sorry."

"No worries. We'll try and make up for it later. I really need to be off, though. Barry should be here any minute, and I have a lot of paperwork waiting for me at the office." He finished his juice and got up, putting his suit coat on. Beverly followed him to the front door.

"What have you got planned today?" he asked.

"Margaret Price has invited me over for lunch."

"That sounds nice."

"I hope so. I haven't been out in ages."

Barry was in the driveway giving his horn a short honk. Beverly and Warren were like nearly all other couples in that they were only a one automobile family. Warren and Barry had made an arrangement to take turns driving, which freed the car up for Beverly on occasion. Warren drove three days one week and two days the next. With Barry only living two blocks away and working at the courthouse, it was a beneficial agreement for the two of them.

"Barry's here, gotta go. Have a good day, sweetheart."

"You too." She gave him a peck on the lips before he was gone.

When Warren had left, Beverly dressed carefully in her best pin-striped gray suit. She felt it was flattering to her figure. The long, fitted pencil skirt hit nearly mid-calf, and the jacket was just the cut to make up for, what she felt, was a short torso. She pinned her hat neatly on her head and surveyed herself in the mirror. The suit was looking a little too fitted, and she ruefully decided that she must start watching what she ate.

She found Keller covered in jam when she went looking for him. He had apparently been drinking it from the glass jar. It made her angry, but there was no point in expressing it. He didn't understand anyhow; his simple little world did not consist of consequences. That was far too complex for him to grasp. All that he knew was that he wanted jam, and nothing else was important. She took a cloth and wetted it, scrubbing his face and hands a bit too briskly out of frustration. It was a struggle to get the dirty shirt off of him. The whole time he was chiding her, "It's not dirty. Give it to me. It's not dirty."

"It's dirty, Kel. We must put a clean shirt on. Don't you want to go bye-bye?"

With the prospect of an outing, he allowed her to put a fresh shirt on. She helped him into the backseat of the car and then got in the driver's seat. It had been months since she had been invited to do anything with friends. She understood why, but she would never verbalize it. It was too painful to admit to anyone. There were times when she feared that she would slip quietly into oblivion without anyone even noticing it.

Margaret was slightly older than Beverly, with a bigger home filled with expensive furniture. She had come from a family that was accustomed to having nice things. Beverly doubted that she had ever worried about money. While Beverly was perfectly content with her own situation, she liked to admire other people's good fortunes. It did not bother her that she and Warren lived in a smaller home, or that she shopped the sales racks, while Margaret had probably never stooped to such levels.

She pulled into the driveway in front of a two-story, traditional brick home with green and white striped awnings above each window. Picturesque, with a well-cared for lawn and meticulously kept flower beds. Keller was out of the car before she could even turn off the ignition. She quickly followed him up the walkway just in time to prevent him from showing himself through the door. "This is not our home, Kel. We must knock before we go in." With that she gave a quick but firm knock. Margaret appeared at the door, all smiles as she welcomed them in.

There were several other ladies sitting in the front room, talking politely to one another in hushed tones over a plate of cheese puffs and mini quiches. Keller eyed the plate for a moment, then reached out and grabbed a handful. Beverly smiled nervously. "He is always such a hungry boy," she offered, mortified within at his animalistic behavior.

While she knew the women from church, she did not know

them well. Laura and Missy were both in the choir. Neither had gone out of their way to befriend her, and Beverly was so wrapped up in her own life that she didn't really care. Now seeing their shocked expressions, she wished to know them even less than she had before. These women did not run in the same social circles as she. They did not associate with just anyone. To be in their group was to be one of the church elite, in with the in crowd. If they did not approve of you, you were simply ignored. They were a fastidious bunch, and not many passed the stringent requirements they had developed as a guideline for membership into their group.

They were not partial to Beverly for several reasons. First, she had nothing to offer. She was not prestigious, nor did she know anyone prestigious, and she did not have unlimited resources when it came to money. She did not come from an old family name, and most of all, no matter how enchanting her company, she had Keller. He was enough to keep her out of the running for good. No one wanted a child like him around, a constant reminder of how horribly nature could foul up. He made people uncomfortable. Those like him, who had not been institutionalized, were generally kept out of the public eye, hidden away in their homes like the dark secrets that they were. It had raised some disapproving eyebrows that Beverly and Warren Vance brought Keller to church, took him on family outings, and that Beverly ran errands with him in tow on a fairly regular basis.

Used to the constant unsolicited advice as to how they should handle Keller, Beverly nevertheless still lacked the tough skin she required to ignore it and not allow the disapproval to affect her. After so many pin pricks she began to resent it, began to feel the bitter sting of it every time she received a withering glance such as the ones that were being directed at her now. She did her best not to scowl at the others as she attempted to divert her young son away from the plate. What would she think in such a situation, if she did not have Keller? She reasoned that perhaps she would have reacted that very way, and she tried to talk herself into giving the two women the benefit of the doubt.

Kind-hearted Margaret took one of the mini quiches and offered it to Keller with a soft expression. "Certainly, growing boys must have lots to eat." Keller snatched it from her hand and crammed it into his mouth.

"It was so thoughtful of you to have us over, Margaret," Beverly offered, sitting across from her on the velvet sofa. "I feel as though I haven't seen you forever."

"It has been awhile. I've just been so busy." Margaret was perched attentively on the edge of her brocade armchair.

"Did you know that she took a trip to New England?" Missy asked.

"No. That's wonderful," Beverly conceded congenially.

"It really was," Margaret said. "It is such beautiful country. We went out on a boat in the ocean and we saw whales! They were just feet from our boat. Dale and I had fresh clam chowder, the likes of which you have never tasted."

"Did you get a chance to go to the beach?" Beverly inquired.

"Oh, yes. It was delightful. I was even persuaded to get myself into a bathing suit. Only I got a sunburn. I suppose with my pale skin I was not meant to lounge in the sun."

"Your skin is perfectly beautiful, Margaret," Missy dutifully claimed.

Up to this point Laura had remained quiet. She eyed Beverly. "I've never been to New England. Have you, Beverly?"

"No, not to New England. I have been East though."

"Really, where?" Laura prodded.

"New York."

"New York? You don't say?" Missy asked, becoming interested.

"Yes. I won an essay contest in college that paid for my expenses to New York."

"Our Beverly is quite the talent with words," Margaret informed the two women. "She wrote for the college paper when she was younger." She had hoped that inviting the two and Beverly over might give them a chance to get to know one another better, might prod Laura and Missy to become more friendly with Beverly. She always seemed so solitary and forlorn, such a lonesome figure. Perhaps this would draw her out, give her an opportunity to visit with the ladies from church and form some new relationships that would make her more comfortable at worship on Sundays. She had other reasons for looking out for Beverly, but it was something that she could never share with anyone, not even Beverly herself. For Margaret harbored a secret, a secret that was in her best interest to keep from everyone else, a secret that smoldered in her chest like a constant heartburn, aching incessantly.

"How nice," Laura replied.

"That was before Warren and I met."

"And you met at the college?" Laura asked.

"Yes, that's where we met. I'm afraid I didn't make it through all the way. I was only there a little over a year when we married. He was just graduating then. He had scarcely gotten back from serving in the Pacific."

"I didn't go to college," Margaret remarked.

"Me neither," Missy added.

"Nor did I," Laura put in with a small laugh.

"Well, it's not for everyone, I suppose," Beverly offered, feeling slightly foolish. "But I enjoyed it. It was a nice change from the happenings of the small town where I was from. There was always something to do and so many interesting people to meet."

"Where are you from originally?" Laura snooped.

"Evans, Ohio."

"Beverly got a scholarship to come to Ball State," Margaret bragged. "That's difficult to do."

At this point Keller had finished all of the mini quiches and cheese puffs. He let out his customary belches and chimed, "S'cuse me."

Margaret laughed. "You know, in some countries that is a compliment. If someone belches after they eat your food it means they thought it was very good."

"It's really a shame Kel was born in the wrong country then,"

Beverly giggled. The other women seemed doubtful but endeavored to give a polite laugh as well. Keller got up and began to investigate his surroundings. There were many lovely things for him to peruse. He walked slowly around the room as the women continued to chat. Beverly got up and began to shadow him.

"Don't worry, Beverly. There's not a thing that he can hurt," Margaret soothed. She really only wanted for Beverly to feel comfortable. She could see the younger woman was somewhat ruffled by Keller's behavior.

"I don't know about that. From my experience, he is very gifted at breaking things."

Keller spotted a carved elephant that looked to be made out of ivory in one of Margaret's curio cabinets. He plucked it from the shelf and inspected it. Margaret went to him, bending down so that she was to his level. "Do you like it, Kel? My husband got it in Europe. Would you like to hold it?"

"That's very kind of you, but it looks expensive. Maybe he shouldn't play with it."

"Nonsense. Dale goes to Europe every few months. He could easily replace it."

"Thank you," Beverly said, knowing full well that Margaret had just told a whopping lie.

"I'll have to show you ladies the new piece of art I just had to have," Margaret stated. "Dale didn't like it, but I didn't care. I told him that he could decorate his study just as he pleased, but the rest of the house was mine to do with as I saw fit." She waited for the three women to congregate around her and then led them through the hall and allowed them to mill around the large canvas. "What do you think?"

"Oh, Margaret, you certainly have exquisite taste!" Laura claimed as she surveyed the painting wide eyed. Laura, in fact, knew nothing of art.

"What do you think, Beverly?" Margaret fished, eager to get Beverly's opinion. Margaret was fully aware that Beverly had an eye for decorating and was especially interested in what she thought of it.

"I think that it fits your personality well. Look at how cheery the colors are." She cleared her throat and suppressed a smile. "I can see why Dale wouldn't like it, though. It is decidedly feminine." They gazed upon the hazy flow of the paint in the impressionistic piece.

Margaret too smiled. "Yes, it is. It was wicked of me to make him live with it, eh?"

As they stood gazing upon the painting, a crash resounded through the hallway. They looked at one anther in surprise. Beverly realized too late that she had left Keller unattended. She felt suddenly sick to her stomach, for she knew what would undoubtedly follow.

"Oh, no, Keller!" Beverly took off in the direction of the noise. As she came around the corner into the dining room, there stood Keller in a sea of broken china, his eyes as big as the saucers he had just decimated. She was dazed for a moment, while the other women pressed in around her.

"Good heavens, your grandmother's china, Margaret!" Missy gasped.

"Keller, what have you done?" Beverly rushed to him, pulling him away from the glass. She could hardly bring herself to look at the mess. Missy and Laura bent down and gingerly began to pick up the pieces. "Margaret, I am so sorry. I don't even know what to say."

Margaret was too stunned to move. She still stood frozen in the doorway. "Let me just get something to put the glass in," she said. She came back shortly with the garbage can. Catching sight of Keller, she had pity upon him. "He looks frightened. Poor thing."

"I should leave," Beverly offered. "I just don't know how to tell you how very sorry I am. I should have been watching him."

"Now, it was me that told you there was nothing he could hurt. How careless of me to leave those dishes stacked on the table where he could reach them. You can't leave yet anyhow. We haven't had our lunch."

Missy and Laura were shooting her looks of outrage as they finished picking up the shattered rose-patterned china. It was obvious from the beginning that they did not approve of Beverly or Keller, but they grew bolder in their derisive glances. Not only did Beverly feel completely shamed and horribly guilty over what Keller had done, but she also felt like the odd man out. "I don't think that it is a good idea for me to stay, Margaret. I should probably take Kel home. I feel just awful that he ruined your china."

"Nonsense. Keller only gave me an excuse to replace that old stuff." Margaret walked over to Keller and took him by the hand, leading him back to the table and sitting him down. "Have a seat, ladies. We'll finish with that later." They obediently sat in their seats, even reluctant Beverly, who could see how futile it was to try and argue with Margaret.

Margaret went into the kitchen and retrieved her everyday dishes and set them neatly before her guests. She was the perfect hostess as she served them the elaborate meal she had prepared. Perhaps sensing that he had crossed a line, Keller sat quietly toying with the elephant, offering no further disruptions. Beverly felt as if she couldn't swallow the food as she took small bites from her plate. It seemed to catch in her throat. So completely forlorn and desperate to be out of the situation was she that she excused herself before dessert. Missy and Laura remained seated while Margaret got up to show her to the door.

The real struggle began when Beverly tried to take the elephant away from Keller. He began to scream and pull away from her. Determined not to let him get the best of her, she pried the ivory carving from his clenched hand. He nearly knocked her down trying to get it back, lashing out with his fingernails, using them as a weapon in his attempt to retrieve the prize he so desperately sought. Bright red scratch marks manifested themselves on her hands, some bleeding where the skin had been broken. Her high heels were a handicap as she fought to get him to leave the house. He was hollering and striking Beverly, putting up a good fight the whole distance from the door to the car in the driveway.

*   *   *

"I've never been so humiliated," she spat out. "I just couldn't believe he did that."

"Beverly, he didn't know what he was doing."

"That's easy for you to say, Warren. You weren't there. You didn't have to face those women. And there was poor Margaret trying to act as if it were nothing to her." Beverly shoved her hands into the sudsy water and vigorously began scrubbing the dishes in the sink. "I wanted to die. Her grandmother's china!"

"We'll replace it, Bev."

"How can you replace a *family heirloom*!?"

"What do you want me to say, Bev? What do you want me to do?"

"Oh, Warren, don't patronize me. I can't ever face those people again, and you act as if you are trying to soothe some silly child who's being unreasonable."

"It probably isn't the best idea to take Keller to a ladies' luncheon. It was doomed from the start," Warren reproached. While he felt sympathy for his wife, he was also very annoyed. "He needs to be watched every moment."

"What exactly is that supposed to mean? What am I supposed to read into that, Warren? You think I don't watch him? What am I supposed to do, just lock him away here in the house and never let him out? Maybe you feel I am simply careless with him. Well, I like that, it is always my fault!"

"That is not what I said, Beverly. You can't expect to take him to other people's homes—especially someone that should have all of their possessions under glass—without anything happening. Dale and Margaret's house is like a museum. All those valuables, they should be taking tours of the place. Everything they own is worth more than what I make in a year's worth of wages. Of course he's bound to break something. They have no children; they don't worry about what is in Keller's reach because they don't have to. Just don't put yourself in a situation like that and there won't be a problem."

"So, I am just supposed to never go out, never have friends?"

"I didn't say that, Bev. You are putting words in my mouth. I'm simply saying that you can't expect Keller to act like other children. He's not like other children. He isn't going to behave nicely or sit quietly. If you don't want him to break Margaret's grandmother's china, then don't let him near the stuff!"

"Well, thank you for your pearls of wisdom!" She shook her hands dry over the sink and stalked out of the kitchen. There was nothing left for Warren to do or say. He went to find Keller. The boy hardly seemed aware of all of the commotion he had set into play. He sat quietly inspecting his post card.

"Hey, son, do you want to go for a walk?"

Keller regarded him with his usual serious face, offering his hand to his father, affirming that he did indeed want to. Warren put his jacket on and held open the door. If there was anything that would make Keller happy, it was being out of doors. He nearly smiled as the sun hit him.

Warren grasped his hand and led him down the street. "You had a busy day. Poor Mother. You shouldn't be so naughty for her."

Keller did not reply, which was not uncommon. He saw the Hartfords' dog up ahead and pulled Warren along. "I see the dog, Kel. Slow down." Keller laughed out loud when the dog ran up to him and licked his hands. He was infatuated with animals, any animals.

"Doggie!" Keller cried. He stroked the dog's fur with great affection. "Good doggie," he cooed, with a soft giggle.

Andy Hartford, a young boy in worn overalls with a generous smattering of freckles on his arms, chest, and face, tore around the corner of his house and ran straight for his dog. He took the dog by the collar and pulled it in the direction of his yard, away from the sidewalk where Keller and Warren stood. "Sugar is playing with me," he said.

"Why don't you and Sugar play with Kel?" Warren asked.

"He don't talk, Mr. Vance. He itn't no fun," Andy griped, eyeing Keller contemptuously.

"That's true he doesn't talk much. He sure likes Sugar, though. Maybe you can show him some tricks with your dog."

Andy considered it for a moment, then shrugged. "All right, I guess so. Just a minute and let me get him some treats." The young boy took off again, disappearing for a few moments before returning with the dog treats. Keller was contentedly petting the animal and was hardly aware that anyone else was about. "Got the treats," he said, waving them in front of Warren.

"Good, now you can show Keller how it's done."

"Look here, Keller." Andy turned to the dog. "Sugar, roll over." He spun his hand in a circle and waited patiently for the dog to do its trick. Sugar obligingly rolled over for his young master and panted expectantly for his treat. "Good dog, Sugar." He threw the treat and the dog caught it in midair.

Keller laughed happily. "Good dog," he chanted.

Andy turned to Warren. "That ain't all he can do. Bark, Sugar, bark." The dog let out a yelp and was rewarded with another treat. "See?"

"He's a very good dog." Warren rubbed the fur coat roughly. "Do you think Keller might try now?"

"Ah, he can't do it. He can't talk, Mr. Vance."

"He can talk when he wants to." Warren hunched down to look Keller in the eye. "Do you want to try, Kel? Do you want to make the dog roll over and bark?" He held out his hand to Andy. "Here, let me have a dog treat." Andy handed them over. "You try, son." He then placed the treats in Keller's small hands.

A grin spread across Keller's face. "Bark, Sugar, bark." On cue, the dog barked. Keller laughed out loud and then threw the whole fist of dog treats to him. Warren couldn't help but chuckle too. The dog frantically dodged from one dog treat to the next, licking them up before anyone could stop him.

"See, he did it."

"He oughtn't to have thrown him all the treats," Andy commented.

"Well, he doesn't know any better. But he certainly did make the dog bark, didn't he?"

Andy was unwilling to concede. "I did it better."

Warren was peeved. "Well, I suppose you did, but this was only Keller's first try."

"I gotta go and I want my dog." Andy took the dog by the collar again and dragged it away, back toward his house. The dog barked and pulled at the collar, trying to get away. "You come along, Sugar, or I'll give you a spanking."

Warren watched the child go with disdain. He sensed Keller's displeasure and tried to make it better. "Say good-bye to the dog, Keller. Say good-bye to Sugar."

"Say good-bye, Sugar." Keller gave a lazy wave of his hand before he turned and headed on down the street. They strolled idly for a few blocks before they turned back. It was getting dark, and Warren knew that Keller would want his bath. His internal schedule would tell him that things weren't right if he didn't have his bath at exactly seven PM. His son needed order, needed regularity. It was when the unexpected happened that Keller lost any semblance of control.

When they returned, Beverly seemed to have calmed. She was quietly knitting on the sofa. Keller burst through the door and ran to her, shouting, "Mama, Mama."

"Hello, baby. Did you and Daddy go for a walk?"

"He played with the Hartfords' dog," Warren informed her. "He told the dog to bark and then gave him a dog treat."

"You did?" Beverly was both surprised and thrilled. "Did you give Sugar a dog treat, Kel?" she asked. It was sometimes the smallest things that brought the greatest joys. Others might think that it wasn't much to brag about, but Warren and Beverly recognized it as a small miracle.

"Doggie, doggie," Keller chanted with a self-humored laugh. He grasped Beverly's hand and pressed his lips hard against her knuckles in a clumsy attempt at affection.

"What a big boy you are," Beverly flattered, hugging him close. He seemed pleased.

"He said, 'Bark, Sugar, bark,' and the dog barked and he fed it the treats," Warren told his wife proudly.

"How did he know to do that?" Beverly marveled, allowing Keller to nestle in under her armpit.

"That little Hartford kid showed him."

"That was nice of him."

"Say what you like about Kel, but at least he isn't a little monster like some children. Let him break all the dishes from here to kingdom come. I wouldn't care, as long as he isn't just flat out wicked."

"What happened?"

"The boy didn't want to play with Kel because he doesn't talk."

"It must be hard for the other children to understand why Keller is so odd. He's really just a baby in this big body of his."

"I suppose, but there's still no cause for him to treat our boy so poorly."

"Shall I talk to Mrs. Hartford?"

"I hardly think it would help, Bev. She can't do a whole lot to change the way the child thinks. It would be just as easy for us to tell Keller not to behave so strangely. Besides, most of the parents are just as bad as their children." Keller left his mother's side and headed down the hall to the bathroom, pulling his shirt over his head and tossing it on the floor as he went. "He wants his bath."

"I'll go run the water," she offered.

"I can do it. You probably deserve a break after your day."

"Thank you, Warren. That's very thoughtful of you."

"I know that it is hard on you, Bev. He is a difficult child and you are dealing with him all day long. It's not fair to ask it of you, but then we have no choice in the matter, do we?"

"I feel guilty thinking of it that way."

"You shouldn't," he advised. "He is very high maintenance and requires a lot of energy."

"It's not that I don't love him . . ."

"Why, Beverly, I know that you love him. You take very good care of Keller. He is happy and fed and clean. I just wish I could figure out a way to make it easier on you. Perhaps it's time that we listen to what Dr. Stephens has to say."

"Warren, he's our son; we can't even consider that option," she reasoned, forcing the annoyance from her response. "He's a child—a living, breathing human being—not some broken toy to discard with the trash. What would become of him?"

From down the hall Keller interrupted their conversation. "Help!" he yelled out. "Help me!" He had grown impatient waiting for his parents and decided that he must be vocal to get his way.

Beverly laughed. "If he doesn't have his bath this minute, the world will end."

"We wouldn't want that to happen. Off I go to save the world," Warren declared, avoiding the consequences of their conversation by quickly retreating down the hall and into the bathroom to aid Keller with his bath. She heard them laughing together, splashing water, playing. It made her feel bad that she had so thoroughly lost her temper over the broken dishes. She would apologize to Warren later, once Keller was in bed and they could talk more freely without distractions.

three

Beverly turned on the television, switching it to CBS. Keller sat quietly on the couch once he saw that it was Captain Kangaroo. Beverly enjoyed sitting next to him during this time and often found an excuse to stay close by, folding laundry or making a grocery list. It was the only time that Keller was ever involved in anything but his own world. She gave a genuine smile when Tom Terrific came on and Kel sang along with Crabby Appleton.

"My name is Crabby Appleton. I'm rotten to the core," he spat out with loud glee. She found it so adorable.

Beverly joined in. "I do a bad deed every day and sometimes three or four." It was difficult for her to understand how Keller could sing a song with so many words and then not speak to her when she asked him a question or when he needed or wanted something. She had resented it at first. Something in her nature craved a conversation with him. What would it be like to have him tell her everything that had been in his head that he had not expressed up to now? What mysteries would he reveal?

She folded a towel and placed it on the towel pile, then paused and watched him sitting there so intently. She scrutinized his face to see if she could read anything from it. When Mr.

Moose appeared and told his joke, Keller knew what was coming. He held his breath, waited until the end of the joke, and then in unison with Mr. Moose, yelled, "Ping pong balls!" as the shower of small white spheres rained down upon Captain Kangaroo in his red blazer. Keller's laughter bubbled up, and he jumped up and down in excitement. "Uh oh!" he cried.

She placed her piles of laundry neatly in the basket. "It's nearly time to go to town," she said, trying to muster interest. He did not acknowledge her. His mind was still on the television program. She stood up and headed for the bedroom. Sitting at her vanity she brushed her hair and put on her makeup carefully. She liked to look nice when she went out of the house. It always made her feel more confident than she really was. Perhaps others would see the perfectly sculpted hair and freshly pressed clothing and never look deeper, to the terribly insecure woman that lay within. When she was finished she went back to the living room to get her basket and quickly put away her folded laundry. She gasped when she saw the tangled towels, shirts, pants, and underwear strewn across the floor. Keller was sitting next to the couch with the bulk of the laundry piled on top of him, only his face peaking out.

"What have you done, Kel?" Agitation welled up inside of her as she quickly went about picking up the laundry and tossing it into the basket. "What were you thinking?" Keller did not move as Beverly took the laundry from him. He simply sat there with his eyes glued to the television. "Every time we are about to go somewhere you do something naughty! *Every* time!"

When she had collected all the laundry and put it back in the basket, she turned to him, unable to keep the harshness from her voice. "I'm talking to you!" She pressed his cheeks between her hands, trying to force him to look at her.

Keller rolled his eyes away from her, using his peripheral vision to avoid looking at her. "Look at me. I'm talking to you!" In exasperation she gave up, dropping her hands to her sides. "Go get your shoes before anything else happens."

Obligingly, Keller got up and went to his room, taking the shoes from his closet. He put them on by himself and then went to find his mother. He had not mastered tying his shoes and for this reason he sought help, for if Keller could do it himself, he did. An independent little man, he did all that he could without having to be inconvenienced by human interaction. Beverly bent down to tie the strings and noticed the shoes were on the wrong feet again. It did not surprise her. She suspected that Keller put them on the wrong feet deliberately, as they were nine times out of ten. She switched feet and tied his shoes.

"Would you like to go to town with Mama?" Beverly questioned as she helped him put his jacket on, feeling remorseful for her earlier treatment of him. When Keller struggled against her, she chided him. "It is chilly out. You must wear your jacket or we will not leave the house." Keller took her threat seriously and relinquished, slipping his arms into the sleeves. He opened the front door and tore out of the house, climbing into the backseat of the automobile. Beverly hastily grabbed her purse and coat and followed him out.

It had only been two years since Warren had bought the car brand new. It was a 1953 Dodge Cornet sedan. The ad had said "dramatic new styling . . . most powerful Dodge of all time." He had been very proud of his new purchase, boasting that it had a V8 engine, and choosing the top-of-the-line model with all of the extras, including white-walled tires and leather seats. It was a cherry red finish with a chrome line that ran down the body of the car, very sharp and very expensive. They had forked out close to $1,800 for it.

Unfortunately, Keller was oblivious to such fancies. In less than a month's time, he had made a hole in the fabric that lined the interior ceiling, and he'd left scratch marks on the leather seats with his fingernails. He had also developed a habit of spitting in his hand and tracing his fingers across the rear window, next to his seat, presumably practicing a new art technique. Therefore the rear window was marred by constant smudge marks, regardless of how often it was cleaned.

Warren was enraged by his son's careless disregard for the new automobile. After attempting to spank Keller into submission, without any success, he vowed never to buy anything new again. Beverly understood and sympathized with his anger. Keller had taken a fountain pen to her sofa cushion once, and she had felt the same rage. She was able to camouflage the blemish by flipping the cushion over. The car, however, remained in disrepair. Warren saw no point in fixing what would surely be destroyed all over again anyhow. It got them where they needed to go, and that was all that Warren was concerned about at this point.

As she drove, Beverly surveyed the scenery. The layout of the town was fairly impressive. There was a college and a hospital, along with schools and churches. Ball Brothers had built a state of the art factory here, producing glass jars and bottles. Then Borg Warner had moved in shortly after the war, providing more jobs and opportunities. With these factories came many new businesses, and the little town was a reasonably modern and well-kept place to live. It was not as large as, say, Indianapolis, but Muncie was large enough to provide comforts one could not benefit from in the rural areas, yet it was small enough to give it a hometown feel. Neighbors knew one another and often ran into each other when they were out and about.

In some ways this made Beverly nervous. Everywhere she went there was someone she knew to witness her inevitable public humiliation. If she thought that she was never going to see them again, perhaps she would not feel so much resentment. It was a constant inner conflict with her. She loved Keller and hated to think that she would change him if given the choice, but she would if she could. As simple as she thought love should be, it was never that easy. Perhaps there was no such thing as unconditional love, because human relationships were all too often far too complex for such a simple notion as that. This was the discord that went on within her on a daily basis. She eyed Keller in the rearview mirror as he contentedly watched life pass by through the window. She supposed that life would always be passing him by.

Dr. Stephens's office was just a few blocks from downtown, which meant it was a short drive for Beverly. She pulled into the parking lot and parked neatly between the lines. The office building was a bungalow-style house, renovated to serve as the doctor's place of business, in what was once a residential area, now part of the business district. She sat quietly for a moment, dreading what was about to come. Keller gave out an alarmed cry. This was not his routine. This was not the ice cream counter at Walgreens. But this was not Thursday. He whined when Beverly opened the car door and attempted to extract him from the leather seat. "Come along, Kel. I'll take you to get ice cream after we're finished here. Don't you want to see Dr. Stephens?"

Keller reluctantly consented. He slid from the seat and stood next to the car for a moment, unsure of what to do. Beverly took his hand and tried to lead him toward the clinic's entrance. He planted his feet and refused to move. "Keller, you need to do as I say," she scolded. "Now come along."

She realized that she should not have spoken to him so insistently. He did not respond well to harsh commands. He leaned in, trying to bite her. She pulled her arm away in time to miss the full fury of his teeth. Keller tried to open the car door to get back in. She blocked his way and grabbed the top of his arm, trying to pull him to the building. He resisted so obstinately, with his jaw set in a stubborn line, that he nearly caused her to fall. She cursed her high heels once again as she stumbled across the parking lot, dodging blows and pinches at the hands of her son.

All the while Keller was yelling, "No, stop. Help me! Help me!" Several onlookers paused and out right stared at the bizarre scene. "That kid's nutty," they said amongst themselves. It always pierced her to the heart to hear such things about her child. She knew that Keller was ignorant of what comments like those meant, but she understood perfectly well. She couldn't understand how people could be so callous. It wasn't the first time she had heard such phrases, and it most definitely would not be the last.

Beverly finally breached the entrance and shoved him in, standing between the door and Keller with her back firmly pressed against it so that he could not escape. He was pounding against her, furious that he had been trapped. She withstood him until he finally seemed to calm down.

A tear streamed down his cheek, and he said, a little desperately, "Let me outta here." When she took hold of him this time it was with a soft and gentle touch, trying to avoid his rage any further.

"We'll go get ice cream as soon as we are finished here, Keller. Please be good," she begged. She checked in at the reception desk, an area that had once been a front living room, and then stood watch over her son as he paced back and forth before the window, like a caged animal. It was only a short time before her name was called. Another scrap ensued as she tried to get him back into the examination room. This time the nurse and receptionist, faces red with indignation, assisted her.

Two bedrooms now served as examination rooms, housing stainless steel examination tables covered with a thin white paper; white cupboards with glass doors, stocked with an assortment of medical supplies; and a stool with wheels. The areas that had once been carpeted had been refinished with gray speckled linoleum.

Dr. Stephens walked in with a sympathetic smile. "Hello, Mrs. Vance. It's good to see you." He was probably pushing sixty, a grandfatherly figure with a wreath of hair on the lower portion of his head and a nice shiny gleam to the skin on the top half. He wore a white lab coat, buttoned all the way up, with his slacks and brown loafers. His appearance was neat, clean cut, and practical.

Beverly had always felt comfortable in Dr. Stephens's presence. He was calm and spoke with a mild and slow voice, which had the effect of being quite soothing. The doctor had delivered Keller and, with a beaming face, pronounced him the most beautiful baby he had birthed in his entire career. He declared the baby to be perfectly healthy before placing the tiny plump body in Beverly's outstretched arms. This same doctor had been there for the birth of her husband. He was a close friend of the Vance family; he was a high school chum that Warren's father had remained tight with over the years.

Now, every time she saw his benevolent face, she sensed guilt.

It was the same reaction Keller evoked from many people. They did not know what to say or how to behave, and it made them feel guilty. There were those who well meaningly tried to overlook the obvious. They tried to behave as if nothing were amiss in the boy and avoided saying anything that might indicate what they were thinking really. Others simply ignored. If you acted as if you couldn't see it, then it was not there. There were still a few who outright gaped at Keller's outrageous behavior. They seemed to have no sympathy or tolerance for him at all. They could not grasp that Keller had little control over his behavior. He was as much a victim of himself as those around him.

"Thank you, Doctor. I am sorry about all of the commotion."

"Think nothing of it," he consoled. "I haven't seen you since we stitched up young Keller's head."

"Yes. It's been awhile. I hope it's not too much of an inconvenience. I know the nurse must think he is an awful child. He looks so normal that it's difficult for people who don't know him to understand that the poor thing doesn't understand what he's doing. He can't help himself."

"He is a beautiful boy, Mrs. Vance, but it certainly must be a terrible burden for you. They have places for children like Keller. I know that we once began to discuss it, but you didn't think that was a possibility then. I can always give you more extensive information if you are interested."

"Please, Dr. Stephens, I don't think that I can talk about that right now." The words caught in her throat as she tried to get them out. Beverly was trying desperately to eliminate the emotion from her speech as she grappled with the discord within. The adrenaline rush from her physical confrontation with Keller had passed, and now she felt nothing but weakness and shame as the tears quietly slipped down her cheeks.

Once they were finished at the doctor's office and Keller had gotten his ice cream, he seemed perfectly contented. But Beverly was completely drained and sat nearly comatose. Mr. Ferrin attempted to make small talk several times, but he gave up once he saw the futility of it. He had three nearly grown children, and he looked at Beverly with the tenderhearted compassion of a father. That could be his Joslyn, he reasoned. And if it were his daughter, he would want others to treat her with respect. He had always harbored a soft spot for Mrs. Vance, and he went out of his way to prove it.

When Keller had finished, the two of them trudged up the street toward Warren's office. Keller seemed suddenly dazed and exhausted from his morning escapades, as if the day's events had finally caught up to him. He trailed behind Beverly in an unusual show of submission. Beverly occasionally had to stop and encourage him to catch up with her. He picked up the pace dutifully until he grew tired and let his footsteps grow slow again.

Upon reaching the office building, Keller was still several paces behind her. She came around the corner and paused to wait for him. Through the window she could see Warren conversing with Miss Clark, who sat at her desk. He was resting against the desktop, his legs stretched out before him and crossed at the ankles, his arms folded firmly across his chest. Barbara was smiling sweetly, provocatively. Beverly felt as if she were watching a television program. For the first time things became very focused and sharp in her mind as she witnessed the blatant flirtation that Barbara was lavishing upon her husband. Why hadn't she seen it before?

Warren seemed at ease, relaxed and enjoying it, a broad grin on his lips. She noted that he wasn't returning her advances, but he was most certainly not rejecting them. Beverly stood, transfixed by their interaction, her heart pounding and her mind racing. Barbara in her crisp lavender blouse, fitted exactly to her curves, touching his arm so gently. Barbara running her manicured nails through her short curled hair, her eyes alight, her head tilted ever so slightly to one side. It was all perfectly easy to recognize once Beverly stepped back to analyze it.

She did not have an opportunity to observe for more than a few minutes because she was shocked back into the real world by the bang of the office door. Keller had caught up with her and without her even being aware of it had run headlong inside the building. She shook her head, as if to clear it, and followed him in. Barbara's enthusiastic smile had vanished completely, replaced by her customary peevish response to Warren's wife and son.

"Keller! What are you doing here?" Warren interrogated. Beverly was close behind, and Warren seemed relieved when he saw her. "Oh, Beverly, for a moment I thought he must of gotten away from home and run here on his own."

"I'm sorry, darling, I had some errands to run and we couldn't leave until we had seen you," she gushed, consciously marking her territory on the man that stood before her.

"It's not even Thursday," Miss Clark observed coolly.

"Well, what a pleasant surprise," Warren conceded.

"Do you have time to grab a bite to eat, Warren?"

"Shicken?" Keller requested with his little eyebrows drawn together.

"I always have time for that," he chuckled.

"Oh good. Perhaps you can hold down the fort for him, Miss Clark," Beverly suggested with feigned graciousness.

"Of course I will, Mr. Vance. You go enjoy yourself."

Beverly felt galled by her overly charming voice. She wondered how it had not been clear to her before. Women's intuition should have told her, but she had assumed all along that it was Keller who made Barbara Clark dislike their visits. How alarming to find that the beguiling, youthful Miss Clark had eyes for her husband.

It was taxing to make small talk or to even enjoy the food as they ate together at Rosie's Diner. She could not even recall what she had ordered. As much as she disliked the idea of Warren going back to work with Miss Clark fawning over him, she welcomed the fact that she would be going home, her haven from the real world. When she walked through the door and into their front room she nearly fell apart, sinking onto the couch and comforting herself with a good cry.

For the rest of the day she wasn't of much use. She attempted to fold the laundry again. It was pointless to try. Keller would knock the piles over as if it were a fun new game that he had discovered. She finally gave up and sat quietly on the sofa, watching him entangle himself in the clothing as he rolled around on the floor. At this juncture he could have torn the house down to the ground, and she would not have cared.

Dinner was a simple affair of cold cuts, leftover yeast rolls, and a platter of carrots, pickles, and black olives. Keller would only eat the yeast rolls, shoving them gluttonously into his mouth, barely able to chew with his cheeks so full. The two adults had grown accustomed to looking the other way in such situations, but it grated on Beverly's nerves this evening.

"Keller, don't eat so much," she scolded.

When the boy began to gag, Warren pounded his back. "You'll choke to death, son." Keller recovered quickly and crammed another roll into his mouth.

"It was a nice surprise seeing you today."

"Really? I was afraid I had intruded," she coyly responded.

"Intruded upon what?"

Beverly shrugged. "I don't know. I just thought you were very busy is all, I suppose."

She picked at her plate with little interest. "Have you spoken to your parents?"

"About Thanksgiving?" he asked.

"Yes," she affirmed.

"I spoke to my mother. She thought that having dinner here would be a good idea."

"Were you planning on telling me?" she snapped.

Warren grew defensive. "Of course I planned on telling you." Beverly got up from the table and, with one quick jerk, emptied her plate into the trash can. She rinsed it off in the sink and placed it in the dish rack to dry. "Have I done something? Why are you upset?" he asked.

"I'm not upset," she said, as she busied herself with wiping down the countertops.

"Do you not want my parents to come? Because I thought you asked me to invite them."

She turned around to face him, leaning against the sink.

"No, Warren. Honestly, why would I be upset over that? Better here than at their home. At least if Keller breaks something it will be ours."

"Well, we agree on that," he responded sharply.

"Wonderful," she replied sarcastically.

Keller had apparently finished his dinner. He took the plate from the table and tossed it into the garbage, then went off to his bedroom. "Keller!" Beverly warned. Warren began to chuckle, which did not sit well with Beverly. "It's not funny, Warren," she cried as she retrieved the dish from the trash.

"Come on, Bev, snap out of it," he admonished as he cleared his own plate. "It's Monday; your favorite television program is on."

"That makes everything better."

"It does for a half an hour anyway." He gave her a peck on the cheek and went looking for his newspaper. As much as he loved his wife, he gladly sought refuge from her anger. It was rare for Beverly to be so out of sorts. He hoped that it would pass quickly. Although she was generally a very amicable person, when she was upset about something, she was impossible to live with.

He sat in his chair with the paper and contentedly read. At one point he heard Beverly giving Keller his bath. She didn't bother him again until her program was on. She brought a bowl of popcorn with her when she came from the other room. Warren hadn't even heard the popcorn popping. He folded his paper with a satisfied sigh and smiled as the *I Love Lucy* theme music began to play.

"This is a great show," he commented, taking a bite of the popcorn she offered him. Beverly sat quietly next to him with a stone face. Usually she very much enjoyed *I Love Lucy*. It was their Monday night ritual to watch the show. But this evening she was not laughing along with him. Warren noticed but chose not to respond to it. He thought that perhaps it would be easier to let it blow over. He had tried to talk to her at dinnertime and she had not wanted to talk then; maybe she had just had a bad day and it was best to let it go. Besides, he didn't want to miss the show.

The program went to commercial and he kept his eyes glued to the set. It was too much for Beverly to suffer through any longer. She got up to leave. At this point Warren felt that his hand had been forced. He saw her get up, saw her start to walk past him, and realized that his plan of ignoring it was not going to work. He grabbed her wrist before she had gotten past him. "Beverly, what's wrong? Don't you want to watch the program?"

"No. I just don't feel like it tonight."

He tugged on her arm until she was sitting next to him again. "Don't you want to talk to me about it? It might help to get it off your chest."

She looked him in the eyes for a moment and then asked, "Are you having an affair, Warren? Are you cheating on me?"

Warren was completely shocked and taken off guard. He sat with his mouth open but was unable to speak. "Are you kidding?"

"No, I'm not kidding. Why would I joke about something like that?"

"Why would you ever think that I was having an affair?"

"Why don't you just answer the question?"

"No, Bev, I'm not having an affair."

"Well, there you have it, case closed," came the sarcastic rebuttal.

"Beverly, I am not cheating on you. Who would I be having an affair with, and when would I have the time, for heaven sakes? When I'm not at work, I'm here."

"Miss Clark."

"She's my secretary."

"Oh, and I suppose men never have affairs with their secretaries. Fifty percent of men have affairs, and I bet you that a majority of them are doing it with their secretaries!"

"How do you know that fifty percent of men have affairs?"

"It was in *Time* magazine a few years ago, if you must know." She looked down sheepishly, avoiding his eyes. "It doesn't matter where I heard it from," she advised. "What matters is that you are being unfaithful to me."

"I never have been, Bev. I've never been unfaithful to you. Why would I want Miss Clark anyhow?"

"Because she's got the figure of Marilyn Monroe, Warren."

"Well, I'm no Joe Dimaggio, Bev. And I'm perfectly content with you." An amused smile played at his lips.

"I saw you," she accused.

"Saw me what?" He was completely confused and bewildered by her confrontation. He searched his brain for some clue as to where it was coming from. Nothing out of the ordinary came to mind.

"Through the window today, I saw you. She was touching your arm and laughing and batting her fake eyelashes at you. I saw it all. And you didn't seem to be objecting to it."

"Now, Beverly, she is my secretary and that is all. I have never touched the woman. Not once," he defended as he felt remorse creep through him. He did not want her to know that they had brushed hands, that his fingertips had rested on her shoulder. It was all innocent enough, he reasoned.

"Why didn't you stop it if there was nothing between you?" she asked. Beverly was seeking a genuine response, something that would help her wrap her mind around his motives. In all of their years of marriage she had never once been tempted by another man. So firm were her loyalties to her husband that she did not even feel comfortable alone with anyone of the opposite gender. Sitting with Warren now, knowing that he saw beauty in someone other than herself felt like the worst betrayal she had ever experienced.

"I love you, Bev. I swear I have never been with anyone else," he insisted.

"How can you say you love me if you want her? You can't love me and all the while want other women."

"I don't want Miss Clark." He took her face in his hands and forced her to make eye contact with him. She looked back with a somewhat shattered and defeated gaze. "I have never encouraged her in any way. I would never do that to you."

"You did encourage her, Warren. You encouraged her by never discouraging her. In my mind the only reason that you wouldn't have put a stop to it is because you liked it."

"Do you want me to fire her? Is that what you want? Would it prove my love for you if I went in tomorrow and told her that she should clear out and that I never wanted to see her again? Come on, Bev. You're a grown woman. You know very well that I can't just get rid of her because you saw her harmlessly flirting and you felt threatened by it."

Beverly, stung by his remarks, jumped from her seat, ready to retreat. The bowl of popcorn sailed from the couch, spilling across the floor. She stopped when she saw the mess she had made and bent to feverishly pick it up. Warren got to his knees and began to help her. His hand brushed hers as he raked the kernels up with his fingers.

"I don't need your help!"

He watched her briefly, as she fiercely scraped up the popcorn and flung it in the bowl. She seemed so pale and her face was strained. She appeared deeply hurt by what he had said. Warren felt ashamed of himself. Even if she was behaving like a goose, there was no need to treat her so harshly. "I'm sorry, Bev. I shouldn't have spoken to you like that."

"Do you want her?" Beverly stayed very still with her head down waiting for his reply, unable to look at him again, afraid that she might betray all that was riding upon the answer to that one little question.

"Of course I don't want her. She is my secretary and that is all."

"Why was she flirting with you then?"

"I think you must have misinterpreted her being friendly as her being a flirt, Bev. Nothing inappropriate has ever happened between the two of us. I'm sure she was just being nice."

"Just being nice? I am a woman. I know what I saw. I know what she wants. Women are not nice for no good reason. I should have guessed with the way she treated me. Who doesn't try to make a good impression on the boss's wife? But every time I come in she is cold and condescending, giving me sour faces. That should have been a major red flag."

"Don't you think you're being a little over sensitive?"

"No, I don't. And the fact that you don't seem to see it makes me very concerned."

"Beverly, you are the only woman I have ever wanted. You have nothing to worry about," he consoled.

"You'd do better with someone else. You know it . . . everyone knows it. I know it too," she cried. "If you hadn't married me, we wouldn't have had Keller. Your life would have been easier. It would have been better. You would have had respect. You would have had some pretty girl like Barbara Clark on your arm. Perhaps she could have given you children to be proud of."

"Don't talk like that. You're speaking nonsense and I won't hear it!" he scolded her with a severe and unyielding voice. He had grown tired of reasoning with her. Surely he had been patient long enough. "I love you. You're my wife and I love you. Now that's the end of it." Far from being comforting, it was an angry retort, defensive and meant to evoke a finality to the conversation.

"I am not finished speaking to you about this."

"Well I am," he told her, his resolve firm. He would not discuss it any further.

"How can you be so dismissive of me?" She got up from her crouching position on the floor in outrage and tried to leave the room. Again he attempted to stop her by holding on to her hand.

"You must know I am telling the truth . . ." he whispered, trying to pull her to him. "Please look at me, Beverly." He tried to hold her close, but she pushed away from him. "What is the matter with you?" he inquired with irritation laced in his verbalization.

"I'm pregnant," she blurted. "I'm pregnant!" she cried out in rage.

She saw Warren's stunned reaction as he tried to process what she had just confessed to him. For the second time that night he felt as if she had punched him in the stomach. Nothing made any sense. He just stood there with his intent gaze upon her, completely confounded by her admission.

"What?" he questioned, unsure that he had really heard what she was saying.

"I went to Dr. Stephens today. That's what I was in town for."

He shook his head, working the cobwebs from his brain. It took a moment for the shock to wear off before he came to his senses. "How far along?" he asked quietly.

"I don't know. You remember how difficult it was to get pregnant with Keller. My cycle is so irregular. The best Dr. Stephens could estimate, probably close to three months." Beverly could see that his mind was working hastily to try and register all that she was saying.

"It makes sense with how tired you've been. I suppose I should have seen it."

"I'm sorry," she cried. Warren realized that she was standing with her shoulders rounded and her arms crossed tightly against her chest, defensive and frightened. He went to her and tried to take her in his arms, cradling her against his chest. At first she remained stiff and unyielding, but the comfort of his embrace broke her resolve, and she sagged against him, weeping.

"It's all right, Beverly. It isn't really that bad is it?" he consoled.

"I can't do it. I just can't do it."

"We always wanted a big family. Do you remember when we were first married and you said that you wanted ten?" He realized that he was grasping at straws, but he did not know what to do for her.

"That was before Keller. What will I do? I just can't take anymore!"

"It will work out, darling. I promise."

"How can you make such a promise? What if we have another retarded child? I couldn't stand it; I just couldn't stand it." That was the first thought that had occurred to him. He didn't have to be told that it was a possibility. "What will people say?"

"It doesn't matter what they say. It's going to be all right, Beverly."

She stopped crying and looked at him with wrath burning in her eyes. "I'm tired of believing that it will be all right. It's not all right. Nothing is ever right," she spat. "I suppose I've lived long enough to figure that out. A few times around the block and you start to wise up."

"Do you not want it?" His question cut her to the quick. It was something that she had been asking herself since she had first suspected that there might be a baby growing inside of her. There was no definitive answer. Beverly had tried so hard to talk herself into believing that it wasn't true, that she was just being paranoid. Now more than anything she only felt afraid.

"What if we have another baby like Keller?"

"What if we have a baby that is perfectly healthy?"

She could not respond. Everything seemed so surreal. How could this have happened, and why? Keller took every ounce of energy, every last bit of her strength. She could not fathom how she would cope with two. There was no movement within, no protruding belly to convince her that it was really real, no tangible evidence that this baby was nothing more than a misunderstanding. Perhaps it was all some terrible mistake. She pressed her face into Warren's chest and cried herself out. Warren waited for a good long time, until he was sure that she was finished. "It's not so bad, is it?"

"I want this baby," she croaked. "I just don't want . . ."

"You'll see, Bev. It will be all right." He grinned like a kid on Christmas day. "We're going to have a baby." His voice sounded eager and excited. It was more than Beverly had thought to hope for. She had suspected that he would be disappointed, maybe even angry. When they had discovered Keller would never be like other children, they had discussed at length what they should do. One of their pacts had been not to have more children.

"I'm so frightened, Warren."

"No," he soothed, kissing her softly, trying to reassure her with his physical contact. "There's no need to be. God knows what he is doing." Somehow when he touched her the world was good. For that moment in time his caresses were all that

47

mattered, and her life, with all of its disillusionment, did not exist. She didn't care about anything but the here and now with him.

Perhaps he was right, she reasoned. Perhaps God *had* played a part in it. In her youth, faith in God had come easily. It seemed logical to believe that he knew her, that he had known her in some ageless, timeless place before this one. In her mind she saw him as a father that clung to her every word, just as she might if Keller would only speak to her. It wasn't until the horrors of life had battered her that she let doubts creep in. An all-powerful God that controlled her destiny gave her hope, gave her a reason to go on, was a comforting concept. But more and more, questions began to cloud her mind, toy with her reasoning. Who was she? Why was she here? What was her purpose? How would it all work out in the end? When she prayed, these were the concerns that spilled from her lips to the mysterious God that dwelt in the outer reaches of heaven.

Now there would be a new plea to send up to him in her petitions. *Please let this child be whole. Please let this child be fit, with a sound mind.* This gave her comfort as she drifted to sleep that night. Surely he would hear her imploring and grant her this earnest request.

four

Beverly was squeezing juice from oranges on the pointed dome of her juicer when Warren came in to breakfast. He slipped in behind her, caressing his hand over her stomach. She noticed that he was in an especially good mood and unable to keep a smile from his face. "Good morning," he whispered against her tangled hair. She felt confusion well up inside of her and did not readily respond to his affection. How could they have such a terrible fight, how could he be so harsh with her, and then act as if nothing had happened the very next day.

"Good morning," she replied, without the usual warmth in her voice. If Warren noticed it, he did not act as though he had. Sitting at the table next to Keller, he gave him a pat on the shoulder. The dark-haired boy was eating his eggs contentedly. Beverly emptied the juice into a small juice glass and set it in front of her husband. The toast jumped out of the toaster, brown and hot. Retrieving it, with minimal contact of her fingertips, she buttered it before cutting it into triangles, and arranged the pieces on Warren's plate with his scrambled eggs. Before taking it to the table, she grabbed the ketchup for him.

He clapped his hands together and rubbed them vigorously. "This looks just wonderful."

"It's the same breakfast you have nearly every day," she informed him.

"And yet it looks divine," he said with a nod of his head. "Has anyone ever told you that you have a way with eggs, Beverly?"

"What a strange sort of man you are, Warren Vance. I don't know if I'll ever figure you out."

"Of the two of us, sweetheart, I am the least complex," he replied with a grin, as he bit into his toast heartily. "Can't a guy be happy?"

Keller got up from the table and promptly threw his plate away, as he had done before. "Kel, you get that plate out of the trash can and put it in the sink," she commanded. He turned around, grabbed the plate, and tossed it with a clatter into the sink. "Thank you. That's a good boy." He took off toward the living room before he was required to do anything else. Beverly sighed deeply. "Do you honestly believe this baby is going to survive him?"

"I don't think you'd let him throw it away, if that's what your getting at," he jested.

"I'm being perfectly serious," Beverly said, shaking her head at him.

"You survived with your big brother. And countless others have throughout the ages as well," was his counsel.

"My brother was not Bluto. Not to mention he was quite a bit older when I was born."

"If you're really that concerned, we'll get him a doll baby and practice with him."

"That's a wonderful idea. I'm surprised that I didn't think of it first," she teased.

"Well, now, Bev, when it comes to doll babies, I know my stuff," he admonished with a thoughtful shrug.

"I knew I married you for a reason."

Warren caught a glimpse of the wall clock. "Say, I'm late. Barry is going to be waiting for me." He jumped up from his chair as if a fire had been lit under him. Beverly stopped him with an insistent tug on his sleeve as he tried to head out of the kitchen. Her face was troubled. He stopped and looked down upon her with a soft expression.

"You won't tell anyone?"

He gave her a questioning glance. "I don't see why not."

"I don't want people to know."

"They're bound to discover it eventually, Bev. Soon enough you won't be able to hide it." He glanced down at her mid section.

"Can't we just keep it between the two of us for now?"

He bent down and gave her a quick kiss. "Our secret," he promised. "Now I really must go. Barry is probably hitching a ride by now." Warren lunged for the table, grabbed the last piece of toast on his plate, and dashed out the door.

Barry had waited as long as he could and then took it upon himself to meet Warren at his home. When Warren came out the front door, his neighbor was leaning against the car, eager to leave. "Morning, Warren," he said pushing himself off of the car.

"Morning, Barry. Sorry."

"I was hoping nothing bad had happened."

"Needn't worry about me. Just running late as usual." Warren unlocked the door on the passenger's side and then went around to get in himself. As he pulled out of the driveway, he spotted Keller standing solemnly in the window. He waved to the boy, but Keller remained statuesque, only moving his eyes as he followed the car down the street, until it disappeared from his view.

Barry was quite a talker and always filled the short time in the car with his rants about politics. Warren had never been one much for political strategies. He voted when it was required, reading up on the candidates so that he could make an informed decision, but nothing had ever driven him to choose a party or an allegiance merely because it was the popular thing to do or because he was Democrat or Republican. Barry's political diatribes bored him. However, Warren was very careful never to show it. He sat quietly nodding his head in agreement every now and then, throwing in a comment here and there so that Barry felt that his pious speeches had found fertile soil in which he could sow his seeds.

Warren preferred the political babble much more than he cared for Barry's other talk. When the conversation turned to women or minority groups, Barry could get downright ugly in a downward slope of tactless oration. It was almost humorous if not so pathetic. Barry, Warren surmised, was more often than not just repeating phrases and words or tidbits of dialogues that he had heard others say. While he would much rather drive by himself, Bev needed the car to get out on occasion, and it helped with the gas as well. He thought he was lucky that anyone had even agreed to ride with him. Very few folks in the neighborhood had even tried to get to know him and Beverly.

It hadn't always been that way, he reflected bitterly. When they had first moved in as newlyweds, the red carpet had been rolled out for them. Several years later, they had Keller. They had gotten their share of dinners and gifts and congratulations at the unveiling of their firstborn. Keller seemed so normal in the beginning, quiet and easy tempered, a beautiful baby that they had considered a blessing. He was quick to smile and giggle. He had appeared to develop just as he should. His little body was round and solid, the pride of his father. It wasn't until he was nearly two that Beverly began to worry. Warren had dismissed her fears. Everyone told him that boys didn't talk as soon as girls. They all presented story after story as evidence that it was so.

As Keller grew older, Warren was forced to admit that Beverly was right. All was not well with their little son. They took him to several doctors before one of them had the fortitude to say that their once bright-eyed little boy was mentally retarded. He would not take over the family business; he would not be the star football player. He would not graduate from high school, go on to college, marry a sweetheart, or give them grandchildren. At that point Dr. Stephens had encouraged Beverly and Warren to put Keller in an institution. He had told them that many couples who had children with such handicaps did that very thing. They should not have to suffer for an unfortunate mistake on Nature's part. Keller would only be a burden to them, and the hospital up in Fort Wayne had professionals that were equipped to deal with him.

Neither Beverly nor Warren would hear of it. Keller was three by then, and as disturbing as his behaviors could be, they could not stand the thought of letting him go. He was their only child, their whole world, their very flesh and blood. It took some time before Warren could discuss it with anyone. Most everybody they knew had already figured it out. But Warren had to tell his parents and Beverly had to tell her father about the doctor's official diagnosis. As Keller grew older and increasingly difficult, more and more of their friends grew more and more distant.

Warren hadn't taken the brunt of it either. He regarded his wife with much esteem for what she dealt with on a daily basis. Sure he had moments when Kel had embarrassed him, but generally he was with his son at home. Any time Beverly needed to run errands or go out, Keller went with her. There had been more than one occasion when she had been devastated by something that someone had said or done. People could be downright cruel and insensitive. There were also those who did not understand Keller's situation. He looked so normal, and when he acted out or misbehaved they considered it the fault of the parent who allowed him to carry on so. They hurt Beverly out of ignorance.

Warren reflected upon the last three years, and he conceded that in some ways it had gotten easier, but it had gotten more difficult as well. Keller had grown in size. He was a very big boy for his age. This had caused quite a few problems for them. They could no longer pick him up and put him in his room if he became unruly or got out of hand.

There was also the aggression. He could become very angry very quickly. Warren was the only one who could physically handle him when he was in an all out tantrum. He kicked, pinched, bit, scratched, and threw things. Overall, he was generally an easygoing fellow that took care of his own needs to the best of his ability. Keller enjoyed cuddling and being close to his parents. He loved animals and was very gentle with them. But when he got set off over something, it was war. How this would mesh with a new baby, Warren could not fathom.

Warren saw the courthouse and slowed down, pulling up next to the curb to let Barry out. He had been lost in his own thoughts the entire ride to work, but Barry had not seemed to notice, assuming that Warren had been hanging on to his every word about the state of the country and the economic impact that was a result of good management on the part of President Eisenhower. Warren gave him a wave as he climbed out of the car.

"See you this afternoon."

"Yeah, thanks, Warren." Barry shut the door as Warren pulled away.

Miss Clark was shuffling through the filing cabinet when Warren came through the door of his building. She looked slightly ruffled, unlike her normally composed self. When she made eye contact with him, she motioned with a nod of her head toward his office, divided from the rest of the room by panels of frosted white glass. The door was open and she felt that she could not speak candidly to him. She discreetly whispered, "The elder Mr. Vance." She motioned for him to come to her.

He leaned in, "Yes?"

"You have crumbs on your lapel," she giggled. And she softly brushed the toast crumbs from his suit jacket, lingering for a moment. "Now you're presentable," she said a little breathlessly. "Very handsome."

Warren straightened, gave her a reassuring smile, and headed in. His father sat at the desk, browsing over several files that Miss Clark had pulled for him. He looked up when his son came through the door. "Hello, there, son. Good to see you."

"Hello, Father." He was leaning against the door jam with his hands formed into fists in his pants pockets. "I hope you're finding everything in order."

"For the most part," he assented. "You do things a little differently than I do, but I don't suppose you care to know how I would do it," he observed dryly. "Still, it all seems completed and all of the paperwork is up to date." He cleared his throat and leaned back in the chair, putting his hands behind his head. "Thought I would just drop in and see how you were coming along."

"And . . ."

"How's that property on Piccadilly?"

"Had a few nibbles but it's not sold yet."

"That's a good location; it should go fast."

"Hopefully," Warren said. The elder Mr. Vance owned Vance & Son, hence the name. He was now in a somewhat retired state. He had not given the business over to Warren yet, although it was in his will that his only child would inherit it upon his demise. Warren had worked with him for several years, learning the ins and outs of it before his father had decided to enjoy his old age and turn everything over to his son, go golfing and fishing, maybe travel a little. He dropped in every now and again to check on things, to keep himself busy.

His continued interest in the real estate business stemmed from the fact that he was finding out the hard way that it was very difficult to fill all the hours in a day with nothing but golf and fishing. It hurt him to be out of the loop, feeling it deep in his bones that old age brought the inevitable sense of worthlessness and decay. Gone were the days when his voice mattered, when his name brought him respect, when life was filled with countless possibilities, and many young women found him irresistible. It hadn't occurred to Warren that the elder Vance was restless and unfulfilled. He surmised that his father's impromptu visits were more to catch him off guard than anything. He did not feel that his father had very much confidence in his abilities to run the place.

Over his thirty-five years of living, he had grown used to his father's apparent disapproval. In his youth it had pushed him to succeed at all costs. But as Warren became an adult, he understood he would never fully please the man. Serving in the war had done much to make him realize that his father's acceptance was not the most crucial factor in his life. Getting home in one piece became the ultimate goal. How disappointed the old man must be in the fact that he had only one offspring, and that child was never good enough. Warren reasoned that he wasn't the only one who had failed the expectations of the man that sat before him. His mother, too, had suffered the same fate. Although he could not remember what she was like when he was very young, Warren was sure that she was not the woman she had become in her middle and later years.

From his earliest memories, his parents had slept in separate bedrooms. When he discovered exactly how babies were made, it was no surprise to him that he was their only child. They did not speak to one another, preferring to live outside of one another's worlds. His mother had turned to social functions, causes, and chasing cocktails one after another. His father pursued sports, work, and redheads. If nothing else, his parents' marriage was a learning experience that had taught Warren exactly what not to do. He had fashioned himself and his behaviors to be anything but what his parents were. Warren knew that their unhappiness was a product of their lifestyles.

Warren studied the man behind his desk. Many people had said that they resembled one another. Perhaps in some respects it was true. They both carried themselves with confidence, squaring their broad shoulders when they walked. Jonathan Vance once possessed the same dark hair, although he was now gray. The two had mirrored steel blue eyes. His father was thicker now than he had been in his youth, yet still fit, and his face was full of the character an older man earns with time. And yet, Warren had a bit of his mother in him too. His full lips and square jawline had come from her. He had unnaturally long and curly eyelashes for a man and a softness to his face that made him very attractive, a masculine beauty.

Truth be told, he was much better looking than his father had ever been. In part the startling contrast may have been explained by Warren's kindhearted nature compared to his father's domineering and manipulative make-up. The elder Mr. Vance might have thrived businesswise by making others insecure, but Warren had grown out of such intimidations. It amused him now to see Jonathan Vance inspecting him and his work in an attempt to illicit the feeling of inferiority from him.

"How are you and Mother doing?"

"Fine, fine."

"I spoke to Mother the other day. It seems you will be having Thanksgiving dinner at our home this year," he informed his father.

"Your mother mentioned that."

"Beverly is quite the cook, as you know. I'm sure she'll do it justice."

Jonathan Vance glanced up with a supercilious grin. "How *is* Beverly . . . and the boy?" He added the last part as if it were an afterthought.

"Faring well."

"That's good to hear." There was an uncomfortable pause before Jonathan hauled himself out of the chair and straightened his tie. "I'm sitting in your chair. I should get out of your way so that you can get some work done. Ten minutes late and now I'm taking up your time." It did not pass Warren's attention that his father had documented his tardiness this morning. "Hope you're not late like that every day."

"Only on the days that you come in, Father."

Jonathan Vance chuckled as if he were amused, although he was not. He approached Warren and stuck out his hand for a handshake.

"Well, I'll be out of your hair, then."

"It was good of you to stop by." Warren grasped his hand firmly. "I'll see you in a few weeks for Thanksgiving."

"Will do," Jonathan nodded.

"Tell Mother I said hello."

"I'll tell her."

Warren could hear his father stopping to talk to Miss Clark in the lobby area. He was charming and generous with women, especially younger women. It was at these moments that he could understand why his mother had fallen in love with the man. He could never see it when they were actually together. The front door closed, and a few moments later Barbara Clark was tapping at his open door.

"Yes, Miss Clark?"

"I'm sorry. I didn't know that he would be in today."

"Think nothing of it. He may come and go as he pleases. I was not put off by it."

"Would you like me to put those files back?" she offered.

"That would be good of you," Warren agreed. She moved across the room effortlessly, bent over the desk, and began to collect the files. Warren glanced up and caught sight of her cleavage as her blouse hung low. He quickly averted his eyes, feeling slightly ashamed. The discussion he had with Beverly yesterday night replayed itself. She would be livid if she were here now to witness this scene.

"Just shut the door behind you," he directed as she left to take the files back to the filing cabinet.

"Of course, Mr. Vance." She gently pulled the door closed, leaving him finally alone.

*   *   *

Beverly washed the dishes in the sink and placed them in the dish rack to dry, periodically looking out the window to check on Keller in the backyard. He was spinning around and around. It amazed her that Keller could seem to do it indefinitely without getting dizzy or sick. He got tired of it and tumbled to the ground laughing. She laughed too. Whenever he showed any emotion she clung to it. Once she had finished with the dishes, she dried her hands on a kitchen towel, giving a quick look out the window again. Her heart stopped. Keller was nowhere to be seen.

Breaching the back door in a rush, she surveyed the backyard but still could not locate him. She dashed around to the front. He was not there, either. Frantically she took her search through the neighborhood, calling out his name. She realized there must be people watching the scene through their windows in scorn. But no one came to her aid. How could she have lost a child? Dread seeped into all of her senses when she could not immediately find him. It had only been a few minutes when she finally spotted Keller, rolling around on the ground with the Hartfords' dog, but it seemed like an eternity. Beverly exhaled deeply, wondering how long she had been holding her breath.

"Keller!" She reached down and hauled him up, marching home with him. "You mustn't leave like that. You frightened poor Mama." He was happily oblivious to her lecture. "Come along home now."

When she got into sight of the house, Margaret Price was pulling into the driveway. *I suppose I can't act as if I'm not at home,* Beverly thought to herself. *She's already seen me.* She approached the car warily, unsure of what would transpire. Margaret had never just stopped by like this. What purpose would she have in doing so? She got out of the car, looking impressive in a pale yellow dress with a fitted bodice and a full skirt. She put Beverly's pedal pushers, gingham blouse, and ballet flats to shame. Beverly realized ruefully that she was still wearing her apron. In her fevered search for Keller she had not taken it off.

"Hello, Beverly. I'm glad to see that you are home."

"Margaret, what a surprise," Beverly said, instantly wary and wondering what this visit was all about.

"May I come in?" Margaret requested.

"Of course you may," she replied, opening the door for her. Margaret ducked down into her car and pulled out a plate of cookies. She followed Beverly into the house with polite patience.

"Cookies!" Keller chirped in excitement. Beverly held him at bay until Margaret extended the plate to him.

"I brought cookies. It's not much, but I thought that Keller might like them. I have something else for you too," she told Keller, reaching in to her handbag. She pulled out a box of Cracker Jacks and handed them to the boy.

"That was very kind of you, Margaret. You didn't need to go to all that trouble," she said as she accepted the plate from the woman. Keller grabbed the box from her with a hungry and excited look in his eyes. "Won't you have a seat?" Beverly offered.

Margaret sat on the peacock blue sofa and waited for Beverly to take a seat. "I suppose I should have telephoned first," Margaret commented.

"Oh, no, Margaret, you're welcome any time you'd like to drop in." She studied the older woman's face to try and get some sort of perception of what her errand was all about. Margaret was nearly forty-five now, but she looked younger. She kept up on coloring her hair and wore all of the latest styles. She also had a nice figure, which Beverly reasoned would be easy if one did not have children.

"I just felt so badly about the way that things went the other day. I wanted to stop by and make sure that you weren't still upset over it." Keller was dumping the contents of the box onto the carpet, looking frantically for the prize that was surely in every box.

"That was very thoughtful, but to be honest I don't think that I will ever get over it," Beverly replied as she fidgeted with the ruffle on the edge of her apron. "I shouldn't have brought Keller along, you see. I could just have died when he broke your china. I wouldn't have had it happen for anything."

"Why, I know that, Beverly. It was an accident. You're far too concerned over it. Look at him. He's innocent as a babe," she said, motioning to Keller who was riffling through the box of caramel-covered popcorn. "He didn't know what he was doing. How could I be angry over such a thing?"

"I just wish that I could fix it somehow, but I couldn't possible replace your grandmother's dishes. Warren wants to pay for them of course, although I'm sure that is small consolation."

"Beverly, I won't hear of it. That is not why I came. I just wanted you to know that there are no hard feelings and that you and Keller must come back to visit me again sometime."

This surprised Beverly. Was Margaret insane? Did she not understand what a risk she would be taking if she were to have Keller back in her home? She couldn't figure what Margaret's reasoning might be for extending such a generous offer. "I don't know if that is such a good idea. It is generous of you to say so, but I don't think that Keller understands how to behave as a guest in someone else's home. It's beyond him."

"Of course he doesn't, dear. He is a child, after all."

"That's not what I mean," Beverly tried to clarify. "He makes people uncomfortable and he breaks things. It's all I can do to control him when we are out. He's not like that as much here. I suppose it would just be best if I kept him home. I know that's what everyone expects."

"Well, he certainly doesn't make me uncomfortable," Margaret insisted. On cue, Keller threw the Cracker Jack box and began to moan and wail. He had not touched the actual popcorn and peanuts. It was the prize which he had centered his attention on. Unfortunately it turned out to be nothing but a ring, which was no good to Keller. He tossed it aside, in obvious disappointment.

"Elephant?" he cried, shaking the box to make sure that it was empty. He sat next to Margaret and pointed at her purse waiting expectantly.

"I haven't got any more," she said, unsure of what she should do next.

"I'm sorry, Margaret. He doesn't understand. He got a box of Cracker Jacks once and it had a little toy elephant in it. Now every time he gets a box he thinks that it should have an elephant." Beverly turned her attention to Keller. "No, Keller, she doesn't have any more. That's all there is."

He looked at Margaret for a moment, apparently thinking hard before he sat next to her, like a diligent suitor, giving her a kiss before he held out his hand. "Cookie, pwease," he begged.

"Oh, Keller. You need to clean up the mess you've made," Beverly commanded, referring to the pile of Cracker Jacks he had left on the floor.

Keller was not to be deterred. He cuddled up close to Margaret patting her hand. "I want cookie, pwease. Good boy!"

Margaret was amused. She laughed at his ploy. "Can't he

have just one? It couldn't hurt. After all he is a good boy."

Beverly was defeated. She picked a cookie from the plate and handed it to Keller, who eagerly took it from her hand before she could change her mind. He was off in a flash, hiding away while he enjoyed his sweets. "I should put these away before he comes back for more," she said, removing the plate of cookies from the sofa table.

"I shouldn't keep you, Beverly. I just felt that I should come by to let you know that I expect you *and* Keller to come the next time I invite you over. I won't take no for an answer."

"Thank you, Margaret." Beverly trailed her to the door. She stopped Margaret before she could leave. "You don't know what it means to have someone be so good to me. You are such a true friend."

"I don't do nearly enough, Beverly," she replied.

Beverly was near tears. "You do more than anyone else. Thank you for the cookies and the Cracker Jacks. You went to so much trouble."

"I didn't go to that much trouble," she confessed. "I bought them at the bakery." The two women laughed together, and then Margaret retreated to the driveway, climbed into her car, and was gone.

After dinner that evening, Warren finished reading his paper and folded it neatly, setting it on the floor next to his chair. He stretched out, yawning and rubbing his face. He looked over at Beverly, who was intently making stitches into a piece of fabric she held close to her eyes. "You need glasses, Bev."

"I do not. I can see just fine."

"What are you working on there?"

"I'm making an elephant for Keller," she retorted.

"Let's see it."

She held it up for his inspection. It was a simple outline of the profile of an elephant, with a U-shaped trunk and two stick-looking legs. She had carefully sewn around the edges and stuffed it with batting. With embroidery thread she had stitched an eye and an ear, as well as a tail. It was small enough that Keller could carry it around with him, even slip it in his pocket if he wanted to.

"What do you think?"

"I think that's a swell idea. One of your better ones."

"Good."

"How was your day?" he asked.

"Keller ran off down the street. I found him at the Hartfords'. He so loves that dog."

"I suppose we know where he'll be if he drops out of sight."

"It nearly scared me to death. What if he had really been lost? He couldn't tell anyone his name or where he lives or who his parents are. It panicked me to think what might have become of him." She continued to diligently work on the elephant as she spoke. "We might never have seen him again."

"Well, it all worked out. No need worrying yourself so."

"When I got back to the house, who do you suppose should pull up into the driveway?"

"I don't know."

"Margaret Price," Beverly stated emphatically. She stuck her finger with the needle and yelped. She sucked on it for a moment and then went on with her story. "She brought a plate of cookies."

"Cookies. Where are they?"

"They're in the bread box."

Warren was confused. "Why in the bread box?"

"Because, if Keller had found them, he would have eaten every last one of them." She put the sewing down and got up from the sofa. "Would you like me to get you one?"

"Bring a couple and a glass of milk, please."

She was gone for a moment but returned with the requested cookies and milk. "Will this do?" she asked, a bit on the sarcastic side.

"That's great. Thank you, Bev."

"It was really quite nice of her."

"I'll say," he agreed with his mouth full. "These are really very good."

"She wanted me to know that she wasn't upset over the china, and she told me that Keller and I are welcome in her home any time."

"I always did like her."

"I just don't understand why she's so nice to me. No one else is. They all behave like Kel has something contagious. I was terrified that she would never speak to me again after what he had done. She had every right not to. Why do you suppose she wants to be *my* friend?"

"Why wouldn't she?"

"Warren, if you haven't noticed, no one else is waiting in line to associate with us. As nice as she is, she still could be just nice and not go out of her way to befriend me. It simply doesn't make sense. Still, I suppose I shouldn't complain. She isn't angry at me, anyway."

"I'm glad that it went well."

"I am too. I was prepared to never show my face at church again. I'll presume for now that all is well."

"I had an unexpected visitor myself."

"Who's that, darling?" Beverly questioned, curiosity peaked.

"My father," Warren told her.

"He was at the office?" she asked.

"Yes. Dropped by to check in on things," Warren reported to her as he rolled his eyes. She laughed at his face.

"After all, the world might stop turning on its axis if Jonathan Vance weren't dictating to it how to spin," Beverly quipped.

"My father has always been a mystery to me. I suppose he's used to being a very important person. It's difficult for him to let the reins go to someone else. I think he secretly misses having so much to juggle. It forces him to have to deal with Mother. He was able to avoid her for all those years before he quit working."

"How did the two of them ever fall in love?" she wondered.

"That is something I have asked myself many times," he said.

"You didn't tell him about the baby?" she pressed, growing flustered at the prospect.

"I told you I wouldn't. I do think that Thanksgiving would

be a good time to do it. They'll be upset if we keep it from them for too long. Are you going to call your father?"

"I don't know. He is very busy."

"Beverly, he'll want to know," Warren advised her.

"Will he?" she asked elusively.

"You haven't spoken to him in quite some time."

"And he hasn't seemed to notice." She grew frustrated with the needle and thread that she was working with and tossed the project into her sewing basket. "What does it matter to you if I speak to him or not anyhow?" He remained silent, thinking it best not to push the subject. "His new family keeps him occupied. What does he need to hear from me for?"

She was twelve when her mother died. Her father had remarried within the year. She had bitter memories of her mother being sick, of her constant pleas for help. She had endured for a very long time before she finally passed away. Her father had always been so generous to Beverly, trying to make up for her inconvenient life. Beverly had felt very close to him, as if they were in it together, until he met a woman, someone that he grew to lean on. Eventually Beverly came to feel that there was no place for her; she had been replaced.

Warren knew that his wife still carried this heavy burden. He rarely spoke of it because of the grief it caused her. While he felt that she should find a way to come to peace with it, he kept his opinion to himself, choosing instead to let her sort it out on her own. There was silence between the two of them until she picked up her sewing again and calmly began to stitch.

"How long did your father stay?"

"Not long. Long enough to aptly point out that I was late and that I was not doing things the way that he would have if he were still working."

"And how is our dear Miss Clark?"

Warren grew cool. "I wouldn't know; I hardly spoke to her. I was very preoccupied."

"Does it make you angry that I asked?"

"Yes, quite frankly it does." He got up and left the room.

Beverly watched him go and felt a pang of conscience. Perhaps she should apologize, but then she reasoned, what for? She was only making sure that what was hers stayed hers. No Barbara Clark was going to charm her way into Warren's arms. *He's my husband,* Beverly thought possessively. *Mine.* It took a lot of nerve for that girl to try and steal another woman's husband, a lot of nerve. She was certainly old enough to know better. A good girl would never behave so brazenly. She finished the elephant before turning out the lights and heading for bed.

five

After painstakingly perusing the pages of the Sears and Roebuck catalog, Beverly had settled upon a doll for Keller. There were several to choose from, dolls that were big and small and all of the accessories that went along with them. While she had not played with toys for many years, she enjoyed looking through the selection. The Nancy doll wore a Swiss dotted dress and had a batch of realistic looking hair upon its head. She carefully filled out the order form and sent away for it.

When her order was delivered through the mail several weeks later, Beverly inspected it with delight. She gently lifted the Nancy doll out of its packaging, stroking its smooth face. The smell of the new plastic filled her nostrils. She straightened its little red and white dress before she went to look for Keller. He was sitting quietly on his bed, playing with the elephant that she had made for him.

"Kel, look what Mama has," she said, extending the doll to him. He accepted it, scrutinizing it carefully. He lifted the skirt to see what was underneath, touched its hair with his index finger, then tossed it unceremoniously onto the floor. Beverly picked it up and tried to hand it back to him. "Keller, don't you want to hold the baby?"

"Nope," he cried, pushing the doll away from him.

"Hold the baby, Keller," Beverly insisted. He got up from his bed and ran from the room to avoid being pressed any further.

When Warren returned home from work, he appeared very tired. He sat down heavily on the couch and loosened his tie. Beverly removed his shoes from his feet and sat down on the floor next to him. He gave her a smile. He was noticing how lovely she looked. Every now and again it struck him, as if for the first time, how lucky he was. She was a Helen of Troy, intoxicating to the point that he would do anything for her. He wondered how married people could grow tired of one another. Beverly had always possessed the ability to hold his interest and keep him coming back for more. She was interesting and often unpredictable. It had become a habit of hers to never choose the same thing on a menu more than once. She reasoned that if she didn't try other things she would never know if it was her favorite or not. She was complex, but just enough so that it was entertaining and not a put off. It was a challenge to him to figure her out.

"I was just remembering the first time I saw you," he told her playfully.

"Really?" She was a little surprised but very interested.

"You were sitting under a tree on campus, reading a book, and a single ray of sunlight had found its way through the leaves. It shone down on you like you were an angel, something not of this world. I saw those rays of light upon you and I thought to myself, if this is the proverbial light bulb, she must be a terrific idea."

"You're crazy, Warren," she teased, although she could not hide the pleasure she felt at his description of that day.

"Possibly," he agreed with a smile playing at his lips. "But you've never seemed to mind."

Keller heard the sound of his father's voice and came running. Before Warren could guard himself, Keller sprung on his father. "Daddy, Daddy!" Warren grunted as the full eighty pounds landed square on his gut. It took him a moment to recover.

"Keller, you must be careful," Beverly scolded.

"And how is our young Keller?" Warren asked as he moved over to let the boy sit next to him.

"The doll didn't go over like I had hoped," Beverly informed him.

"No? You didn't like the doll, Kel?" Keller was fiddling with Warren's neck tie and did not respond to his question.

"He wouldn't have a thing to do with it."

"Well, he's a boy. Perhaps he just did not want to play with a doll. He probably found it insulting. Boys don't play with dolls, do they, Kel?"

"What do you mean? It was your idea," she said accusingly.

"I'm the first to admit my folly. Next time we'll get you a baseball glove, Keller. Would you like that? Would you like to learn to play baseball?" he asked rubbing Keller's thick hair affectionately.

"Well, how do you like that? I thought we were going to show him how to care for a baby, Warren."

"It will be fine, Bev. Stop worrying so." He playfully tickled Keller again, who laughed loudly. He tried to mimic his father and, not so gently, tickled him back. "Keller, where is your elephant?" Keller jumped up and disappeared down the hallway. He returned shortly with the elephant in hand looking proud as he showed it to Warren. "Did Mama make that for you?"

Keller offered it to his father. "Elephant," he replied earnestly.

"Yes it is, son." He handed it back to Keller, who sat down next to Warren once again and contentedly held the elephant in his hand, running a finger over the eye and the ear stitches, reverently.

"He really loves that elephant, Bev. That was a swell idea."

"I'm glad you approve." She waited for a moment, her brain working furiously to try and figure out how to broach the next subject she was stewing over. "I was hoping that I could go to town alone on Saturday," she stated nonchalantly.

"What for?"

"Thanksgiving is in two weeks, and, well, I was hoping to get some clothing to wear."

"You don't think you could properly try things on with Keller in tow?" he teased.

"Would it be too much trouble? I haven't got any maternity things. I got rid of it all. And even if I hadn't, Keller is nearly six, they'd be out of fashion by now."

"I suppose we could swing it. Would you like to spend the day with your old man, son?" Warren asked, draping his arm around Keller's small shoulders. Keller snuggled in to him, still gazing down upon his elephant without the slightest indication that he had heard his father's question.

"I think he would prefer to spend the day with you over me any time. He gets tired of me. You're always fun. I'm always making him wash his hands, and comb his hair, and all of the other things that he hates to do."

"Oh, Bev, the two of us couldn't survive without you."

"So you say," she scoffed.

"Don't be so jaded, darling," he joked.

"If you would like dinner you mustn't upset the cook. Otherwise it will be leftovers for the two of you."

"I'll try and keep that in mind."

"Speaking of which, do you have any requests for dinner? I am too spent to think of anything with my own brain. My creativity has gone right out the window," she told him, standing up and stretching. "Keep in mind I haven't been to the butcher in a week."

"Let's just go get a hamburger. Maybe Keller will let us go to the drive-in. Are you too tired to catch a movie?" he offered.

"I am tired, but never too tired to see a movie." She was actually relieved by his suggestion. She never felt that it was her place to propose such a thing. She knew that Warren, quite often, did not want to go out again once he was home from work. She also knew that it cost money. They did not have any real issues with their budget, but Beverly felt somewhat inferior to her husband when it came to financial decisions because he brought home the paycheck and she did not. He had allocated what her spending should be for groceries and other such necessities and she had stuck to it precisely. This was the reason that she had asked so reluctantly to purchase new clothing.

Warren did not put much stock into such things. He dressed with conservative taste, wearing suits that were not top of the line or made by a tailor, but they were of good quality and professional looking. He knew that his image was important in his line of work, but he never went overboard. In truth, he felt that Beverly was far too concerned with such matters. Still, he liked to please her and he rarely commented on the subject. As much as Warren did not like to spend his pay on such frivolities, he took pride in her appearance when she was about town. He wanted others to know that he took good care of her, that she had all of the things she wanted and needed.

"Let me just get Keller's shoes and we can go," she offered. "I might need to run a brush through my hair. I probably look a fright." She rushed off to her tasks.

She returned shortly, carrying Keller's shoes in her hand. Bending down, she helped him put them on, double tying the shoe strings. The three of them piled into the car and set out on their adventure. When Warren pulled up to the McDonald's, he was good and hungry. He parked the car and got out, walking to the window to order. He was on his way back to the car, brown paper bags in hand, when he heard someone call out his name.

"Warren, Warren Vance?"

Mildly surprised, he looked about to see who was calling for him. Before he could determine who it was, a strong hand clapped on his shoulder. Warren spun around quickly, feeling a little caught off guard, until he saw who it was. "Ron!"

"Well, it's been a good long while, old boy."

"Yes, it has. What a surprise to see you here," Warren said with a grin.

"Where have you been keeping yourself?"

"Oh, I've been about," he offered weakly. "Keeping busy."

"Are you still working at your father's place?"

"Yes, I am. I've been running it for nearly four years now."

"How is Beverly?"

"She's good," he offered without much conviction. Warren was inwardly hoping that Ron would not be asking any more questions. He had not seen his friend since shortly after he and Beverly had gotten married. It would be easier if Ron did not know about Keller, he reasoned.

"Well, is she here with you?"

There it was. The words fell on his ears like a death sentence. He couldn't avoid it now. "Yeah, she's . . . uh, she's in the car over there," he replied with a nervous chuckle, motioning over to where the car was parked. He pointedly did not offer to escort him over to talk to her.

"I have to go say hello." Ron trotted over to the red Dodge Cornet, tapping his knuckles on the glass of the window. When Beverly recognized the man before her, she smiled warmly and rolled the window down. It only took Warren a second to catch up, when he came to his senses.

"Look who found me, Bev," Warren offered, with mock delight. If only they had run into each other on a work day, when Warren felt confident and at his best. Many people knew of his son, knew of their trouble, but to have Ron feel pity for him was too much.

"Ronald. It's good to see you," Beverly gushed with a pleasant tone in her voice.

"Beverly Keller, you are a sight for sore eyes. I don't think you've changed a bit. Why, Warren, you lucky dog, you got yourself a looker."

"Always the flatterer," she chastised. "How have you been?"

"I'm good. I was telling Warren here that we don't live that far away. We ought to see each other more often. I was the best man, for pete's sake." He spotted Keller in the backseat and the beam on his face grew broader. "Is this your boy?" he asked turning to Warren.

"It is," Warren conceded. "This is Keller."

"I wanted to name him after my father, but Clifford wasn't exactly our favorite choice, so we named him Keller instead," Beverly explained.

"Well, he's a good looking fellow." He looked over Beverly's shoulder. "Hello, there, Keller," he greeted with a friendly wave. Keller did not respond. He had his eyes firmly planted on the bags his father held.

The boy's patience was beginning to wear thin. "I want food pwease," he begged.

"We'd better feed him. He's got quite an appetite," Beverly suggested trying to avert a scene. She knew that Keller was on the verge of a meltdown. He hadn't the patience to wait beyond a few minutes, and those few minutes were up.

"Now, be polite, son, and say hello to your father and mother's old friend," Ron ordered good-naturedly.

Warren stood there dumbly holding the bags. He didn't know what to say or do. Beverly recognized the look of panic on Warren's face, like a deer caught in the headlights. She reached through the window and took one of the paper sacks from his hand, rummaging through it to pull out an order of french fries, which she then gave over to Keller, deterring a tantrum for the time being. He was content at once and began to eat several fries at a time. "He doesn't talk much, Ronald," Beverly offered as an explanation.

"The silent type, huh?"

"Like his father," she joked, trying to remain good natured as she and Warren exchanged glances. She knew that he was embarrassed. She knew from the hollow look in his eyes that he felt lost and ashamed of his own feelings. Warren was a strong man, a rock to lean on. His character was nearly fault proof, but even he had a tender spot here and there that could be tested and exploited.

All of those years that he had tried to please his father, tried to make him proud, had left a residue on his soul. Ron had witnessed her husband in his glory days, had gone along for the ride on many of Warren's adventures. To allow Ron to see what his life had become was not something he wanted to face. It would be merely one more story to add to his book of shame. Beverly sympathized. She too had been very humbled by the child sitting in the backseat of the car, wolfing down french fries.

"I hate to break this up, Ron, but we were on our way to the drive-in," Warren offered, once he had come to his senses. "Don't want to miss the show." He handed Beverly the other paper sack and stepped back onto the curb, hoping that Ron would follow. He did. "It was good to see you again."

"Well, I don't want to hold you up, but we really should get together sometime. Don't have the missus with me or I'd have you come say hello. I told her I'd bring dinner home, and she's probably wondering where I am. I got four of my own little ones now," he told Warren. "And they're all probably as eager as Keller is to get their dinners."

"You say hello to Mary for me, would you?"

"Sure I will."

Warren gave him a quick handshake. "Take care, Ron."

"Will do." He turned toward Beverly and waved. "Good to see you again, Beverly. You take good care of Warren here."

"Good-bye, Ronald," she called, waving back.

Warren left Ron on the curb and climbed into the car next to Beverly. Their old friend watched them drive away, perplexed by Warren's odd behavior.

Warren was silent as they set out for the drive-in theater. Beverly sat quietly for a moment then softly asked, "Are you all right?"

"Who, me? I'm fine." He did not take his eyes off of the road. "Imagine seeing Ron like that after all these years."

"That *was* an unlikely meeting," she agreed.

"Same old Ron."

When they pulled into the drive in, Keller had already consumed all of his food. He sat quietly in the backseat observing everything that was going on around him, the cars and people and sounds. Beverly and Warren ate their meal as they watched the screen in front of them. When they had finished, she slipped across the seat next to him. "This is that Indiana boy," Beverly informed him. "He's from Fairmount, I think," referring to the actor on the screen.

Warren chose not to reply. He was trying to watch the film,

and Beverly always had an annoying habit of starting a conversation with some worthless fact that quickly became a tangent and then grew to epic proportions. Once she started, she was hard to stop. She could talk a politician under the table. Generally, he did not mind her verbalizations. It was part of what made her appealing, but he certainly did not want to carry on in the midst of *Rebel without a Cause*.

He found the smooth and cool manner in which the lead carried himself, and his soulful, mournful expressions, mesmerizing. The film was so gripping that when it came to the end he hardly noticed that Beverly was crying. He cleared his throat and wrapped his arm around her shoulders. "What's the matter?" he soothed.

"It's just so sad. So dreadfully sad," she wept.

"Now, darling, it's just a silly picture."

"I know," she agreed, trying to get herself under control. "I suppose I'm just being foolish."

Warren raised himself up from the seat and, with his free hand, reached into the back pants pocket of his slacks and pulled out a handkerchief. He offered it to her, and she accepted it gratefully. "There now," he comforted, rubbing her arm.

"Thank you."

"Certainly." He twisted in his seat to check on Keller. "Looks like Kel didn't like it as well. He's fast asleep."

Keller's head was slumped forward and his chin was resting on his chest. He had been quiet throughout the length of the film, so neither of them had noticed him doze off. He was snoring softly and drooling out the side of his mouth. Beverly laughed. "Wouldn't it be nice to be able to sleep so soundly? It'll be the devil getting him to bed."

"Yes, well, it's not exactly easy to carry him in any longer. I'm afraid I'll put my back out."

She blew her nose informally into his handkerchief and wadded it in the palm of her hand. "Why does life have to be so tragic?"

"It was bound to happen sometime, Beverly. All children get bigger," he teased.

"You know that's not what I meant."

"Next time we'll have to catch a comedy. No more drama for my girl." He put the speaker back and rolled up the window. "Best get home. It's getting late." He put the car in drive and pulled out of the parking spot, following the line of cars exiting the outdoor theater. Once he pulled into the driveway, he held the door open for Beverly, then went to extract Keller from the backseat.

Keller whimpered and resisted, until Warren had his feet planted on the ground. He guided Keller up the walkway and into the house. Beverly removed his shoes, opting to leave him in his clothing. If she put him in his pajamas, it could wake him, and he might remain up all night long. She and Warren moved him onto his bed then covered him with his bedspread. Beverly looked down on his relaxed and sleeping face, smoothing his hair and kissing his brow.

"He's such an angel when he's sleeping. It makes you forget what a difficult boy he can be, when you see him like this," she murmured before leaving him alone to his dreams.

When Saturday finally came around, Beverly was past being patient. She had looked forward to her shopping excursion eagerly for several days. Although she had a hint of guilt over leaving Warren alone with Keller, it was not enough to keep her from happily anticipating her time away. She dressed with great pains, wearing a blue floral three-quarter length sleeved dress, with flared skirt. The bodice was fitted, with three dark blue ribbons running parallel to one another on the bodice. One was just below her bust line, another at her waist, and the other ran evenly between the two. The same ribbon edged the hemline. She pulled on her white cuff-length gloves and selected a handheld clutch before slipping into her high heels. The dress was bulging at the seams, but the flared skirt helped cover much of her troubled area.

Warren let out a low whistle. "Maybe I shouldn't let you out looking like that," he jested lightheartedly. "You may never come back, darling."

"Don't be silly, Warren. We both know I look like a stuffed goose. Did I show so soon when I was going to have Keller?"

"I don't recall," he lied. As a matter of fact, her waistline was a concern. Perhaps she was having twins. The thought made him a little more than sick to his stomach. Beverly had always been trim and attractive. It wasn't that she didn't look good now, but it was impossible to overlook the rate at which her tummy was beginning to protrude.

"I left some cold cuts in the icebox for you. And don't let Keller outdoors. He'll run off again. Ever since he found he could go beyond the yard he won't stay for anything. Oh, and make sure that he doesn't get into the kitchen."

As if being subconsciously summonsed by the mere mention of his name, Keller came strolling into the living room. Beverly was surprised and pleased to see that he was carrying the Nancy doll. "Well aren't you a darling?" she gushed. When he came to her and offered her the baby doll she gasped. "What have you done, Keller?"

The baby's soft plastic skin was covered with scribble marks, but, worst of all, the very culprit that had made those marks had been jammed into the socket where once a glass eye had been cradled. She plucked the fountain pen from Nancy's face, which only made the doll look worse, for it had a hollow hole where once the pen had been.

"Do you see what he's done to this poor doll?"

Warren was suppressing a grin. "It's only a toy after all."

"He's ruined it."

"It's still perfectly good, even if it is missing an eye."

"Poor Nancy."

He couldn't resist any longer and laughed out loud.

"What is so amusing?"

"You just called it Nancy."

"Well, that was its name in the catalog."

"I think you're making too much of it, Bev."

She reluctantly agreed. "I suppose you're right. But I spent good money on that doll."

"It wasn't enough that you need to carry on so."

"You don't find this the least bit disturbing. We purchase a doll baby to try and train Keller for the real baby that will be coming along, and he stabs the thing in the eye with a fountain pen? That doesn't worry you?"

"Well it is a bit concerning, but it isn't a real baby, now is it?"

"He's all yours," Beverly declared in exasperation. "I am going shopping." She handed Warren the doll before she made her exit.

It was with relief that she walked into J. C. Penney, alone and relaxed. Without Keller there would not be any uncomfortable situations or distractions. She could shop at her leisure, inspecting the garments with ease. A sign that read "Maternity Wear for the Modern Mother" was displayed in a small corner where the maternity clothing was housed. She went to work searching the racks for what she was looking for.

Beverly was a very particular shopper. It was difficult for her to find the exact items that she wished to purchase. Everything she owned had much thought put into it. She enjoyed browsing through magazines and looking at the fashionable women that graced their pages, and she strove for the same elegance in what she wore and how she looked. She found a matching dove gray skirt and blouse with white french cuffs and collar. The buttons were pearl shaped and the back of the blouse had a pleated panel. The waistlines of many of the maternity items were cinched with a drawstring, so that you could make the waistline as big or as small as needed according to how far along you were. Such was the case with this skirt. There were also waistlines that buttoned, the buttons being spaced at regular intervals, making it possible to let the waistline out as you grew.

Beverly studied the fabric and held it up to herself. She decided it was a wise buy and hung it over the crook of her arm as she continued to look for other items she might like. When she had found several things she liked, she made her purchases and headed for Sears and Roebuck. A thorough searching unearthed a few more outfits that she thought would work.

Feeling somewhat triumphant, she stopped in at Walgreens and got herself a soda before she continued on her errands.

Mr. Ferrin was as agreeable as ever. He sat the glass in front of her and asked, "How are you today, Mrs. Vance?" He noticed the packages and bags and the light and pleasant expressions she bore. Generally she appeared strained and nervous. It was a nice change, he thought.

"I'm just wonderful, Mr. Ferrin," she replied earnestly.

"And where is young Keller?"

"He's with his father today. I've been given permission to go out shopping . . . *alone*."

She sipped leisurely at her drink, savoring the fact that she did not have to hurry. When the straw had nothing left to transport, Mr. Ferrin took the glass from her. There were other customers, but he was quicker to see to her needs.

"Would you like a refill?"

"Oh, no thank you. I shouldn't." She paid him, collected her things, and headed for her automobile. She dropped her purchases off in the backseat and headed down Walnut again. Ball Stores was beckoning to her. She passed through the doors and headed for the women's clothing. En route Beverly passed the jewelry counter. She stopped suddenly and ducked behind a display of handbags, crouching low so as not to be seen.

Her heart pounded as she watched the sales clerk assisting Barbara Clark with a necklace. She was quietly transfixed, watching the exchange. Barbara fixed the clasp behind her neck and regarded herself in the small round mirror on the countertop. Beverly felt like she was intruding or spying as she observed the younger woman at her task. The secretary admired the necklace for a few moments, tipping her head to one side, and then the other, in obvious rapture, before she removed it and handed it back to the clerk. She apparently was only looking and not in the market to buy. She thanked the clerk and then walked away. Still unmoving behind the handbags, Beverly waited until she saw Miss Clark leave the store through the large doors that she herself had just entered.

Afraid she might return, Beverly stood hunched over, unwilling to afford a chance meeting. She nearly jumped out of her skin when a sales assistant tapped her on her shoulder and politely asked, "Looking for something in particular, ma'am?"

"You startled me," she gasped, trying to regain composure of herself. She feigned interest in a black leather hand bag, scrutinizing its quality. "No, I was just browsing, thank you."

He nodded politely and wandered away. Beverly dropped the bag back to the shelf and stood up straight, glancing around to try and discern if anyone had seen her. She edged her way through the aisles.

When she stood before the jewelry counter, she felt a bit paranoid. What if someone were watching her as she had watched Miss Clark? They would surely know what she was up to. Seeing no one that she knew when she looked around suspiciously, she petitioned the clerk. "May I see that necklace?" she asked, pointing to the very one that Miss Clark had tried on.

"Certainly. This must be a very stunning necklace. I seem to have a lot of interest in it." She opened the glass case and extracted it from its perch on the velvet-covered throat. Beverly handled it carefully, examining it painstakingly. "It's a seventeen-inch triple strand of pearls. Very high quality," the clerk informed Beverly.

It was a stunning necklace, Beverly admitted to herself. The pearls in the center of the strands were larger and then slowly grew smaller as the necklace tapered out. She checked the price tag that dangled by a string. The debating over whether she should spend so much on a necklace lasted only a moment. She knew that Barbara Clark wanted this necklace but couldn't have it. "She has excellent taste in jewelry and men," she muttered to herself.

"Excuse me?" the clerk asked, unable to make out what Beverly was saying.

"I'll take it," she replied firmly.

After looking through the maternity clothing, she was able to get a handsome navy suit set, a few blouses, and some undergarments, as well as two pairs of slacks. It was on her way to be

rung up that she spotted a cocktail dress on one of the manne-
quins. It was a sensational dress, one that she couldn't seem to
take her eyes from. The skirt was full with layers of chiffon and
netting. The bodice was fitted with a scoop neckline and an over-
lay of Chantilly lace that hugged the clavicle bone and tapered to
fitted see-through sleeves.

Beverly knew that she should not buy such a dress, what with
the baby, but she found it on the rack and took it into a dressing
room to try on. She smiled at herself in the mirror when she saw
her reflection, thinking it would make an elegant dress for a hostess on Thanksgiving Day. She disputed with her inner self, until
finally she decided she must have it. "Hello, Jonathan. Hello,
Doris. Won't you come in?" she mouthed as she extended her
arm in a sweeping circle. She laughed at herself, hoping that no
one was passing by to see her role-playing.

It was without hesitation that she put the dress on the pile of
clothing she was paying for at the counter. She suspected that the
sales clerk was wondering why she was getting maternity clothing
along with a cocktail dress, but he smiled pleasantly as he rung
her purchases up. He wrapped the garments in tissue paper and
placed them carefully in a bag for her. She left the store swinging
the bag ever so slightly, in eager anticipation of wearing the dress
and the necklace.

Not until she was driving home did she begin to feel a small
hint of remorse for those two frivolous buys. She wondered if
Warren would be upset with her. She considered hiding them,
stuffing them somewhere deep inside her closet, but eventually
she would have to wear them, and he would know then anyhow.
When she pulled into the driveway, she was apprehensive about
taking her bags in. It was Keller that made the decision for her.
He was watching from the window and burst out of the front
door screeching, "Mama, Mama!" Warren followed him, went to
the backseat, and gathered all of the packages and bags to help
her in with them.

She took Keller's hand and came in behind him. Warren set
the packages in a heap on the couch.

"I was afraid you really wouldn't come back," he said.

"Is our boy too much for you?"

"I'll be the first to admit it," he agreed.

"What did you and Daddy do together, Kel?" Keller was seeking affection from her, much the same way a cat would. He rubbed his face against her gloved hand and wedged himself beneath her armpit.

"Wuv you," Keller mumbled, planting a kiss on the back of her hand.

"Did you enjoy yourself?" Warren inquired.

"I did, darling. Thank you so much for letting me go."

"Well, let's see what you got," he began to rummage through one of the bags. Beverly quickly interceded. She would rather show him on her own terms.

"Sit down and I'll show you," she commanded. She waited until he had planted himself in his chair. "How about I do a fashion show for you?" She collected her bags and headed for the bedroom. She unzipped her dress and slipped it down around her ankles, laying it out on the bed before trying on the navy suit. When she came back and spun around, Warren seemed gratified.

"You look very nice, Bev," he complimented, with an impressed tone.

"Thank you."

"Where did you get that from?"

"Ball Stores."

He continued to compliment her with the next several outfits that she tried on for him, until finally she unwrapped the black cocktail dress. She held it up for a moment, wondering if she should simply take it back. But the temptation to keep it was too great. She dressed herself carefully in it and then took out the strands of pearls and put them on too. When she emerged from the bedroom Warren seemed surprised.

"Say, that looks great!"

"You really think so?" she asked shyly.

"I certainly do." He got up from his chair and took her hand, spinning her around. "Is this maternity clothing?"

She did not answer him right away. "Well, no. I got a size larger than I generally wear. I thought it would be nice to have for Thanksgiving, for when your parents come over."

"Is this new too?" He picked the strand of pearls up in his hand and eyed them closely.

"Yes. Do you like them?"

"I think you look just great," he confirmed once again.

"Consider them a gift from you to me," she replied sweetly.

"I have excellent taste."

"Yes, you do."

"Speaking of Thanksgiving, Bev . . ."

"Yes?"

"We're agreed that we'll be telling my folks about the baby, right?"

The pleasant expression was replaced with a sulk. She had the hint of a pout on her lips as she asked, "Why must we tell them so soon? I just don't know that I am ready to tell anyone. And if we tell them, you know that it won't be long before everyone knows."

"It concerns me that you won't tell anyone about the pregnancy. You're beginning to show, Beverly. People are probably speculating anyhow."

"Let them speculate. It's really none of their business. Why can't we just keep it between us?"

"I think you are being unreasonable."

"That's a fine thing to say. Is it so wrong to want to feel a little joy over it before everyone else makes judgments about it and ruins it?"

"What are you talking about?"

"I see the way they all look at us. I know what they think about Keller and why he is the way he is. They think that it's somehow or other our fault, that we did something to bring it upon ourselves. Now they'll think that we shouldn't have had another child. They'll wonder what we were thinking to try again," she responded with heated conviction.

"You don't know that."

"I do. Don't you think I know how painful it was when you

had to tell your father that Keller was never going to be normal? You had to have a boy to carry on the great Vance name. Then that boy turned out to be unsatisfactory, and according to your father's way of thinking, it's an embarrassment that he even carries the family name at all. That name is only for the cream. What happens now, Warren? Will they be happy because maybe there is still a chance, or will they be upset because there might be another child that is unworthy of your ancestry? Either way it is going to make me good and mad and I don't want to be."

"Gosh, Beverly, I didn't know you felt that way. I know that my parents can be difficult, but are you really that resentful?"

"Yes, I am. Do you suppose that your mother shows off pictures of her only grandchild at the club, or that your father brags on him in his social circle? They're ashamed of him. They don't want to admit that our inferior little Keller somehow belongs to them. It just stews inside of me. I know that they think it's my fault. It certainly didn't come from your side of the family, now did it?"

"I'm sorry you feel that way, darling. You might even be saying nothing but truth, but they are still my parents. I think the best thing to do is tell them about the baby when they come over for dinner."

"Suit yourself."

"I wish you wouldn't be so upset," he soothed.

She removed the pearls and unzipped the side of her dress and stalked off toward the bedroom. Warren let her go. He knew that she needed to cool off. He had tried to remain true to his promise that he would not tell anyone about the pregnancy, but she was becoming unreasonable. Surely she had to know that people would figure it out and in a very short time.

A sudden realization that things had become very quiet brought Warren to attention. Looking around, he saw that Keller was not in the room. Hurriedly he began to search the house. He didn't have to look far before he found his son in the kitchen. Keller had pulled out a dozen eggs one by one and busted them on the floor. He was running his fingers through the thick, slippery liquid, when he looked up at his father and cried, "Ping pong balls! Yuck!"

six

Giving up on attempts at sleep, Beverly lay in bed, scrutinizing the ceiling above her while contemplating the situation she found herself in. Once upon a time it had been Warren who had requested that Beverly tell no one. She remembered the day vividly, for how can you forget the day your heart is broken? The funny thing about a broken heart is that it's not fatal. Though you wish in vain that it were, life continues on and you have no choice but to continue on with it. You take the hand that fate has dealt you and you press forward because there is nothing else that can be done.

That same heart that lay within her breast had known for months that something was not right. Keller was a part of her, made from some mystical sphere that bequeathed him with a portion of her genetic make-up. Instinctively, that core tissue that had helped sustain his life during the nine months she had carried him had recognized the deficiency within. She knew him beyond his cherub round face, knew him beyond his sturdy little body, beyond his blue eyes and dimpled smile, to a depth that alerted her to any danger her offspring was in.

As many times as she was told nothing was wrong with Keller, she would hear a whispering within that it was not so. *He is not right,* the voice would counsel. *There is something wrong with him,* it would insist. After persistent attempts at trying to sort out the truth, it finally came to them, much as a train comes barreling down the tracks. Although her heart had earnestly sought the truth, when the moment arrived she tried to reject it. How could it be that in one moment lives could be changed forever so drastically? How could she look upon this child she had borne as if he were a stranger to her, when just a moment ago there was no one who knew him better?

Even as the doctor's words fell upon her ears, she did not understand how any of it could be so. Too stunned to shed a single tear, she had sat next to Warren in numbed silence. Keller was on the floor, quietly spinning the wheels on the toy car he was playing with. His eyes were so intently focused on those wheels, as they rotated, that he didn't seem aware that anyone else was in the room with him.

"Your son is retarded," the doctor declared with matter-of-fact frankness. "I don't know how anyone couldn't have seen it up to now."

"But he can't be. He was talking once. And he does things . . . things that require intelligence," she defended. "He is very resourceful when he wants to be."

"Mrs. Vance, he can't even play with his toy car properly. He is not using it for its primary function. He simply likes to see the wheels spin. I can assure you that is not the way a typical child plays with a car." She looked over at her small son spinning his wheels, holding the car like a turtle on its back. "He has no useful language. Why, he's not even aware that we are here in the room with him," he countered.

"He's not always as oblivious," Warren informed the doctor.

"Are you saying there is no hope for our boy?" Beverly questioned with a strain in her voice. She recalled the countless hours she had worked with Keller to try and get him to speak. How hard it had been to go over and over each object she presented him with and repeat its name over and over again. He would grow impatient with her and launch the objects across the room, but she persisted. She believed, she *hoped*, that it was going to pay off eventually.

The doctor sat quietly, clasping his hands together as he attempted to find the right words for such a delicate situation. He was not a man who possessed much sympathy. He had been doing what he did for many years. His ability to break hearts had become decisive. But there was something in Beverly Vance's heart that made him hesitate. "I couldn't tell you that for certain. We aren't positive what the cause of his retardation is. We could not say if it is heredity or if he has suffered some sort of brain damage. We couldn't say if it was in the womb or after birth. Sometime before or after he was born, his mind stopped growing. That is all we really know.

"Now, whether you want to pursue other treatments or not is for you to decide. That is not a decision I could even begin to make for you, but I would discourage it. I personally feel that you should not waste your time and resources on anything of that sort. That boy may never speak and will likely need to be cared for just as a little child would for the rest of his days. In situations like these I would suggest you put him in an institution. You should not have to bear that burden. With him in such a place you can go on with your lives."

"Abandon him?" she cried indignantly.

"I understand that this is a terrible shock, Mrs. Vance, but you must realize that to keep this child would be a terrible strain that is far greater than you can imagine." His voice was somewhat stern and commanding this time, with an authority that made it difficult to argue any further.

Keller dropped his toy and wandered over to where they sat, hoisting himself onto his father's lap. Warren looked down on his little son with eyes clouded by the knowledge that he was somehow a different child than the one he had brought to this place earlier. Life had been altered beyond recognition in just the space of a few short hours. A battle raged within him, a striving to understand what was happening, to make sense of what he had just been told. Warren held Keller with a fierce embrace, unwilling to let him go even when the boy began to squirm.

They thanked the doctor for his time, shook hands, and left the clinic to climb into their car just as the sun grew low in the sky. The drive home was in darkness. Neither spoke, unsure of what to say, unwilling to break the silence that was a refuge from what needed to be discussed. As quickly as their minds were spinning, there were no cohesive thoughts to be shared.

It was Beverly who voiced the word that was running through both of their heads, like a record that was skipping. "Why?" she asked. There was no answer. Perhaps it was luck of the draw, perhaps God's infinite plan. No matter how long they lived, they would likely never have any solid solution that would help them fully understand or be at peace with that question. Nothing would ever be a balm that would soothe or heal those broken hearts.

Warren kept his eyes on the yellow lines in the center of the road as they flew by, carefully avoiding Beverly. He cleared his throat after some time. "I don't think we should tell anyone just yet."

Beverly studied him closely, perplexed by his comment. "Why not?"

"He may grow out of it. Just like everyone keeps saying. After all, we don't know anything for sure. That was just one opinion."

"Opinion? Every doctor we've taken him to has agreed that there is something the matter with him. No one would tell us what, but they all said he wasn't developing normally. Dr. Rolf is just the first to give it to us straight."

"He's an intelligent boy, Bev. I've seen him do things that a feeble minded child couldn't do. How do you explain that?"

"I can't," she replied softly as she choked back tears. There was no arguing the point. Keller had an incredible ability for problem solving. He had many capacities that had been overlooked in his testing because they were not testable in an IQ sense. Still, she could not dispute what the doctor had said. Keller was not as a normal three-year-old should be. She had seen it herself. She had witnessed what the other children were doing, and she knew that Keller was far different.

"We just wait. We wait and see if he grows out of it." But waiting did not make it go away. Waiting did not remove the agony that burned within them. And they eventually were forced to face it, despite their wait.

Sleeplessly agonizing as she remembered back on that day, the irony did not escape Beverly. She was striving desperately to hold on to the joy of this child she carried before the scrutiny of others picked it apart and endeavored to destroy it, just as Warren had attempted to shield Keller from the same lot. As hard as her husband had tried to hold on to their son, he had been forced to let go. She realized she too would be required to give up her secret.

When things were still in the quiet of the night and she was left only to her thoughts, they inevitably turned to Keller. Sometimes she wished that she didn't have to think, didn't have to feel. It had been several hours now since she had first awakened. If she chanced to stir in the night it was rare that she could go back to sleep, for thinking. One thought led to another, until her brain was burdened with a plethora of churning thoughts. Growing uneasy as she tossed and turned in the tangled sheet, she decided that she could not stand it any longer and swung her legs over the edge of the bed to tiptoe on bare feet into Keller's room.

Although a youngster, he snored as proficiently as an old man. His mouth slightly open, face relaxed, she deemed him perfection when he was sleeping. She liked to watch him this way, for it reminded her of how much she really did love him. It renewed her resolve to be the best mother she could be to him. She tucked the blankets more closely about him and tiptoed back out.

It would be dawn soon. Beverly knew that she should try and get some sleep while she could, but as tired as she was, she knew that sleep was an elusive thing and would probably not come easily to her. If only her mind had an off switch. There was a semblance of peace in the darkness and silence. Very few such opportunities presented themselves in Beverly's chaotic life. When they came, she relished them.

"What are you doing up?" Warren asked from the shadows.

She looked up, surprised by him. "I couldn't sleep," she replied with a lazy smile. "What are you doing up?"

"I can't sleep, either. Without you next to me, I can't rest."

"I suppose you can't get rid of me then, now that you need me."

"I suppose not."

"So what do you suggest we do, if neither of us is sleeping?"

Warren walked over to the record player and shuffled through their small collection. He pulled out Jo Stafford's album and took great care with removing it from its sleeve. He had purchased this record for Beverly several years before. They had been young when Jo Stafford sang on the big-band scene shortly after the war. She had performed with one group or another until going out on her own just a few years later. It was her song "You Belong to Me" that had impressed Beverly so thoroughly. Warren had bought the record for her birthday and she adored it.

With the record on the spin table, Warren painstakingly put the needle to the vinyl, adjusting the volume before he went and collected his wife from the sofa. He held his hand out to her and she accepted. The strains of "You Belong to Me" in Stafford's smoky voice streamed faintly from the speaker. There were no words between them as they danced slowly to the music in their living room. Warren gave her a little spin and held her close to him, their fingers still connected, with his arms wrapped around her, her back pressed against his chest. They swayed together as he touched his lips to her neck, then dropped his hands from their clasp and ran his fingers over the silk fabric of her nightgown, stroking her tummy with tender affection.

In just her gown, it was very obvious that she was expecting. When she was wearing her regular clothing, one might wonder if she was just putting on some extra weight. However, when her waistline was not inhibited by the fitted confines of her daily wear, she had a nice round form. Warren felt a certain sense of pride over her blooming figure. Although it wasn't a conscious thought, this baby represented his ability to produce a viable heir, a child that would tell the world that he could do it right. He and Beverly had tried for years to conceive Keller. All the while they got the standard teasing and prodding that comes when a young couple doesn't have a baby in a timely manner.

It had hurt Beverly deeply. "We're trying. Can't they cut us a break?" she would fume. Then their little boy was not right, once he did make an appearance. Warren felt that it was somehow a flaw that he had a hand in, even if he had no control over it. In part what Beverly spouted off the other day had been truth. He had felt it too, the unspoken shame that had been pasted on the two of them. But now, there was a new hope. Perhaps this baby would be the proof that he so longed for, the proof that it was not him, that he had not been the cause of Keller's problem. Not only would it be proof to himself, but to others, those wicked sinners who passed judgment upon him and his sweet wife.

"What will we name it?" she inquired, still resting against him.

"I think Jonathan if it's a boy," Warren answered in a believable, serious voice.

"How do you like that! I don't think Jonathan's the right name at all," she protested.

"Well, then perhaps I should leave it up to you," he suggested.

"We left it up to me the last time and no one seemed too keen on my choice. As I recall, you couldn't be serious about a name then either, teasing me right up to the end."

"Keller is a fine name," he assured her.

"What if it's not a boy? Have you thought about that?" she speculated.

"A little girl with her mother's good looks. I wouldn't mind that a bit."

"Her mother's looks?" Beverly scoffed.

"You look just like Grace Kelly in *Rear Window*." They had seen that picture last year at the drive-in, and he firmly believed that she bore a striking resemblance to the actress in her haircut, her fine delicate features, even her style in clothing.

"You are a flatterer," she told him modestly, although she liked it very much when he spoke of how pretty she was. "Grace Kelly?"

"I mean it," he affirmed as he let his lips graze against her hairline. "I don't know any other man who is as lucky as I am," he told her in a mock Jimmy Stewart accent. She giggled at his playful antics.

"I think you need to go back to bed, Warren Vance. You are getting quite silly. Is that what happens to you when you are deprived of sleep?"

"It's your perfume, darling. It renders me incapable of any coherent thought."

"I'm not wearing perfume," she laughed.

"Are you positive? I thought that surely must be what your intoxicating smell was." All the while his fingertips glided over the fabric of her gown.

"Such talk. You can certainly spin a girl's head. Handsome good looks and pretty words as well. How could I ever turn away such a package?" She turned in his arms to face him.

"That's my aim . . . to be irresistible," he admitted as he kissed her tenderly.

Beverly felt lucky that her husband was still the source of weak knees for her. He was still able to evoke such sentiment and passion that she found she was completely unable to withstand him. Warren brought out her vulnerability, made her feel exposed, drew emotions to the surface that she was forced to repress with everyone else in her life. As frightening as it was to be so defenseless, Warren had never betrayed that trust, but nurtured that tender, unguarded spot, liberating and fostering it. Here was a soul mate that knew her in every sense and still accepted her and loved her, flaws and all. She clung to him, needing his healing. He made her strong. If it had not been for the support he offered, she questioned whether it was possible to even continue on. Surely if a day ever came that he was not there, life would end.

She caressed his face with her small hand, feeling the coarse whiskers pressing their way through the pores along his jawline. "It's late," she breathed.

"It is," he agreed.

"We should be in bed."

"I couldn't agree more."

*   *   *

Saturdays were happily satisfying days in the Vance home. No work, no commitments or obligations to tie them down; they did as they pleased and made it fun. Before Beverly and Warren had Keller, they spent it with friends. They took turns hosting dinner parties, playing cards, and enjoying other such activities. Now they spent Saturdays alone. When the weather was nice, they might enjoy a trip to town or a walk on campus.

One of their favorite spots to visit was not far from where they lived, in Anderson. It was Mounds State Park, established as such in 1930. During the 1920s it had been somewhat of a local attraction, with a roller coaster, carousel, shooting gallery, skating rink, and boat rides. There was an impressive restaurant and dance hall as well. It was Indiana's small-town equivalent of Coney Island, a place where the young folks could go to have some fun.

As popular as this destination was, it did not survive the 1929 crash on Wall Street. The enterprise went belly up. The Madison County Historical Society came to its aid by purchasing the land and donating it to the state. There was something mystical about this place, a plot of land that embodied the primitive people who had lived here before, where they had left their mark with giant, man-made mounds of earth. When a person roamed over this place, remnants could still be found, such as arrowheads, tools, and other such artifacts.

It was a place that suited Keller to perfection. He was a bit of a primeval little savage himself, and he took to this wilderness, just as the original inhabitants might have. It astounded Beverly and Warren that he seemed so calm and at peace in the outdoors. Nature was his element. And so on that Saturday after-noon, despite the cold, they dressed themselves warmly, bundled in wool hats and flannels with jackets, and headed out. Beverly packed a basket with a thermos of hot chocolate and some cold sandwiches for a midday meal, and they drove to the park, eager to get one last trip in before the snow fell.

They had no definite plans as they wandered over the crude trails, enjoying the wilderness, their breath forming in clouds of white. Keller wore an expression of contentment, sometimes forging a path just within their view and far ahead, sometimes lagging behind with a lazy pace that allowed him to take every-thing in. He picked up a tree limb and struck tree trunks as he walked by or stirred up the decayed, crisp brown leaves on the ground. Sometimes he chose to walk with his parents, holding his mother's hand, with a faint smile on his lips.

No one else had thought to come out on such a chilly day. The place was all theirs. Even with the bare branches of the trees, exposed and dark against the sky, this spot held a beauty that was irresistible. In the autumn it was breathtaking, a patchwork of color. Keller knew his way around, memorizing every step they took, remembering all the places they had been on previous trips. He headed for the barren old farmhouse that stood solitary among these trees. His parents watched him shuffle around, inspecting the grounds, laughing at his seemingly curious examination of an ant hill close to the eastern wall. Keller could be quite ador-able, with the inquisitiveness of a small child discovering the world around him. He took his stick and poked at it, watching the minuscule creatures scatter, some climbing up the very thing that threatened to destroy them. A few of the ants made it to his fingertips, where he observed them in fascination.

"Those are ants, Kel," his father told him, squatting next to him. Keller looked at his father with his customary troubled expression, as if he were thinking hard, and then turned his attention back to the ants.

"His nose is bright red. Perhaps we should go," Beverly sug-gested. "I don't want him to get sick."

"I hate to make him leave. He enjoys it so much here."

"Well, just a little longer then," Beverly consented. "We still have lunch in our basket back at the car."

"Come along, Keller. Let's head back to get some food." That's all he needed to say to get the boy's attention. Keller stood up and went back the way they had come, without assistance from his mother or father, searching for their car. When he saw it, he willingly climbed in and waited patiently as his parents followed behind him.

"Are you hungry?" Beverly asked him.

"Pwease."

"Here is a peanut butter and jelly sandwich just for Keller." She reached back and handed him his sandwich, which he accepted and took an enthusiastic bite from. "Do you want ham or chicken?" Beverly asked Warren.

"I think I'll take the ham if you don't mind."

"I don't," she assured him, handing him the ham sandwich. "Would you like some hot chocolate to go with that?" Keller nodded his head yes since his mouth was full. "There you are."

He accepted the cup she offered him. "He really is content here, even with cold weather."

"I have always secretly wondered if he was born to be an Indian and was sent to me by mistake, several hundred years off schedule."

"Could be," Warren agreed.

"Drink, pwease," Keller piped up from the backseat.

"He wants a drink," Warren teased, stating the obvious.

"What will we do with him during the winter? He won't want to be cooped up in the house for the next several months. I am going to run out of things for him to do," she commented as she handed Keller his drink.

"Maybe you should take him to visit your brother."

"My brother and I haven't spoken in ages, Warren. What am I going to do, call him out of the blue and tell him I'd like to visit him? I am sure his wife would be very pleased with the prospect of uninvited guests, more unhappy when she found out that it would be Keller who was coming. Besides it's a four-hour drive. Can you imagine Kel in the car for four hours? I hardly think that would go well."

"Just a suggestion," he said.

"Well, I don't think that he and Kel would get along so well anyway. They would butt heads. He's very set in his ways."

"Who, your brother? He seems pretty easy to get along with."

"How would you know? You've only met him three times. When we got married, when we had Keller, and when he came through town the year before last."

"And I got along with him every time," he insisted.

"He's a mystery even to me, Warren. I have vague recollections of when he'd come home to visit every now and again. I remember that last time, when my mother died. He was so mature, and it fascinated me to hear he and my father talking about his life and what he was up to."

"How did he take it when your mother died?"

"I think he was in shock. He seemed so distant and didn't say much. But he held me when I cried at the funeral. He put his arm around me and held me and comforted me. My dad was in a daze and didn't even notice that I was upset. It was Stan who took care of me then."

"I'm sorry, Bev. I know that must have been hard for you."

"Yes, well, it was a long time ago, and life goes on. Darn it, he just poured his cup of hot chocolate onto the floor." Agitated, she took a napkin from the basket and half crawled over the seat to try and sop it up. "Keller, that was not nice."

"He's a terrible little runt," Warren observed.

"Why would you dump it out on purpose?" she ranted, expecting no reply. Keller ignored her, as he shoved the rest of his sandwich into his mouth.

"All done," he chirped, sliding to the door and pulling the handle to get out. So that was it. He assumed that if he finished quickly he would be permitted to return to his errand of exploring.

Warren jumped from the car and headed him off at the pass. "Get back in the car, Keller. It's time to go home."

Keller went to pieces, throwing himself down and crying. "No, no, no!" he protested. Warren grunted when he tried to pick his son up off the ground, as Keller continued to object loudly to leaving.

"Keller, get in the car. We must go now," Warren said firmly, hardly able to keep the annoyance out of his voice. He stepped back, giving Keller a chance to make the decision on his own. Keller grabbed hold of the stick he had abandoned when he had gotten into the car and began to swing it at Warren. This really got Warren's blood boiling. He furtively tried to grab the limb as it struck him in the lower leg a few times. He finally got a grasp on it and ripped it from Keller's hands, throwing it long and high away from Keller.

He somehow managed to shove the boy back into the car and shut the door. Keller waged a full out assault against the closed door, kicking it and screaming. This posed a problem. Warren did not know how he could safely climb into the car and drive away. If he let go of the door, the child might try and open it. The only choice that was left to him was to wait while Keller tired himself out. His wails finally quieted to a dull roar and Beverly leaned over, locking the door. Warren hurried to get behind the wheel and drive off before Keller decided to try and escape again.

Once the car was in motion, his plaintive objections began anew. He was kicking the back of their seat, jarring the two adults that he was most unhappy with at the moment. It made Warren more than a little angry. "You stop that right now, Kel, or I'll pull the car over," he threatened through clenched teeth. He was quickly coming to a point of being infuriated. The warning did nothing to calm Keller. His tirade continued. Warren pulled the car over to the side of the road, jumped out, opened the rear door, and began to spank Keller, all in one quick movement.

"That's enough!" he yelled through gritted teeth, slamming the door violently. He got behind the wheel once again and drove toward Muncie, taking a few deep breaths to try and calm himself. The reprimand did little to help the situation. Keller began to scream at the top of his lungs. If he was mad before, he was furious now. He didn't calm down until they were nearly home.

Beverly remained silent, sick from the conflict. She hated confrontation; it made her upset and nervous. It seemed to her that life with Keller was one unending altercation after another. She remained that sober for the remnant of the day, even once he was in bed. She made popcorn and sat with Warren on the sofa, as they watched the *Jackie Gleason Show*. They, like the rest of America, were hooked on him. Beverly couldn't remember missing an episode in quite some time.

"You all right, darling?" Warren inquired.

"It started out to be such a good day. It seems a shame it had to end that way."

"Are you upset that I tried to discipline him?" he questioned, defensively.

"No. I'm just . . . I don't know, bothered that he had to be spanked."

"What am I supposed to do, ignore him kicking the back of my seat? He's out of control, Bev. I didn't really have much of a choice."

"I know." She paused, trying to get over the emotion she was feeling. "We just had such a good time at the park and things were going so well, and I'm just disappointed that it turned out so badly."

"What do you suggest that I should have done differently?"

"He's just a baby. He looks like a grown boy, I know. But his mind is just a baby's. I don't think he understands what he is doing. It's like a toddler throwing a tantrum. I don't know what to do differently, but I feel sorry for him. He couldn't see that it was time to go. He can't be reasoned with."

"Well, if we don't punish him, he'll never understand. He's lucky we put up with his fits. A less strong man would have put his foot down by now, and put him where he rightfully belongs."

"What are you saying?" she wondered in shocked disbelief.

"Nothing," he spat. "I'm not saying anything!"

"Don't be cross, Warren," she cowered.

"Of course not," he replied in frustration, and he allowed the conversation to come to an end before it escalated any more, as they turned their attention back to their program. He knew that there would be many more times in the future that this same discussion would come back up again, and he wasn't in the mood for it tonight.

seven

The day Beverly had dreaded had finally arrived—
Thanksgiving. With great care and preparation she had planned
a menu and composed a shopping list, as well as a list of things
to do. Going over and over each item to make sure that she had
gotten everything that would be required for the meal was essen-
tial, in her mind. There would be no shops open, and if she by
chance neglected to get an item she needed, she would be out of
luck. That morning she got all of her ingredients out, stuffing
the turkey and putting it in to bake so that it would be ready
by late afternoon. Beverly took the pies from the icebox that she
had baked the night before, smiling to herself, pleased with how
beautifully they had turned out. She mixed the rolls and set them
out to rise, covering them with warm towels. Preparing the other
side dishes would come later, closer to dinnertime.

Cleaning and scouring came next. The bathroom first, before
she took a shower. Then, Beverly set the table with deliberate pre-
cision, centering each of the plates, folding the cloth napkins,
arranging her mother's polished silver, and distributing the gob-
lets. Keller's place setting was not as fancy; no knife, and a small
plastic cup instead. While she was about her business, Warren

kept Keller busy. He dressed his son in the detested blue button-up oxford shirt that was only brought out on Sundays. Keller moaned and wailed when he saw his father pull it out of the closet. He hated wearing anything that was long-sleeved. Once the boy was dressed, he ran from the room, pulling at the cuffs.

When he found his wife, Warren couldn't help but express amusement as he caught sight of her wearing the black cocktail dress, her best attire, with an apron over the top, furiously vacuuming the floor in the living room. She saw him laughing at her and scowled. "Why don't you make yourself useful and go put the dinner rolls in the oven for me?" she commanded over the roar of the vacuum cleaner.

Doing as he was told, he retreated in to the kitchen, inspecting the pies before he removed the towels from over the tops of the rolls, where they were rising in their pans, and went to open the oven. Behind the first door, a large succulent bird stewed in its juices in a roasting pan. Although it looked like the most divine turkey he had ever seen, and he couldn't help but let out a "Mmmm," in anticipation, he thought it had an odd smell to it. He shut the first door and opened the next. Before he could shove the pan of rolls into the pre-heated oven, his eyes grew wide as they beheld a truly horrific sight.

"Nancy!" he gasped, dropping the rolls with a clatter onto the floor. He lunged forward, trying to pull the doll out with his hand, but he quickly realized that was a mistake. The hot plastic burned his fingers and he pulled back, shaking his hand wildly to cool it down. In panic he grabbed one of the towels Beverly had used to cover the rolls. As he dragged the doll from the oven, her hair brushed across the heating coil at the bottom of the oven and burst into flames. Warren let out a holler as he ran across the kitchen with the blazing toy, launching it into the sink, where he extinguished it with the faucet. The vacuum was switched off in the other room, and Beverly came running.

"What's the matter?" she asked with concern. Warren turned to her, holding the doll by an ankle. It dangled there, one eye missing, hair scorched and smoking, plastic melted in the shape of the oven rack. The smell of burning synthetic hair had permeated the entire kitchen, leaving no room for the more pleasant smell of turkey. "Good heavens! What has he done to Nancy?"

"She was in the oven!" he fumed.

"What was he thinking?"

"He could have burned the whole house down!" Warren blew past Beverly in search of his son. "Keller! Keller!"

There sat Keller quietly playing with his animals on the floor in his bedroom. To make matters worse for himself, the floor was scattered with buttons. Keller had ripped them off of his shirt and had taken the thing off, wadding it up before discarding it in the corner. He had redressed himself in his Davy Crockett T-shirt and now appeared to be completely content. He seemed oblivious to the goings on around him, despite all the noise and commotion.

Beverly held Warren back with a hand on his arm. "There's no point. It won't do any good to scold him." Warren took a few deliberately deep breaths, turned around, taking the abused baby doll with him, and stomped back to the kitchen. He pressed the trash can lid open with his foot and chucked the doll in with enough force that it nearly knocked the can over. His sense of justice had not been appeased, and it took every bit of restraint he had not to kick the thing in.

Beverly crouched down and picked up her pan of rolls, forlorn by the flattened dough. She tried to salvage them but quickly surmised that it was futile. They too met their fate in the trash can. If this were any indicator of what the rest of the day held for them, she had already spent the last of her patience. She tried to convince herself that it could only get better. At least she had the foresight to prepare two pans of rolls; now there would be one to serve at dinner. A few rolls were better than none at all.

At six o'clock, Warren opened the door to his parents, who stood side by side on the front step with false smiles spread across their faces. His mother, dressed in a crisp floral taffeta dress and fur coat, handed him a casserole dish as she crossed the threshold. "I brought a little something to contribute to the meal," she explained.

"Wow, Mother, you didn't need to do that," he responded, meaning that she *really* did not need to do that. His mother was not known for her culinary skills. When he recognized the under-cooked, lumpy potatoes, his heart sank. He invited them in and hurried to put the potatoes on the table with the rest of the food Beverly had already set out, then came back to take their coats. His mother handed her sable coat over to him and helped herself to a seat in the living room. She looked around for a moment, slightly confused.

"Warren, would you mind if I make myself a drink?" she asked, unable to locate the wet bar herself. She had quite a nice wet bar herself, an oriental black lacquer cabinet, fully stocked.

"We don't have liquor, Mother."

"What?"

"He said they don't have any, Doris," Jonathan injected.

"Thank you, Jon. I heard what he said," she snapped. "What do you mean you don't have any?" she pressed Warren.

"We can't keep Keller out of anything, so we don't keep any of the stuff around. We were afraid he might get into it. The only thing we keep is a bottle of cooking sherry in the kitchen. I think Bev has made punch to go with dinner." He took his father's coat and made a beeline for the bedroom, leaving his mother to some privacy so that she could panic properly. Warren had tried to convince Beverly to at least buy some wine, but she grew up in a home where there was no drinking. She did not believe in it. As much as he had tried to explain that his mother hadn't functioned a day without it for the past twenty years, Beverly did not understand how she couldn't go just one evening without it.

He heard her speaking to his parents now. She must have emerged from the kitchen. "Jonathan, Doris, it's so good to see you again." He ruefully threw himself back into the mix.

"Everything smells delicious, Beverly," his father offered.

"Thank you."

"Something smells funny to me," Doris admitted.

Warren shuddered. His mother certainly didn't pull any punches. Even if she did detect the remnants of the burning plastic, she could have kept it to herself. "Bev, here, has been cooking all day, and she's made an impressive spread," he informed them, putting a protective arm around her shoulder.

"Where is young Keller?" Jonathan questioned.

"He's playing in his bedroom."

"Is he doing any better?"

"He's all right, I suppose," Warren told him.

"Well, you mustn't blame yourselves," he consoled, thinking he was doing them a great service by saying so. Warren could feel Beverly stiffen with indignation. It amazed him that she could get so angry over such a silly comment, when they had heard worse, and on many different occasions. "I tell you what I would do," he began.

"No one wants to know what you would do, Jon," Doris snapped. She was obviously on edge, because she generally gave Jonathan the courtesy of arguing with him confidentially. His mouth was open and his eyes wide, amazed that she had spoken so harshly to him. "I think the best thing to do is let them lead their own lives." As she spoke, the hatred she felt for the man was noticeable reflected in her eyes. As every year passed the woman became more and more bitter, until the love that she had once felt for him was now a loathing and contempt she could hardly suppress.

"Maybe we should come sit down to dinner before it all gets cold," Beverly suggested.

"That's a good idea," Warren agreed. He could see that Beverly was uncomfortable with their quarrel. It did little to ruffle him. He had grown up with these two. War was a common occurrence between them. It actually amused him because his father was rarely put in his place by anyone but his mother. Jonathan did not like to be contradicted; it was not a habit of others to do so, either. He was a man that took respect whether it was given willfully or not. Perhaps after years of being treated so, his mother had gone in full out rebellion against the man who had dictated over her.

Beverly went to find Keller and left Warren to usher his parents to the table. He let them pick their own seats, as far away from one another as possible, then he slipped into the kitchen. The punch was in a crystal pitcher on the kitchen table. He poured some punch into a glass and brought it back into the dining room, handing it to his mother just as Beverly returned with their son.

"Try the punch, Mother. Bev makes a delicious punch." Beverly shot him a confused look, for there was nothing really magnificent about the punch. His mother took a little swallow, then set the glass down, looking thoroughly disappointed.

Beverly pushed Keller's chair into the table and tucked his napkin into the front of his shirt. He fiddled with his silverware while they waited for Warren to return. Warren handed his mother the drink and then sat down to the table as well. "Father, would you bless the food?" he asked.

Jonathan was only too happy to. He liked to hear his own voice, and in a sermon-long prayer he remembered to bless everything but the food. It seemed like an eternity to Beverly, who knew that Keller could only sit for so long. When he finally graced them with an "Amen," Keller grabbed for the basket with the dinner rolls and helped himself.

"He's got quite an appetite, it would appear," Jonathan commented.

"Yes, he does. You're a big boy, aren't you, Kel?" Beverly put a few slices of turkey on his plate and cut it for him before spooning on a heaping pile of green beans. That is all he liked out of the feast that was laid before them. As an afterthought she put a few yams on his plate.

"Nooo!" he cried. "Put it back. Put it back!"

"He must not want yams," Warren observed, trying to smooth the situation over with humor.

"I should say not," his mother assented, with a hint of bewilderment.

Beverly raked the yams onto her own plate without a word. She sat down and eyed Warren, who knew what her silent communication meant. She was not enjoying the visit. He picked up his mother's potatoes and passed them on without helping himself to any. His father did the same. When they came to Beverly, she politely portioned some out for herself and then passed them on to Doris, who also decided against them.

Once the food was all passed around and everyone was eating, there was very little to say. The only noise was the sound of the forks and knives clinking against the china and Keller's occasional belching. Every time he let one slip, Doris looked at him with an outright horrified expression. She took the napkin from her lap, twisting and untwisting it with slightly shaking hands, appearing agitated with a vacant expression.

"How are you doing, Mother?" Warren asked, feeling nothing but pity for her.

"Such a good son," Doris replied, unable to control the emotion in her voice. Warren thought for a moment she might cry.

Beverly tried to politely eat the potatoes. She took one bite and wondered how they could be lumpy and yet watery at the same time. It took a good portion of her will to swallow it, and the rest was spent trying to keep it from coming back up. She was envying Keller for being able to speak his mind when he didn't wish to eat something. If she could, she would refuse this dish. After a few bites she gave up trying and did not finish them.

"How are things at the office?" Jonathan asked, trying to seem casual in his interrogation.

"Seems to be going well."

"No one wants to talk business over dinner," Doris threw in.

Jonathan chose to ignore her. "And Carl Trip, you spoken to him lately?"

"Yes, as a matter of fact, I just spoke to him on Tuesday."

"Things to his satisfaction?"

"They seem to be. I try and get with him once a month to make sure that he is happy with the property he's leasing."

"Once a month won't do, Warren. You should be calling him more often than that, and you should be asking him to the golf course or fishing," Jonathan advised. "You leave him to himself and he's going to start wondering what he needs you for."

"He seems pleased with my abilities so far," Warren replied dryly.

"I'm not saying you aren't doing a fine job . . . but now you go the extra mile with these people, and you'll have 'em eating right out of your hand. You make a good impression and they'll refer you to a friend, and so on and so on until you have some connections. If I was you, I'd be taken 'em to lunch, asking them out for a drink . . . well, you get what I'm saying." All the while he wore a broad smile across his face. It was his way: patronize with that all-knowing grin. He talked sort of slow and drawn out, each word emphasized as if everything that came out of his mouth was of great importance.

"Yes, well, I'm sure you're right about that," Warren conceded. "You know the business more thoroughly than I do. I'll see that I am calling Mr. Trip more often."

"You do that, and I promise you, that will impress him. But now if you invite him to dinner, you should probably take him out by yourself, so you can talk business . . . if you know what I mean," Jonathan said, and his meaning was unmistakable. He cleared his throat and with a wry grin and a twinkle in his eye said, "How's that Miss Clark?"

Warren could have fallen off of his chair. He knew his father very well, well enough to know that he had probably checked the secretary out every time he came in, but to mention her in front of his wife and Beverly was a step above even his usual boldness. Warren carefully avoided Beverly's hot and furious eyes. "I suppose she is all right. I don't know; you'd have to ask her."

Keller was finished. He pushed his chair out, picked up his plate and silverware, and went in to the kitchen. Beverly stood up to follow him. "Excuse me," she said as she went after him. "I don't want my mother's silver to end up in the garbage."

"What was that?" his mother asked in confusion.

"Still doing all right, Mother?"

"Fine, just fine, son." Her answer was anything but convincing.

"What's the matter with you, Doris?" Jonathan questioned sternly.

"Nothing, Jon. Nothing at all!"

"I don't know what's gotten in to you." She rolled her eyes at him, getting up from the table and going to sit in the living room alone.

Beverly returned with a pie in each hand. She looked somewhat frazzled. "It seems Keller has put his hand in both of my pies," she complained.

"I'm sure it won't affect the taste," Warren offered. He got up and took one of the pies from her hand and set it on the table. "I know they'll be just swell."

"Where's your mother?"

"She went to sit in the living room. Probably just ate too much," Jonathan lied, which was apparent from the untouched food on her plate.

"Maybe we should have dessert in the living room. We can just leave all of this here and I'll clean it up later."

The pilgrimage to the living room began. Beverly was busy serving pie to her guests and to Warren. When she finally sat down with her own piece, every nerve in her body was strained.

"This is delicious, Bev. You've really outdone yourself," Warren commented.

"That's good of you to say, darling," was her grateful reply. They seemed to have run out of conversation topics. The pie was eaten carefully and deliberately, in an attempt to seem as if they were concentrating on something else so that they wouldn't have to speak to one another. Warren's mother looked bored and ready to bolt. She wouldn't even look in Jonathan's direction.

"How are things with your ladies' auxiliary group, Doris?" Beverly probed, trying to stimulate a conversation. Doris was a member of the Daughters of the Revolution, with a pedigree to prove it. She was one of the aristocracies who could authenticate that they had a place with that society.

Suddenly Doris was at attention. She sat up a little straighter when she responded. "We're organizing a coat drive. After all, it is getting cold and there are some who cannot afford coats. We especially would like children's coats."

"Perhaps I can give Keller's coat from last year," Beverly offered.

"It would be a worthy donation," she informed her daughter-in-law. "It's just terrible that there are children suffering from exposure. Anything we can do to help the less fortunate."

"I'm a firm believer in helping oneself," Jonathan grumbled.

"How can a little child help himself, Jon? They have no means to provide for themselves," Doris scoffed.

"Then perhaps their parents shouldn't have had them. If they can't take care of their own, they just shouldn't have them." Again that know-it-all smile. It was enough to drive poor Doris mad.

"No one asked for your opinion." And she turned away from him with her full body.

"The ladies always sponsor a food drive around Christmas too. They've done it every year since I can remember. We always have a good turnout for that one." Her face grew pleasant as she told Beverly, "Warren used to get out his little wagon and go around the neighborhood with me to collect canned goods. He was so darling that no one could say no to him. He was always such a good boy."

"Oh, that's so sweet," Beverly said, sending a sentimental sort of look to Warren.

"He had a girl in high school that helped one year too. What was her name, Warren?" She did not wait for him to answer, for she already knew the girl's name. How could she forget? She was the girl Doris had wanted Warren to marry. They had been serious enough for her son to think about buying a ring, but then they went their separate ways in college. "It was Charlotte. You remember her, don't you? Well, I thought for sure they would get married."

Warren saw this as very dangerous territory. First his father with Miss Clark, and now his mother with Charlotte. Were they intentionally trying to make Beverly insecure? He knew his wife was a very jealous woman and that their words would have a lasting effect upon her. This was something that she would hash over and hash over for months. He was in a hard place. Should he cut his mother off and appear insubordinate in order to prove to Beverly that he would not stand for her ill treatment, or should he give the older woman free range to say whatever she pleased and then try and make it up to his wife later?

"You remember her, don't you, Warren? I really liked that girl. She was so pretty and pleasant. She came from a good family as well. He gave her up when he enlisted. He didn't think it fair to keep her waiting for a boy that might never come home."

"That was a long time ago, Mother. We were just kids."

"Old enough," she countered.

"You know we went on a cross country trip with her parents, Ted and Janie Winston, to California. Now Ted is the bank president down there at the credit union. He gave me the loan when I got that office there in town. His father was the deputy mayor back in, oh, around '28. He was a big fella. Sold all his property there over by Riley Street. Made a pretty penny on it too," Jonathan said.

"Yes, she came from good stock," Doris muttered.

"Do you remember the O'Briens that lived just up the street from us?" Jonathan asked Warren.

"It wasn't the O'Briens, Jon, it was the O'Bannons," Doris corrected.

"Now I don't believe it was. It was Sam O'Brien, and he came from Virginia."

"It was Sam *O'Bannon*," Doris argued. "His wife, Millie, and I were dear friends. We were bridge partners in the garden club, I tell you." Doris was a member of the garden club, a group of women who met together to have coffee, fancy desserts, discuss gardening, and play cards at the local Methodist church. Not just anyone was allowed to be a member of their group; you had to have a formal invitation in order to attend their get-togethers."

"Oh, it doesn't matter anyhow, Doris," Jonathan said directly to her before he went on to address the whole group. "I was just going to say that he passed on last month. They found him at his office desk, just slumped over dead. They said it was his heart, but I don't believe it. That man was as fit as anyone. Strong as an ox, I tell you. He had a cabin up at the lakes that he had us visit every now and then."

"That's too bad, Father," Warren offered, because he wasn't sure just exactly what to say.

"Well, I will miss going to the lake," Jonathan lamented.

"Let me get these plates out of the way," Beverly offered, as she went around and collected all of the dishes scattered with pie crumbs. She went into the kitchen and placed them in the sink.

Leaning against the counter with her hands, she sighed deeply. Perhaps they would not notice if she hid in here for the remainder of their visit. She doubted they would care, at any rate.

She went back through the dining room and into the living room, where the real circus was to begin. Without realizing it, seven o'clock had come around. When she sat back down, she wasn't there for long. Keller came from his bedroom and stood in the hallway, as naked as the day he was born, looking innocently from his father to his mother, expectant.

Doris saw him first and uttered a shocked, "Good gracious!"

The group turned in unison to catch a view of the boy standing patiently, waiting for some attention. "Bath?" he petitioned.

"Keller, go to the bathroom," Warren commanded.

"He's taken off his clothes," Doris declared, bewildered.

"It's his bath time," Beverly defended. She had come to the end of her rope. Doris's attitude toward Keller all evening had been one of disdain and scorn. At least Jonathan had attempted to ignore his behaviors.

"Doesn't he know any better than to parade around exposed like that?" she shot back incredulously. She seemed horrified by the very thought of it.

"You act as if you've never seen a bare bottom before, Doris. I know for a fact that you have had to have seen at least two from the head count in this room, so why do you act so shocked?" Beverly couldn't keep the sarcasm from her voice. If his own grandparents couldn't accept him, then who would? She chose to ignore Jonathan's roaring laughter as she got up to go assist Keller with his bath. She turned around vehemently and threw in, "By the way, Warren and I are expecting another baby." Then she turned on her heels and was gone.

eight

One week into December and she supposed there was no point in trying to hide it any longer. Beverly selected one of the maternity outfits that she had purchased and dressed herself in it. Thinking about exposing her secret made her a bit uneasy. Still there was no point in pretending. She knew that Warren was right, but it didn't make it any easier. She pulled the pearls from her jewelry box and fastened the clasp before slipping her shoes on. She applied her makeup, pressing the smooth tip of the deep-red lipstick to her lips, rubbing them together, and blotting on a tissue. When she looked at herself in the mirror, she knew that no one would be able to mistake her condition any longer.

It had become quite cold. Enough so that she would not be able to go to town every Thursday. Only those days that she had the car. Walking in this weather, even just eight blocks, would be a silly thing to do. She bundled Keller in his coat, hat, and scarf. He would not keep mittens on. She had given up on that two years ago. Once she had him ready to go, she helped herself into her coat and gloves. When she had her purse, she was ready to go. She opened the door and let Keller run ahead.

The drive to town was a short one, but she turned on the radio and adjusted it until a station came through. It was the beginning of December, and Frank Sinatra was singing "Jingle Bells." This particular version was old, but Beverly liked it and sang along. "J-I-N-G-L-E bells. I love those J-I-N-G-L-E bells . . . It's going to be Christmas soon, Keller. Do you want to see Santa Claus? Do you want to sit on his lap?"

Keller was solemn as he met his mother's gaze in the rearview mirror. When they had taken him last year to wait in line to see Santa, they didn't make it. The line was too long and he could not stand to wait. After some crying and a few scuffles, Beverly gave up and took him home without the landmark visit with Santa. It was better that way. He would only have terrible memories of it if she had forced him. Besides, after the fit he threw, he was likely to get a big lump of coal instead of the customary candy cane.

She parked the car and helped Keller out; then the two of them walked to Walgreens, hand in hand. The bell jingled above the door as they walked in, and Mr. Ferrin was quick to be of assistance when he saw who it was. If he noticed that she was wearing maternity clothing, he did not let on. He was simply his usual pleasant self. He served them their drinks, chatting as he did so.

"You ready for Christmas?" he asked.

"Not really. I console myself with the thought that I still have two and a half weeks left. I suppose that will go quickly, though."

"What does young Keller, here, want?"

"To be perfectly honest, I haven't a clue. He's not one for talking, and he's so picky about what he will play with. Maybe I should just get him socks and underclothes." She laughed. "Would you like that, Keller?"

"I know he don't talk much, but he's a smart one, that boy," Mr. Ferrin said with a nod of his head. "He's always watching. I bet you money he could do my job and do it well."

Beverly did not know what to say. No one had ever called Keller Vance smart. Generally, when she had him out in public, they called him nuts or crazy, but never smart. She really wasn't sure if Mr. Ferrin was saying it to be kind or if he meant it. Surely he knew by now that Keller was retarded. According to the doctors, he would never be smart; he would never be anything.

Mr. Ferrin was perplexed by her nervous reaction to his comment. He realized he had said the wrong thing. He did not want to risk offending her. That was the last thing that he wanted to do, so he let it drop and didn't say anything else. He busied himself with transferring a small portion of what was left from a large tub of ice cream into a new one that was full and replaced it into the freezer behind the counter.

"Ice cream," Keller observed, pointing to the freezer.

"You're right, that's where I keep the ice cream," Mr. Ferrin agreed.

"Now that it's cold, we won't be in every week. We'll only be able to come when we have the car for the day. I don't think it would be wise to walk in below-zero temperatures."

"No, not wise. It'll be snowing soon and there won't be a sidewalk to walk on. Boy, I dread it. Shoveling just itn't my cup of tea."

"I'm lucky to have been born a woman, I suppose. I'm not expected to do that anyway," she said with a little laugh.

"So what'll you and Mr. Vance be doing for the holidays?"

"It will be just he and Keller and I. I believe his parents are going to Florida. They'd rather spend it warm than stuck here in the cold," she mused. "I can't say that I blame them. Sunny Florida or freezing Indiana is not a terribly difficult choice."

"I guess," he agreed unconvincingly. "So nothing fancy, huh?"

"No. Warren said we would likely be getting the tree tonight when he comes home from work. We're probably crazy for trying that again. Keller wouldn't leave it alone last year. I can't tell you how many times he tipped it over."

"Our children did the same thing when they were little ones. My wife had to put it in the play pen. Imagine putting the tree in the play pen to keep the babies out." They both chuckled. "Once they outgrow it you'll miss it though. You miss them being babies." Their conversation was interrupted by the bell above the front door. Mr. Ferrin greeted his new customers with a smile and a "Good afternoon to ya."

Beverly swiveled on her stool and looked over her shoulder. She was a bit surprised to see Missy, from church, and another woman, Ginger, who was holding her little son coming their way. She felt instantly uneasy.

When a look of recognition passed over Missy's face, she politely said a quick hello. "Beverly, it's so good to see you." As unconvincing as it was, it was better than not being acknowledged at all.

"Hello, Missy."

"Ginger and I were just going to grab some sandwiches. You know Ginger."

"I think we've seen one another at church," Beverly offered.

"We were just going to go over the Christmas program, you know. She's in charge of planning it. Has been for—how many years now, Ginger?"

"Seven," Ginger informed her, the superiority she felt shining through. The baby squirmed in her arms.

"That's very good of you," Beverly replied. "It must be quite a demanding task."

"I don't look at it that way. It's my way of giving back to God. You can never do enough for the church, if you ask me," Ginger advised them. "It's a small inconvenience compared to the joy it brings to others." She tried to manage her squirming child by shifting him to another hip.

Inwardly, Beverly found it amusing. The Christmas program was hardly audible to those in the congregation, due to a lack of proper acoustics, and inevitably Ginger would cast her own son, Teddy, in the lead role. The boy was neither good looking nor proficient as a thespian. If anything he was gifted in evoking yawns. He often missed his cues, and when he looked out onto the crowd he was performing in front of, he would forget what he was saying and stand there, dazed and confused, until his mother "whispered" his lines to him. Her whispers where more like soft shouting, loud enough for everyone to hear. The worst part of it all was that the congregation was forced to endure the program sitting on the hard pews at the expense of their tail ends, and the yearly program perpetually ran over the allotted schedule.

"Well, you do such a lovely job. They couldn't possibly find anyone to replace you," Missy flattered. Ginger's baby began to fuss.

"It is something I look forward to every year," Beverly lied. "And your son always brings tears to my eyes," she assured. *For I really am bored to tears*, she thought. After such a program, you were left to question whether you really did have the faith and fortitude it took to attend services each Sunday.

Keller finished his drink and got up from his seat, ready to go. He caught sight of Ginger's little one and his eyes suddenly became bright and engaged in a way they seldom did. He smiled and spoke softly, "Baby."

Ginger was trying to coax the baby into submission, but he continued to fuss. Keller drew closer, clasping his chubby fingers over his eyes. "Peek-a-boo," he said, pulling his hands away and brushing them gently over the baby's round cheeks. The baby stopped fussing, his attention diverted. "A-boo," Keller repeated. At this point the baby began to laugh, watching Keller attentively.

Keller laughed too. "A-boo," and he pulled his hands away from his eyes and fluttered them against the baby's soft skin again. This time the baby's giggle was more enthusiastic. Beverly watched in pleased fascination, struck by the tenderness of Keller's interaction with the little fellow. She felt something close to awe as her heart began to pound a little faster. Her eyes wandered from her little boy to the baby he was entertaining and then they fell upon Ginger, who wore revulsion quite candidly upon her scowling face. She didn't want Keller touching her baby.

Beverly hastily scrambled for the change to pay Mr. Ferrin. "Thank you, Mr. Ferrin," she said. She turned to the ladies, grabbing her and Keller's coats. "It was good to see you. I do hope that everything works out well with the Christmas program." She wanted nothing more than to get away from there, away from them, away from their poisonous rancor. She took Keller by the hand and tugged him toward the door.

"See you, Beverly," Missy called after her with a little wave. As if a spell had been broken, once Keller was out of sight the baby began to fuss again. Ginger and Missy sat down to the counter and ordered their sandwiches. Ginger balanced the crying baby on her hip as she took out a pad of paper and pencil. They waited until Mr. Ferrin was at his task of preparing their sandwiches until they began to speak.

"How do you like that? I think she's going to have a baby. Did you notice?" Missy declared, horrified.

"Oh, I noticed all right."

"I don't know why she insists on taking that boy everywhere; it's just horrible the way she parades him around. I told you about how he broke Margaret's china. He never should have been there in the first place, if you ask me. A sensible person would keep him home so that he doesn't bother anyone."

"He's so disruptive during services. Don't you think? I mean, how can the rest of us worship with him making a lot of racket? I'll tell you right now, he's never going to be in my Christmas program. Can you just envision what he would do up there in front of everyone. Why, he'd ruin it. That's what he would do."

"Oh, I hear you. And now she's having another one."

"Imagine!"

"And did you see him?" Missy gasped. "He has the worst manners. Burping out loud, just vulgar, and his face was filthy . . ." She pursed her lips and shook her head disapprovingly. "Huh, Laura will just die when I tell her Beverly Vance is on the nest."

Mr. Ferrin handed the two of them their sandwiches, a look of sorrow in his eyes. No wonder Beverly seemed such a fragile and defensive woman. How could she be otherwise? She never knew when the next assault would come. This was a new side to the single-dimensioned lady that he chatted with on Thursdays and knew very little about. The poor woman would have been heartbroken if she had heard the conversation that had just transpired between these two hens. He vowed he would never be the source of distress for her again.

And they're supposed to be good Christian women, he thought.

Beverly anxiously pulled the door open to her husband's office building, savoring the thought that she knew what would most certainly come next. She had waited until she felt that the moment was right to wear her pearls to Warren's work place. Today was that day. Keller tried to make a dash for his father, but Beverly held him back for a moment. "Is he with anyone?"

"No, he's not," Barbara confirmed, with agitation. She was busy, too busy to be bothered by Warren Vance's ball and chain.

Beverly let Keller out of her grasp, allowing him to go to Warren's office. She held back, lingering in the lobby area near Miss Clark's desk. Barbara Clark couldn't have been over twenty, in Beverly's estimation. She was young, as were most secretaries, working only until they got married and then crossing over to housewives. She was certainly pretty enough to have snagged a husband by now, with her dark hair, long eyelashes, and slender oval face with pale, unflawed skin. But she didn't want just any man, Beverly reflected. Miss Clark seemed uncomfortable. She tried to busy herself with typing in an attempt to avoid Beverly altogether. Beverly, however, had other plans for the fresh-faced secretary. She was in the mood for a little cat and mouse.

"Have you any plans for the holidays, Miss Clark?"

Barbara Clark stopped typing and looked up at her rival with skeptical eyes. What should this woman care what plans she had made? "None of particular note. I'll just be spending it with family . . ." Her last words trailed off into silence when she caught sight of the necklace Beverly was showcasing around her slender neck. "That's an interesting necklace. Where did you get it?" Although Miss Clark knew exactly where the necklace had come from. It was the very necklace she had eyed for nearly six weeks, asking different sales clerks if she might see it, might try it on, always being careful that it was never the same girl behind the counter. She had hoped to purchase it once she got her Christmas bonus. She would never own the necklace now.

"I don't know where it came from. Warren got it for me," she bragged, touching the pearls with a delicate stroke of her gloved fingers. As she spoke, Warren emerged from his office with his coat in one hand and Keller's hand in the other. "Miss Clark likes my necklace," Beverly told him, giving him a peck on the lips. This surprised Warren. He was not use to Beverly displaying affection in public situations.

"It's lovely," Barbara Clark admitted without any conviction in her voice.

Beverly's smile was genuine, but Warren could see the cattish expression in her deep blue eyes, and he wondered what she was up to. "You have excellent taste, darling," she told him, replaying the inside joke they had exchanged several weeks ago when she had bought the necklace.

"So I've been told," he replied, quickly donning his scarf and coat. He was feeling slightly threatened by these two women fraternizing together. He had the feeling that he should retreat before they began an all out war. He could see this awkward situation ending badly if he didn't do something now. "Are you ready to go to lunch, Bev?"

"Certainly. I always have an appetite these days," she teased. "Have you told Miss Clark our news?"

She saw, with an inner delight, Miss Clark's face register confusion. She looked from Beverly to Warren, waiting for the big unveiling. Better than the confusion was how completely caught off guard and shocked she seemed to be when Beverly told her, "Warren and I are expecting." Her design had been to make it perfectly clear that not only did she possess the pearls that Barbara Clark had coveted, but she also possessed the man. She smiled sweetly at the wide-eyed girl. "Well, we should let you get back to your work. Warren, let's get out of poor Miss Clark's hair."

"I'll be back in an hour or so, Miss Clark," Warren said, shutting the door behind him. He fell in to step next to his wife with a curious sideways glance. "What are you up to, woman?"

Her reply was anything but innocent. "Just making sure that our dear Miss Clark has a very clear picture of where her proper place is." She put her arm through his and clasped his hand.

"Now and again you still surprise me, Bev."

"That's a very good reason to stick around and find out what happens next, darling," she retorted with a tempting lift of her eyebrow.

nine

Picking a tree was the easy part. The more troublesome half
of the equation was putting it up and decorating it. Keller would
not let the box of ornaments alone. He rummaged through them,
retreating only when he was told to get, running away until his
parents had their backs turned. Then he would pop up again
at the same mischief he had previously instigated. Before it was
finished, he had broken several of the bulbs. Beverly picked up
the bigger pieces and kept him at bay until she was able to get the
vacuum cleaner to dispose of the rest.

Once the tree was finished and the lights were plugged in,
he lay beneath the tree with his hands behind his head, looking
up in awe with a huge grin spread across his face. Warren and
Beverly watched him from the couch as they sipped hot chocolate. "What do you think he's thinking?" she mused.

"He likes the lights," Warren guessed.

"He's so content laying there. It's funny how the oddest
things seem to calm him."

"It'll wear off soon enough," was his all-knowing reply.

"The baby's moving."

"Where?"

She guided his hand to where the persistent nudges hammered within her womb. They both sat still waiting for another movement.

"Did you feel it?" she asked. She could see from the overjoyed expression on his face that he had. He pressed his hand more firmly against her bump.

"That's a strong little baby," he boasted.

She took his hand from that spot and relocated it higher up. "Feel here."

"Maybe we'll have a little football player."

"Do you remember how active Keller was?" she recalled. "I could hardly sleep for him moving so much. Remember that night when we were sleeping and you had your arm around me and he nearly kicked it right off."

"I remember." He smiled broadly with the recollection of it. "There's another one," he said, referring to their unborn child. "How do you go about with all this going on inside there?"

"I don't know; you just get use to it, I suppose. It's funny to me how small this baby is and how much it lets you know that it's there." She looked over at Keller, still gazing up at the tree. "Keller, come feel the baby move," she urged. He ignored her, choosing the tree over the baby. She got up, went over, and sat next to him, taking his hand and pushing it against her. When he felt the ripple just below his fingers, his eyes met hers in surprise and confusion. Just as quickly as he had made recognition of it, he pulled his hand away, annoyed by the control she had exerted over him, and shoved it back under his head, turning his attention once again to the tree.

"He felt it," she observed. "Keller, there is a baby in there."

"Baby?" Keller echoed.

"I've thought of the perfect name if it's a girl," Warren remarked.

"You have?"

"Nancy."

She got up and took one of the throw pillows from off of the couch, beating him with it. They were both laughing, although she insisted, "That's not funny! I really would like you to stop teasing me so and get serious about it."

"Well, I think it's a perfectly good name."

"I like Joyce."

"Joyce?"

"You don't like it?"

"Not particularly. It sounds too grown up for a baby."

"I guess there's plenty of time to come up with something we can both agree on." Keller moved closer to her and laid his head in her lap. "He's getting so big," she lamented, running her fingers through his thick, unruly hair.

"I know. The other day I was wrestling with him and he nearly bested me," Warren agreed. "If he doesn't slow down, he'll eat us out of house and home."

"It frightens me," she said. "It just brings us closer to the inevitable."

"What do you mean?"

"I can't sleep at night for worrying about things. Who will care for him if something happens to us? Maybe my brother? But he hardly knows Keller and he is so much older than I am. If we are gone, then chances are he would be too." Her brother was twelve years older. She had only been six when he left home to strike off on his own. They were friendly with one another but not close. Certainly not close enough to ask him to be Keller's guardian in the event of Beverly and Warren's untimely demise.

"What if someone treats him mean or is unkind to him? What if someone hurts him?" she questioned soberly. These issues were always pressing their way from the depths of her mind, causing a panic she could hardly keep under check, if she dwelt on it for too long. "There was a man I knew growing up. He was not right in the head. Not smart, you know, and he was taken advantage of and treated badly. This woman convinced him that she was his girlfriend, and he spent much of the savings that his parents had left for him buying things for her. She just left town with all of the things she had tricked him into buying, just took off. There is always someone that will prey on the feeble minded. Heartless, cold people," she fumed.

"Now, Bev, you are wasting your energy needlessly. We'll just worry about that when we come to it," he consoled. "We won't let anything like that happen to him."

"You never think about those sorts of things?" she questioned defensively.

"Well, certainly I do, but I just don't dwell on it. There's no point in getting upset over something that may or may not happen."

"I suppose you're right," she conceded. There was no point in pushing the issue. Warren had always been the type to avoid fretting over what-if scenarios. It was difficult to think about the future when you had a child with a handicap. It merely reminded you of how fragile life was, and there were so many possibilities as to what might happen, none very appealing.

She remembered reading an article in the paper only a few years back about a husband and wife who were aging and had chosen to take their own daughter's life for fear of what might become of her once they were gone. Out of desperation they had concluded that no one would care for her or love her or treat her as well as they had, that she would be better off dead than to face the world alone. Beverly did not wonder if her son would become a doctor or a lawyer or a butcher. With a child like Keller you wondered who would care for him when you were gone. Where would he go? Was there enough money stashed away to support him for the remainder of his days?

Beverly moved Keller's head, getting up to climb back onto the sofa and snuggle in next to Warren. "Should we invite your parents over for his birthday?"

"That's nearly a month away. Do we really need to plan that now?"

"Less than a month, and I would like to know in advance so that I can make arrangements," she replied. "It's sad that he's never really had a proper birthday party. All the other children his age are having their little friends over and playing pin the tail on the donkey."

"Thank heavens that we don't have to suffer through that, huh?" he joked. "All the little kids screaming and crying, everyone crazed on sugar, too many children to keep track of."

"I wouldn't mind," she said.

"Come on, Bev. What's gotten into you tonight?"

"Nothing."

"Snap out of it."

"I'm sorry, Warren. It's just that some days are harder than others."

"Well, you're welcome to invite my parents if you'd like to, but after Thanksgiving I'm not sure if they'll come." She laughed because there was nothing else to do. Warren had a way of evading issues through humor. Not that he was the funniest person, but he did have a dry sense of humor, a wit that was endearing. "I got something for Keller for Christmas," he said, changing the subject.

"What did you get him?"

"A livestock hauler with animals." There were some perks to having a child like Keller; you could freely converse in his presence without having to worry about if he was paying attention. Christmas gifts were not off limits, for he probably was not listening. In general, adult conversations were not something that registered with him.

"How many animals?" Beverly wondered with a hint of disapproval.

"I don't know."

"He'll probably have them all over the floor. How big is it?"

"It's pretty big," he replied, holding his hands up to show her about how big he estimated it to be. "I saw one just like it in the Sears and Roebuck catalog."

"Show me," she told him, getting up to retrieve the catalog, and then presenting it to him.

He shuffled through the pages until he landed on the page he was looking for. "This one right here," he indicated with his index finger.

She scanned the page and read the description aloud. "Big

cattle truck with separate compartments for cattle, pigs, and sheep . . . just like transporters on the highway. Die-cast metal, chrome-plated aluminum cab. Trailer of heavy-gauge steel. Fourteen die-cast metal wheels with rubber tires. Includes ten realistic, hand-painted animals of die-cast metal. Big cab and trailer are twenty-four inches long. Six dollars and ninety-eight cents."

"He won't be able to destroy that. It's all die-cast metal," Warren bragged.

"I don't suppose he will, but it will be loads of fun keeping all of those animals picked up. It seems rather big too. You don't think he'll hurt himself on it?"

"That boy never gets hurt. *He's* made out of die-cast metal, if you ask me. Besides, you're just sore that you didn't pick it out."

"I have a few things in mind myself. I don't care that you got something for him."

"Good, because I think he's going to flip when he sees it. He loves animals. I can picture it now, with the cows and pigs and sheep."

"Where did you put it?"

"I left it in the trunk of the car so he wouldn't find it."

"That's a good idea."

"It's the only place that's safe around here anymore. He's always rummaging through everything, and he's figured out all of our other hiding places." Warren was surprisingly annoyed just from the thought of it. Keller had an uncanny ability for problem solving, especially if it was something he very much longed for. The boy had learned to undo locks, climb, and break whatever stood between him and the objects of his desire.

"I know what you mean. He went into our bedroom and rifled through my vanity this afternoon and got into my jewelry. Sometimes I believe that God made him cute so that when I look at him I can't help but forgive him."

"Interesting theory," he mused.

"And what should I get you for Christmas, darling?" she inquired.

"I don't know. I don't really need anything."

"You never help me out. You always say that same thing and then you're completely disappointed with what I choose."

"I'm not," he insisted.

"Yes, you are. At least give me a general idea so that I'm in the same ballpark. Don't set me up for failure again."

"I need a new satchel for work," he offered.

"Well, then I will pick you out a new satchel. See how easy that was. You told me what you wanted, and now I can pick something out that you'll really use."

Keller got up and wandered away, taking his shirt off as he pointed himself in the direction of the bathroom. "He wants a bath," Warren noted. He did not move to get up.

"I suppose I should go bathe him then." She left Warren to himself. He very happily got out the paper and opened it, with a rattle of the pages. Time for his evening wind-down.

The next morning when Warren came into work, Miss Clark was employing a small stepladder in her attempts at decorating the Christmas tree in the front lobby. She turned with a bright, eager smile when Warren walked in and put his coat and hat on the coat tree by the front door. He cleaned his shoes off on the doormat and looked up to her with an equally engaging grin. In truth he was amused by the scene before him.

"Looks like you're keeping yourself busy," he observed.

"Trying to anyway, sir," she replied with an attractive laugh. She finished draping silver garland on one of the upper branches and turned to him with her hands on her hips. "Well, are you going to just stand there, or are you going to make yourself helpful?" she teased.

"Help with what? It looks as if you have everything under control to me," he appraised.

"Now that you have come I won't have to climb up and down this silly thing," she said, in reference to the ladder. She pointed to the box of decorations. "There, hand me those ornaments," she commanded.

"Yes, ma'am," he said, fetching two ornaments and handing them to her.

"I knew you could be useful to me," Barbara told him with a lift of her eyebrow. Her flirting carried a double meaning, and it was crystal clear.

The alarm bell was ringing in his head, telling him that this was a dangerous game. He should leave now, but he didn't. He watched her hook the ornament over one of the branches. She was stroking his ego, and he didn't want to leave. It felt too good to leave.

"Here's another," he offered.

"So, Mr. Vance, will you be on Santa's naughty or nice list this year?"

"Oh, I'm a good boy," he replied.

"Even good boys can't be good *all* the time." She held her hand out behind her back without looking. "Pass me another, would you?" she requested.

Warren obliged, handing her the last ornament in the box. "That's the last one," he informed her.

"I need the star," she advised.

"Ah, yes, the star." He grabbed the silver star and put it in her outstretched hand, brushing her fingers with his. She stretched on her tip-toes, rotating her hips so that her round bottom was prominent at his eye level, and settled the star on the top branch.

"How does it look?" she asked.

Warren couldn't help but notice her derriere in the snug fitting dress. He cleared his throat. "I think it looks quite fetching."

"Good. I'm glad you approve."

Miss Clark turned and began to descend the small ladder, stumbling on the last step. She was flung forward with little grace; Warren was able to quickly catch her in his waiting arms. The palms of her hands were pressed against his broad chest, her upturned face just inches from his in a clumsy embrace. She smelled faintly of jasmine, he thought to himself, feeling his heartbeat accelerate. Her breath was fast and heavy, perhaps winded from the fall. He watched as her eyes traced a shy path from his slightly open lips to his startled eyes, holding his gaze with an appetizingly seductive glance.

It was possibly only a second, but it seemed like an eternity to Warren, as he became aware that she was moving in closer, in an attempt at kissing him, before he came to his senses. He nervously placed her back onto her feet with one quick motion. Angry at himself for nearly giving in to the temptation, he buried his balled up fists deep into the pockets of his trousers.

"Careful there, Miss Clark," he cautioned. "Wouldn't want to hurt yourself."

"It's lucky you were there to catch me, Mr. Vance. Thank you," she purred.

"No problem."

Warren stood awkwardly until he could take it no more. "Well, I should be getting to work. Lots to do," he offered. And then he escaped to his office, hiding there for the remainder of the day, wondering over what had taken place.

It was disconcerting to Warren that he had been so enticed by the young Miss Clark. Didn't he care at all for Beverly, he asked himself. If he truly loved her, how could he have contemplated betraying her so? But it would have been so easy to touch his lips to hers, so red, so ripe. Shame burned his face, made him feel weak and wretched. Some part of him feared that his wife would somehow know what had transpired. He half expected the telephone to ring, to hear her voice on the other end, sour from his betrayal as she wept. But she did not phone him, and he reasoned, how could she possibly know what had transpired?

While her husband was grappling with his inner demons, Beverly was being industrious. Unwilling to wait for her husband to become motivated, Beverly took it upon herself to begin cleaning out the spare room. With Christmas just around the corner, she had far more pressing matters to think about, but she could not banish the thought that she was running out of time. The baby would be here in a matter of months and she had not prepared in the least. Beverly was a woman who took immediate action when she got something into her head. She wanted the room ready and she would do it herself, rather than depend on anyone else.

The room was being used for storage, with stacks of boxes lining the walls and in the closet. She toted one box at a time to the garage, pushing the ones that were too heavy for her to lift down the hall, through the kitchen and laundry area, to their final resting place in the garage. At one point she came across a box that had housed her mother's things. She sifted through it, looking over pictures and memorabilia that she hadn't seen in years. Her mother had been very pretty. Beverly did the math in her head and realized that she must have been in her early forties when she had passed away. That seemed so young. Even more so the older Beverly got.

Memories floated through her mind of when she was a girl. Her mother used to read to her before she went to bed each night. Her favorite was a book of children's poetry by James Whitcomb Riley. Beverly had attempted reading it to Keller once. He enjoyed the illustrations, but he was not patient enough to wait for her to read through the pages before he would turn them to see the next picture. She had put the book away, not wishing for it to be destroyed. It was one of the few things that she had left from her childhood, a fond reminder that she had been loved.

Many times she had wished that she could ask her mother for advice, or unload her woes upon a sympathetic ear. Many times she had wanted to ask for help, or have a shoulder to cry on. Looking at her mother's picture, she felt sad and a little lost. The woman staring back had never known Keller and would never know the child she carried now. She quietly slipped the picture back into the box and shut it again before moving on to the next box. There was no point in hashing over old memories.

Warren got home from work later than usual, feeling the weight of the world on his shoulders, his tie loose, his hat pulled low on his brow. There was no one to greet him when he walked through the door. He looked around the house until he found the empty spare room, with Beverly and Keller. Keller was looking out the window, an odd sight. He looked as if he were contemplating some great truth, some fundamental concept of space and time and the universe. He turned and his face lit up when he saw his father standing in the doorway.

"Daddy!" he squealed.

"Hello, son. It's good to see you too," Warren said, taking him into his arms in a hug. He went over to Beverly, with Keller hanging on his leg and gave her a peck on the cheek. "What's all of this?"

"I am just getting it ready for the nursery," she explained. "I've gotten it all cleaned out so that I can paint it and put some furniture in."

"Couldn't it have waited? I would have been able to help."

"Well, this way you won't have to think about it."

"I don't want you doing too much. Some of these boxes were very heavy."

"I didn't lift the heavy ones."

"You are in such a hurry. I told you that I would do it later."

"Warren, you said that three weeks ago."

"We have nearly four months," Warren complained. "You're always so determined to make a big something out of a little nothing. You're just as bad as he is," Warren accused, referring to Keller. "Getting something in your head, and it must be done right away or the world might end."

"I would like to have it done before then," she said defensively. "Four months isn't very long to get everything ready that needs to be done." She smoothed the side of his face with her hand. "What are you angry about? It's just one more thing you won't have to worry over." In actuality she felt guilty, like a child that had done something wrong and was now trying to appease the adult for her shortcomings. Beverly had known that Warren would be displeased with her attempt at trying to work on the nursery. She knew that he would say it was not a priority until closer to when the baby was to come.

"You really are a wonder, Bev. Just relax a little. There's no point in pushing yourself to get everything done all at once," he admonished her, trying to calm himself down.

She shuttered inside, because she knew that he would be annoyed by the next bit of information that she was about to divulge. "I went to the hardware store and picked up a can of paint. Wait till you see the color I chose. It's a very pretty butter yellow, very soft and subtle."

He groaned. "We'll take care of the paint later. Right now I'd just like a hot meal and a rest in my chair. I'm beat."

"I'll just go and quickly throw something together," she appeased, making a fast exit for the kitchen. Truth be told, she hadn't thought a thing about it. She had been so concerned with the nursery that dinner was the last thing on her mind.

She rummaged through the icebox and the cupboards, searching for an easy fix to her problem. By the time she had gotten dinner in the oven, she was feeling a little over extended. She cleaned up the dishes in the sink and set the table before going to see what was going on elsewhere in the house. Warren was sprawled in his chair, watching the news on television.

"Dinner will be ready soon. Sorry I didn't have it done when you got home," she apologized. "I got a little carried away, I guess."

"You just get something in your head and it's got to be done right away. I would have helped you with the boxes."

"I know. I'm sorry. I just didn't want you to have to do it."

"I tried to call my father about Keller's birthday, like you had asked, but I guess they already left for Florida. The housekeeper said that they decided to go early."

"I wonder what they do while they're on vacation," Beverly speculated.

"What do you mean?"

"Do they spend the whole trip doing things separately?"

"I suppose. I don't know," he snapped.

"Does that make you cross?" she asked, a bit incredulously.

"I don't talk about your family that way," he pointed out.

Beverly shut her mouth. Warren appeared to be in a very bad mood. She realized that regardless of what she was to say he would take offense. She went back to the kitchen, thinking she would prefer to leave him alone rather than get into a quarrel with him. Keller came in after awhile, tugging at her apron. She shooed him away a few times, busy with other things, before she finally gave him her attention.

"What is it, Kel?" she cried, in exasperation.

He took her hand and tried to pull her along with him. She resisted. "I'm busy. I can't play right now." He persisted until she gave in and followed him. He towed her along behind him until he reached the room she had just cleaned out for the nursery. He stood quietly in the doorway, waiting for her to see what he had brought her to see.

"What's the matter?" She felt a cool breeze touch her face as she waited expectantly. It was then that she realized that the window was wide open. "The window is open," she stated to Keller, as if to tell him that she now understood what he had been trying to convey. Crossing the room to close it, she had her hand on the latch, ready to pull it shut, when she saw the real reason that Keller had summoned her. Looking out over the window sill, Beverly beheld a disastrous sight. Her can of yellow paint lay down below on the ground. It had apparently exploded upon impact, sending butter yellow paint in splatters across the snowy landscape and upwards along the side of the house, a painfully obvious contrast to the brick exterior.

Beverly gasped when she saw the wreckage. "Oh, no! What have you done?" For a moment she debated what was best to do. Should she tell Warren? He was already in a bad mood. She loathed to make it worse by exposing what Keller had done. She knew that she would also take some of the blame for purchasing the darned paint in the first place. Oh, why had she been so driven to buy the paint today? But then, if she didn't tell Warren, he would most certainly find out anyway. How could she hide such an obvious blemish on the front of their home?

Warren did not look up when she went to tell him what had happened. She was hesitant as she said softly, "Warren, there's something I have to tell you."

"What?"

"I, I just went into the nursery and the window was open," she began to explain.

"Well, then shut it. Do you need my help to do that?"

"I wasn't finished. You see, Keller opened the window and threw the can of paint out of it." Beverly braced herself for the fall out that would surely follow. Warren seemed disbelieving at first.

"He did what?"

"He threw the can of paint out the window."

"That's surprising," he replied. "Those things weigh a lot."

She cleared her throat. "I don't think you understand, darling. You see, there is yellow paint all over the side of the house, outside where he dropped it."

"Are you kidding me?" he bellowed in his rage.

"No, I'm afraid I'm not."

Warren jumped up from his chair and ran outdoors to try and survey the damage. Just as she had described, the paint had splashed in an arc, directly under the window, across the face of their home. He hastily went for the hose and turned it on, only to find that it was frozen. He threw it to the ground in disgust. Not wasting any time, he pulled the garage door open, searching out a pail. He took it in and filled it at the kitchen sink. Beverly stayed out of his way. She knew better than to cross a rampaging bull.

Warren hastened back to the paint mess and threw the bucket of water against the wall. While some of it was flushed away, the majority stuck stubbornly to its spot. He went back to the kitchen for more water and repeated the process. It was actually more detrimental than helpful, with the water freezing just moments after hitting the brick. Warren saw Keller watching him from the window and fairly growled, peeved beyond his ability to keep control of himself.

He went back in to the house and grabbed his keys on the table near the door, remembering at the last minute to get his coat as well. Beverly timidly came to see what had happened. "Did it come off?" she questioned. He did not answer but put his coat on and headed back out the door. "Where are you going?" she asked before he had shut the door completely.

"To the hardware store to get some paint thinner," he spat.

"I'm sorry, Warren. I didn't have any idea he would do something like that."

"You just had to have that paint. You couldn't wait, could you?"

"Please, I didn't mean to—," she began.

"It doesn't matter," he replied, in a voice that said otherwise. He slammed the door behind him before there were any other exchanges between them. He did not come home for some time, leaving Beverly to fretfully wait for him. She had dinner finished and put it on a plate covered with tin foil to stay warm in the oven. When she did hear the car pull into the driveway, she did not attempt to see if he was all right. Better to let him work on it by himself and let him cool down, rather than to worsen the already difficult situation by hounding him.

He finally came in some time later, looking grim and defeated. He flung his keys back onto the entryway table and put his coat in the closet. Beverly rushed to take his shoes off when he sat down, and then hastily went to retrieve his plate and put it on a tray for him. Keller heard him come in too. He came running with an eager grin on his face. "Daddy!"

Warren did not look pleased to see his son. His eyes were smoldering as the little boy wrapped his arms around his father's neck. Beverly presented him with his food, and he took the fork from her, jabbing it into his meat vehemently. He noted with disapproval that it was dry and must have been in the oven warmer for a long time. It figured. He didn't see that complaining would do any good, so he dug in and ate without any further ado, filling the empty stomach that had been plaintively speaking to him since he had returned home from work.

As was his custom, he would keep his displeasure to himself. He saw little point in voicing his anger. He knew that Keller did not understand, and he wasn't sure that Beverly cared much. She would simply try and smooth it over, make it seem like no big deal. That was her way. It was much easier for her to avoid conflict and act like nothing had happened rather than deal with his displeasure. He knew her well enough to know that she probably felt responsible anyhow. What was the point in make her suffer anymore?

"Did it come off?"

"It came off." He chuckled sarcastically. "The brick is several shades lighter in that spot, but it came off."

"I'm very sorry, Warren. I really am."

"I know," he sulked.

"Please don't be mad at me," she begged.

"I'm not," Warren lied. "Could I just eat my dinner in peace?"

"Certainly, darling."

Beverly could always tell when her husband had reached his breaking point. He grew unnaturally quiet, choosing to hold it all in, rather than discuss it. She knew not to push him any further when he was in such a mood. She had never been able to get him to voice his feelings when he was in such a temper; it was as futile as trying to engage him in a conversation about the war. He would suddenly become very reserved and get that guarded look she knew so well. As good and kind as her husband was, he was not a man that could put into words what he was thinking or feeling when he was most frustrated. It was best to let him keep it to himself, and work it out on his own.

If she knew the real reason for his foul mood, she would not have been sympathetic at all. But how could she know that he was secretly still out of sorts about his encounter with Barbara Clark that morning? How could she know that he blamed her and Keller for his momentary weakness? If he didn't have such a difficult life, perhaps he could have resisted the urge to put himself in temptations path. After all, he was merely a man.

Beverly took Keller by the hand and led him to the bathroom, trying to keep him busy with a bath until it was bedtime. She washed his back and hair, which he hated, despite his love of water. He always let her know that he was upset with her when she put the soap in his hair and rinsed it out. "Help me!" he would squeal. "Get me outta here."

Once the dreaded part was over, he played happily. He put

his mouth to the water and blew against it. His laughter was contagious. He would blow against the water and then say, "Bubbles, Mama. Iss bubbles."

She dried him with a towel and dressed him in his pajamas, putting him to bed slightly early; all the while he was kissing her hands. He must have realized, on some very simple level, what a predicament he had put her in. It was hard to stay upset with him; he looked so innocent, peering up at her with his head on his pillow. She kissed his brow and pulled the covers up to his chin before leaving his room. It was a terrible thing, she knew, to be so relieved when he went to bed, but she was nonetheless pleased. There were times when the only peace she felt was when he was asleep. In the moments of silence when he was slumbering she could recuperate from the trauma of the long day. She comforted herself with the thought that tomorrow might bring happier times.

She discovered that Warren had gone to bed early when she emerged from her self-imposed exile. She cleaned up his dinner plate and went to the living room to read quietly until she was sure he was asleep so that there would be no need for conversing. When she slipped into bed, her husband rolled over and tucked an arm around her. It left her feeling somewhat comforted. Perhaps he wasn't so mad at her after all.

ten

Christmas came in its usual fashion. Warren and Beverly did not have to worry about Keller waking them in the wee hours of the morning. He slept as if it were any other day. When he did wake, he was perplexed by the gifts under the tree. They had not been there the night before.

"It's Christmas, Kel. Do you want to open your presents?" Beverly baited. She pulled a gift from beneath the tree and scooted it across to him. He looked at it for some time, wondering what he was to do with it. Beverly tore some of the paper to start him. Once he saw there was something hidden under the paper, he ripped it away without hesitation.

"I told you he would love it," Warren lectured, as Keller's eyes grew round with excitement when he saw the truck and animals.

"It's as big as he is," Beverly observed.

"Do you want me to help you get it out?" Warren offered Keller. He took the box to open it, but Keller grabbed it back and held it tight, afraid that it was being taken away from him.

"Mine!" he protested.

"I know that it's yours. I was just going to help you open it."

He moved closer to Keller and opened one end of the box, while his son did not let up on his grip. Warren slid the trailer and the animals from its packaging so that the boy could clearly see it. Keller knocked the box away and dove for the toy.

He seemed quite content as he loaded the animals into the trailer. Beverly and Warren watched him for awhile, and then Beverly went for another gift. "Kel, here, open this one." Keller ignored her. She pushed it more persistently into his hands. Again he denied it, pushing it back, and then returning his attention to his animals.

Beverly thought that if she were to start to open it, as she had the truck, that she might arouse his curiosity. She tore away some of the paper and tried to give it to him again. He resisted. She put the gift back. "Looks like he doesn't want anything else," she said with a disapproving click of her tongue.

"We should have just gotten him one thing."

"What, your truck?" She couldn't help but be caustic.

"It's plain to see that he is quite happy with it."

Beverly watched him line up the animals in a meticulously straight row, happy with his new treasure, and chose to let it go with that. She reached over and grabbed a large box from among the gift wrapped packages and handed it to her husband. "Merry Christmas," she offered, giving him his present.

Warren tore away the paper in the same energetic way that Keller had. Beverly had to smile to herself; he could still resemble a little boy at times. He opened the box and pulled out a leather briefcase. "It's very handsome, darling. The nicest one I've ever had." He unbuckled the straps that held it closed and inspected the interior compartments. "Plenty of space," he commented, and nodded his approval.

"Do you really like it?" she asked, fishing for more compliments.

"It's a fine satchel."

"It's what you wanted, isn't it?"

"Yes, yes, it's the very thing."

"I also got you this," she said, eagerly handing him a hat box.

He accepted it and removed the round lid. He seemed impressed with its contents. He pulled out the dark gray fedora with a wide black band, looking over it carefully.

"Do I look dashing?" he asked setting the fedora at a jaunty angle on top of his head.

"Very," she laughed, finding the sight of him in his navy pajamas, wearing a hat, an amusing sight.

"My other was getting a little worn, huh?"

"It was."

"Well, Beverly, are you ready for your gifts?"

She nodded eagerly. "I think so."

"Santa brought you something and put it in your stocking," he hinted.

Beverly jumped up from the floor and went to her stocking to dig for her gift. Her fingers brushed against a long, thin velvet box. She pulled it out and opened the hinged lid. She gasped as she took hold of the bracelet and held it up. "It's stunning!" she declared. The bracelet was a double row of painted beads with a small silver charm, shaped like a square box. She rushed over to him and pressed her lips against his.

"You like it," he observed, pleased with himself.

"I love it, darling," she gushed.

"Well, your other gift is a little more practical."

She went over to the tree and sifted through the few remaining gifts that were for Keller. She pulled out the one with her name on it. It was very small in size, and she wondered to herself what it might be. When she opened it, a little white card was the only thing she found. She held the card up with a confused expression.

"What's this?" she wondered.

"Read it."

"It says, 'Look in the garage,' " she read.

"Perhaps you should go look in the garage," he offered.

She hastened to get to the garage through the laundry area. Swinging the door open wide and flipping on the light switch, she was surprised to find a buggy with a large red bow waiting for her. She ran out, her bare feet cold against the concrete floor, to admire it. It was a deep green with ivory trim, chrome duchess gear, four bow hood folds, gray rubber tires with L-shaped brakes and large plated hubcaps. She tried it, rolling it back and forth before she rolled it inside, back to the living room, where Warren was waiting.

"It's wonderful, Warren."

"I thought you might be able to use it soon."

"I can take Kel and the baby for walks."

Keller's attention had been diverted. He went over to the buggy and took hold of the shiny chrome handle, running it up and down the length of the room. Warren and Beverly were amused. They laughed at him as he sped back and forth.

"I don't think it is a good idea to let him push the baby— ever," Beverly said, as he recklessly ran it into the wall. Keller grew tired of the buggy and went back to his animals after awhile.

"You should probably put it back in the garage, where it's safe from him."

"Don't you think I could keep it in the nursery?"

"It's up to you, but I doubt he'll leave it alone in there."

"I guess you're right," she agreed, going to put the buggy back where she had gotten it. She relished it for a few more moments before shutting off the light and closing the door behind her. It was exciting to have some tangible object to remind her that a baby was coming. It made it all seem more real. When she went back to the living room, she saw the other gifts that Keller had refused to open.

"Looks like we have enough left over for his birthday," Beverly said, collecting them and taking them back to the bedroom, where she stashed them in her closet. With the gift unveiling over, Beverly went to the kitchen to begin breakfast. She had prepared some dough for breakfast rolls the night before, and she took it from the refrigerator to let it rise while the oven was warming.

Beverly felt that the breakfast for Christmas day was very important. She remembered her mother preparing a feast each year, until she had grown too sick to carry on the tradition.

During an interval, between making the bacon and the eggs, Beverly peeked in on Warren and Keller, still playing in the living room. Warren was pulling the trailer around and making truck noises while Keller followed after it on his hands and knees.

She smiled to herself, content with the fact that he seemed very happy with his Christmas gift. When breakfast was ready, she called them in, yelling loud enough that they could hear her from the other room. She put the plates and silverware and glasses on the table and waited for them to file in. Keller was clutching his truck and trailer and doing his best to juggle all of the animals in the other arm. He sat down in his customary seat and waited patiently.

"Kel, can you put that down while we eat?" she requested, trying to take it from him.

"NO!" he cried, yanking it away from her reach. "Mine."

"It's time to eat breakfast, Keller. Put it down and you can have it again when we are finished," she promised. She reached out to claim it again. He grew all the more defensive and began to slap her hand.

Warren, who still wore his pajamas and hat, interceded. "It won't hurt to let him hold it this once. He'll get tired of it soon enough and then it won't be a problem."

"Fine," she said, slightly defensive. She sat down to the table and spread her napkin across her belly, it being closer to any spillage than her lap, and bowed her head. "Let's bless the food," she ordered.

Warren hastily removed his fedora and said a quick prayer before he set it back on his head and dug in to the eggs. He helped himself to a cinnamon roll and some bacon before he began to eat. "Everything tastes great, Bev," he complimented.

"Thank you," she replied. "And thank you for the lovely gifts, Warren. They were very thoughtful."

"It pleases me that you like them."

"You were right on the money with Keller. He certainly seems to love that animal hauler," she commented, motioning to Keller, who was trying to eat his breakfast with his hands full.

"You can't go wrong if it has animals," Warren said modestly.

*   *   *

After returning from his Christmas break, Warren had more than enough work to catch up on. He tried to eliminate one file at a time until he finally reached the top of his desk again. At lunchtime, Miss Clark rapped softly on his office door. "Come in," he allowed.

She was wearing a new dress with a dark green ribbon tied in her hair and smiling brightly. "Will you be going to lunch, Mr. Vance?"

"I don't suppose so, Miss Clark. It seems that I have more than enough to keep me busy. But you may leave for your break, if you'd like," Warren proposed.

"Thank you, Mr. Vance." She went back toward the lobby area and came back with a small package, wrapped neatly with a bow on top. "It's late, but I got you a small Christmas gift," she explained, placing it on the desk before him. He eyed it warily. "Aren't you going to open it?" she pushed.

He took the present in his hands and unwrapped it carefully, feeling uneasy and a little trapped. When he opened it, he found a gold plated money clip with his initials etched on it in a swirling cursive calligraphy. Warren held it for a moment, his mind racing to try and figure out what he should do next.

"That was very generous of you, Miss Clark, but I cannot accept such a gift," he admonished.

She was not about to take no for an answer. "Mr. Vance, you are a very good, very dear employer to me. I was only trying to say thank you for all that you have done on my behalf. Besides, you can't give it back. It has your initials on it. What would I do with a man's money clip that has the letters WFV on it? I don't know any other Warren Franklin Vances."

"Miss Clark, I appreciate what you were trying to do, but—," he protested before she cut him off.

"I insist that you keep it. You would deeply offend me if you did not," she coaxed.

142

Warren put it back in its box and smiled weakly. "Thank you, Miss Clark. It was very thoughtful of you," he conceded. "I am grateful for the gesture."

She smiled triumphantly. "It was the least I could do," she replied, then went back out the door to get her coat and handbag to leave for lunch.

Warren opened his desk drawer and dropped the small box in, sliding it to the back. As far as he was concerned, the money clip would never see the light of day again. He could just imagine what Beverly's reaction would be if she ever found out. He was not going to risk making her upset beyond reasoning. He shut the drawer with a bang and tried to return his concentration to the work that lay before him.

eleven

January eighth, the anniversary of Keller's birth. Beverly steadied the cake she carried, moving slowly so that the candles would not go out. She couldn't help but grin as Keller belted out "Happy Birthday" in unison with her and Warren. She was very pleased that he knew the song, although she was sure that dogs would be howling if they could hear him singing it. As Beverly set the cake carefully in front of him, they finished their rendition before she told him, "Blow out the candles."

He seemed so excited, so happy, as if he really understood what was going on. He took a big breath and then endeavored to blow them out. She helped him get the last one when he ran out of steam. "Happy birthday, Keller," she gushed, as she pulled out the cake server and cut his cake up into eight portions. "You're six years old today," she informed him.

She dished each slice up onto a plate and passed them around the table, then sat down to enjoy her own. Now that Beverly was getting along in her pregnancy, food was a great source of pleasure for her. She made sure that every last morsel of cake had been licked from her fork before going back for another bite. Warren observed her in amusement.

"Good cake?" he asked, mockingly.

"Very good cake," she agreed, unwilling to let him sour the experience.

"Just think, six years ago we were keeping track of your con-tractions."

"I didn't think I would ever have him. Two weeks overdue, and no end in sight. I was so miserable." She laughed. "And big."

"I was certainly concerned about the prospect of you going on indefinitely. I didn't think that I would ever have my old wife back. I was never as much afraid of anyone as I was of you then," he mused with a mischievous grin, as he took another bite of cake.

"Did you blame me, Warren? I was uncomfortable and in quite a lot of pain," she said.

"More, pwease," Keller begged, extending his plate to her.

"It's your birthday, so I won't say no," she told him, cutting a slice in half and putting it on his outstretched plate. He accepted it eagerly and dug in. His face was smeared with chocolate, but he seemed very satisfied.

"Do you want to open a gift?" she asked. She left the kitchen for a moment but came back with his gift, still wrapped in Christmas paper.

"You didn't rewrap it?"

"Well, what's the point, Warren? He doesn't care."

Keller took the present in his hand and unwrapped it. Beverly helped him open the box, and he pulled out a drumming bear. She wound it up and the bear began to sway as he beat the drums. Keller was very amused. He clapped his hands and laughed. When the motor stopped, he wound it himself.

"He likes it, Bev," Warren congratulated.

Keller took his bear and ran the fur against his cheek before he jumped down from his seat and ran off to play. He often took his treasures to his room, where he could savor them. He kept his stash under his bed. Beverly always looked there first if she was missing something.

"Did you see the nursery?"

"No. Why?"

"They delivered the furniture today. Come see," she begged.

Beverly showed him into the nursery and switched on the lights. Although the room still looked bare, it now had a chest of drawers and a crib, where once it had been completely vacant. It was a small room, but Beverly had taken advantage of the space by placing the furniture so that it was utilized to its fullest potential. With the walls painted and the two new pieces, it was beginning to look very warm and inviting.

"I used my S & H stamps to get the chest of drawers," she explained, pleased with herself. "And the crib was on sale." The pale yellow walls complemented the robin's egg blue baby bed, which had fuzzy baby animal decals on the end panels and colorful beads on the rails. The chest of drawers was a simple model, all white.

"Very nice, with the little bunnies and the beads to keep the baby occupied."

She could tell from his voice that he was teasing her. "I'm sorry if I bored you. I was just excited that it's nearly finished."

"I am too," he insisted. "It really does look nice in here."

"I just need to get some curtains, a few pictures for the walls, a rocking chair, and I'll be done."

"With time to spare," he added.

"I know that I can be a bit extreme, but I want to be ready. If it was left up to you, the poor baby wouldn't have a place to sleep until it was Keller's age," she defended.

"Won't it be in the bassinet for the first few months?"

"Yes," she acknowledged.

"So why does it matter?"

"Because once the baby comes, when will I have time to work on it?"

"That's a legitimate point," he admitted.

"Well, how do you like that? Warren Vance just agreed with me."

"How could I not? You're rationalization skills are far better than mine, darling."

"For some reason that doesn't exactly sound like a positive thing," she said with mock indignation.

"I do wish that you had chosen a different color of paint."

"You'll never forgive me for that, will you?" she asked, remembering back to when Keller had dropped the gallon of paint out the window. It had been a nearly a month, but it had not been long enough that they could laugh over it yet.

"I realize that it wasn't your fault. I was just upset that it happened."

"It certainly seemed as though you thought it was my fault."

"I was angry. What do you expect?"

"I expect you to control your temper, Warren. I know that Keller can be difficult, but it would help very much if you didn't blame me for everything he does."

"Good grief, Bev. Are you going to make a federal case out of it?"

"I was just trying to say that it is hard enough to deal with his behaviors without you turning on me. I know that I am the laughingstock in town, but to have you desert me too . . ."

Warren seemed surprised. "Don't you feel that I support you?"

"I often feel that you disapprove of me. That you think I do everything wrong."

"On the contrary, Bev. You are the most perfect person I know."

Her mood suddenly changed. "I'm so alone," she whispered, with a far-off look in her eyes. "I'm so lonely. I feel like there's no place for me. That I exist in my own world, apart from everyone else. Or rather Keller's world. It's Keller's world I live in." She met Warren's perplexed gaze. "When you are angry with me, I feel like I don't belong anywhere."

He didn't know what to say. He patted her arm gently, as if to tell her with unspoken words that he sympathized, that he understood. In a small way he did, but then he wondered if he could ever grasp fully what she must be suffering. In college she had been bubbly, outgoing, sure of herself. She had a gaggle of girlfriends that she went to movies and dances with. Something in her disposition drew people to her, a magnetic pull that others gravitated toward. He knew that she once had her choice of beaus; she could have married other men, many that had turned out to be more successful than he had. Warren had always counted himself lucky that she had deemed him worthy. Seeing her like this made him resentful.

Why couldn't he give her happiness? Why couldn't he give her the life that she deserved? It made him feel less of a man. Worst of all was the fact that he never knew what to say to her, how to comfort her. Warren tried to be sensitive to her needs, but he had within him an alien element that he could never quite overcome. There had not been any proper example for him, and he often felt himself fighting the more callous expressions that sprang so easily to his mind. It was with resolute determination that he fought his natural man, fought it just as earnestly as he would a foe in battle.

"Am I speaking nonsense again? I'm sorry that I get so emotional sometimes."

"I don't think so, darling. I apologize for my bad behavior. I should have been more thoughtful," he conceded.

"Tell me you love me?"

"Of course I do!"

"I want you to say it."

"I love you."

"Say my name. Say, 'Beverly, I love you.' "

His voice softened, and he touched her face tenderly, running his thumb along the outline of her bottom lip. "I love you, Beverly." They exchanged longing glances, feeling for the moment that they were on the same page, that they were of one mind, connected in a deeply spiritual sense. It seemed good and right. She took his hand and entwined her fingers with his, pressing his knuckles to her lips.

"You have such strong hands," she commented, as she studied them. "It always makes me feel so secure. If you hold me in those hands I will never fall; your strength will support me."

Those words pulled from him the desire to be better, to make her proud. He wanted so much to be as strong as she believed him to be. He would do what was right. He would be the man she longed for. This was his resolve, his pledge to himself as he studied her face. It was slightly rounder, now that she was getting along in the pregnancy, but still beautiful nonetheless. He marveled to himself that she could change so radically in her appearance and remain so alluring.

"I won't let you down, Bev," he pledged. "You can always count on me."

*   *   *

Taking Keller to the supermarket was a difficult chore. Beverly inevitably left the store with more than what she had intended to purchase. Keller simply would not take no for an answer. If he wanted something, he would toss it in the cart, with little regard for what his mother's reaction would be. Sometimes she squabbled with him over it, trying to put things back, but there were also times when she didn't bother. It was easier to let him have his way when they were out.

Marsh Supermarket was a large and modern place, with a wide variety of produce and plenty of tall shelves with lots to choose from. Their cuts of meat were top quality, and they were cut to your specifications right in front of you so that you knew exactly what you were getting. The only problem she had with the place was the grocer's uncanny ability to put everything that Keller would find appealing right at his eye level. Beverly intentionally tried to skip some of the aisles she knew would be most difficult to get him through.

As she wound through the aisles, selecting her groceries, Keller tagged along, eyeing the shelves for something he might want. He spotted the Cracker Jacks and grabbed one of the boxes before Beverly could stop him. He turned his back to her so that she couldn't take it from him, shielding it with his body until he could open it. He knew that it was too late for her to take it away once he had opened it.

"Keller, that is not nice," she scolded. "We haven't paid for that yet."

He dug through the box, spilling some of the popcorn onto the floor, attempting to find the prize. It was not what he wanted. It was a small green army man with a parachute neatly folded into a little pack with the strings wound around it. He threw it down when he realized it was not the surprise he had been hoping for. Beverly picked up his mess and stuffed it back in the box, situating it in the cart so that it did not spill again.

"No more. You come along with Mama." She took his hands and forced them upon the handle of the cart, securely under hers, so that he was unable to do anything but come along with her. "You need to be a good boy for Mama," she chided.

They zigzagged through the rows of shelving, checking off the things they needed from her list as she got them. When she got to the butcher's corner, she asked him politely for a pot roast. He was a friendly sort, tying the strings of his white apron behind him and washing his hands before he began her order.

"How big would you like it, ma'am?"

"Oh, I think a pound and a half will do," she told him.

"Would you like anything else with that?"

"I think some pork chops would be nice, four or so."

"Will do," he said, going to select the meat from the refrigerator.

She was watching him cut the meat behind the counter when her son, seeing she was distracted, took off in a flash. Beverly panicked. "I'll be right back," she said quickly to the butcher as she darted off after Keller. She had a hard time keeping up with him. As if in replay, the boy wove his way along the same route that they had just come from. He skipped the aisles that they had skipped, propelling himself back to where the Cracker Jacks had been. Beverly would catch sight of him disappearing around the corner of an aisle and try and pick up her pace to reach him, calling out his name all the while, only to see him vanish around the next corner.

When she finally did catch up to him, he was sitting in the

middle of the aisle with three boxes of Cracker Jacks opened and spilled onto the floor. He had not found the prizes satisfactory and had gone back for another, in hopes of acquiring the one he desired. "Keller, get up off of the floor this minute!" she rebuked. He ignored her request, mumbling, "Elephant," and tried to go for another box. Beverly grabbed his hand to try and stop him. "No more!"

He lay himself flat upon the ground, unwilling to move from the spot. "Help me!"

"Please get up, Keller," she begged. "Please."

"I want elephant, pwease."

"There is no elephant." She bent down to try and hook her hands under his armpits, in an attempt at getting him up from the ground. His body was completely limp, and she realized right away that she would not be able to lift him. She was concerned more for her condition than she was for teaching Keller a lesson.

"Kel, be a good boy for Mama and get up," was her last try at coaxing him.

"I want elephant, pwease."

She sat down next to him on the floor and took a box of Cracker Jacks from the shelf, turning it over in her hand, she opened it from the bottom and peaked in. A false tattoo, the kind you wet and press against your skin. She set the box down and seized another, tearing it open from the bottom of the box; a small plastic compass. She set that down with the others. The next prize was a ring. Then came a magnifying glass and another tattoo. She ripped the next box open, exposing yet another tattoo. In desperation she took another off the shelf.

A Marsh employee, under the guise of straightening the shelves, approached them with a curious expression upon his face. "Can I help you, ma'am?"

"No, thank you," Beverly answered, not bothering to look up from her chore. She was determined, at this point, to get it over with so that she could leave the store. That was her goal, to get out of this place as quickly as possible.

The man counted to himself the eleven boxes that had been

pilfered through and lined neatly before her. He was somewhat concerned. "Do you intend on paying for those?"

"I certainly do," she returned, a little more hostile than the situation warranted.

The twelfth box was the lucky one, as she pried a small plastic elephant from its cardboard tomb. When she thrust it toward Keller, his face lit up. He snatched it from her hand with glee, holding it so that he could inspect it carefully. "Elephant!"

Beverly got up from the floor and pulled Keller up with her. She turned to the grocer, who had not left the scene, but stood resolutely where he had been observing, and said with a sweet smile, "Could you please see to it that those are taken to the front for me. I will be up shortly to collect them." She took Keller by the hand and dragged him back to her cart, which was waiting by the butcher's counter. Gathering the meat, wrapped in white butcher's paper, from the counter, she placed it in her cart and took the most direct way to the cash register.

The same man that had taken such an interest in her Cracker Jack looting stood behind the round conveyer belt, and without saying anything, only giving her a disapproving eye, began to ring her up. Keller was quietly content with his elephant. He remained oblivious to the adults around him, one frowning in displeasure, the other red faced from shame, as he ran his fingers over the smooth plastic as if he were petting it. It did not matter what they thought, only that in his little world everything was as it should be.

"That'll be twenty-two dollars and thirty-seven cents."

Beverly rummaged through her coin purse, pulling out a package of neatly folded bills. She handed him the money and waited for her change. He put the change in her outstretched hand, then gave her a few S & H trading stamps. She pulled out her little stamp book and stuck the strip of green tickets into the folds of the pages before leaving. She didn't bother saying thank you because she didn't know what to thank him for. She was still frustrated and annoyed over the Cracker Jack incident.

The bag boy was waiting for Beverly with her groceries. He

followed her as she headed for the doors. On their way out, Keller caught sight of the coin-operated horse at the front of the store and tried to deviate from his mother's chosen course. Beverly held fast to his hand, unwilling to allow him to ride on it. If she let him climb on top, she had serious doubts as to whether she could get him back off. She was sure that one ride on the horse would turn into a plethora, and there was no guarantee that it would ever end.

"Keller, I'll take away that elephant if you don't come with me right now," was her stern admonition.

It may have been the look in her eyes or the tone of her voice, but Keller took her at her word and followed along. Once they were to the car, she put him in first before opening the trunk of the car for the bag boy to load the groceries. He stuffed the paper bags laden with groceries into the empty cavity with the carelessness of youth. Beverly hoped her eggs were still intact. When he was finished, the boy smiled politely and bid her, "Have a nice day." He seemed genuine.

Beverly gave him a decent tip, which he thanked her for, and then she climbed gratefully into the safe confines of the automobile and headed home. Each time she took Keller some place, she vowed to herself that she would never do it again. Unfortunately, out of necessity, she was forced to break that resolve again and again. How was she to get groceries if she did not take him with her? How was she to accomplish anything if he was not accompanying her? It was an unhappy fact of life for Beverly, no alternatives for it. Whether or not she liked it, Keller was an appendage, forever attached to her. The tears burned in her eyes, but she swallowed hard and refused to let them spill.

That evening, Warren seemed pleased when Beverly proffered the bowl of Cracker Jacks to him. He accepted it, taking a handful, and popping it into his mouth. "What's the occasion?"

"No occasion."

"This is an awful lot of Cracker Jacks," Warren observed.

"Twelve boxes, to be exact," she admitted.

"Why'd you buy twelve boxes?"

"I had to," she replied.

"On account of?"

"On account of your son refusing to get up from the ground until I found him an elephant in one of them. I can't lift him anymore, what with the baby, so I was forced to do what he wanted. It took me precisely twelve boxes to locate that toy so that I could get out of the supermarket to bring him home," she explained in a huff.

Warren laughed. "You opened twelve boxes of Cracker Jacks right there in the store?"

"Yes, yes I did." She did not seem to find it as amusing as he did.

"I'm sorry, Bev, but you have to admit that is a pretty funny story."

"No, I don't have to admit it."

"Come now, darling, just think about it. They must have thought you were completely nuts when you paid for twelve opened boxes of Cracker Jacks. Can you imagine what they were saying to themselves?"

"If you think it's so funny, perhaps next time you can take him shopping," she challenged. "See how funny it is when you're the one sitting on the floor rummaging through that stuff to find a darned elephant. I doubt that I will ever be able to eat Cracker Jacks again."

"I'm sorry it's got you so upset. I suppose I shouldn't have laughed."

"I suppose not," she agreed and left it at that.

twelve

It was sometime after lunch that Miss Clark received the phone call from Mrs. Vance, on an afternoon that seemed doomed to boredom. Warren had been out for most of the morning with a prospective buyer, and she had been alone all that time. Still, it was not Beverly Vance's voice that she would have liked to hear when she asked, pleasantly, "Vance and Son, how may I help you?"

"Miss Clark, I must speak to Warren. Is he in?" She sounded as if she were in a panic. Her voice shook and it seemed as if she might cry, quite distraught to say the least.

Miss Clark was not one for theatrics and was naturally annoyed by the emotion that she detected. It was not good of Beverly Vance to be calling her husband at work anyhow. He was a busy man, without time for unnecessary telephone calls. Beverly had him all to herself when he got home from work. Why couldn't she simply wait until then to speak to him? Barbara Clark had far too many things to do to concern herself with playing page for Warren Vance's wife.

"He's not back from lunch. I believe that he was meeting with a client." She had given the information, but she would not go as far as offering to take a message.

"Could you please tell him that I need to speak to him as soon as possible?" she begged, desperation sounding in her voice.

"I can do that, Mrs. Vance."

"It's urgent. Please tell him to telephone me as quickly as possible."

"I understand, Mrs. Vance." Without even saying good-bye, Beverly hung up the phone. "Good day to you too," Miss Clark fumed into the disconnected receiver. Warren did not return for another half an hour. He took his mail from the corner of Miss Clark's desk on his way through the lobby area and went into his office. As he sorted through the envelopes, Miss Clark came to the open door.

"Did you need something, Miss Clark?"

"Just wanted to see how your lunch appointment went."

"Very well, thank you."

"I'm glad to hear it." She continued to stand in the doorway, hovering without any real purpose in being there. Warren tried to ignore her, thinking that she might go away, but she didn't. He looked up from what he was doing, waiting expectantly.

"Was there anything else?"

"I nearly forgot. Mrs. Vance telephoned and asked that you call back when you had a moment," she said, making it sound trivial.

"When did she call?"

"Close to half an hour ago, sir."

Warren picked up the receiver and dialed his home telephone number. The telephone rang for some time before it was finally picked up. It was not Beverly who answered but a decidedly male voice. He cleared his throat. "I'm sorry, I must have the wrong number." He hung up and dialed more carefully this time. Again a man's voice was on the other line. "Sorry, me again. I'm trying to dial my wife, and I have somehow mistakenly called you twice now."

"Are you looking for Beverly Vance?" the voice on the other end of the line asked.

"That's right."

"You called the correct phone number, Mr. Vance. This is Albert Johnson with the sheriff's department. I'm here at your home on account of we got a phone call and responded to an accident here."

Warren's stomach dropped to his feet. "Say again."

"There's been an accident, and your wife was hurt. Seems she went to the neighbor's house for help and your neighbor alerted us."

"What happened?"

"Your wife was injured, but she'll be all right. Still, we got your family doctor here, and it would probably be a good idea if you came home," Deputy Johnson advised.

Warren did not wait for any further direction. He was off the phone and out the door before any more time could pass. He was in such a hurry that he neglected to get his coat. Dashing into the lobby, he told Miss Clark, in a rushed blur of words that were hardly discernible, "I'll be out for the rest of the day."

Pulling onto his street did little to pacify his fears. He could see the sheriff deputy's patrol car parked in the driveway, and another car, which Warren assumed was the doctor's, parked at the curb. He scarcely had parked his own car, forgetting to turn off the engine before he rushed through the front door, with dreaded anticipation of what might come next. Keller's screams accosted his ears. His son was in the living room, looking more like a caged animal than a little boy. The deputy stood guard over the hallway entrance, apparently relieved to see Warren.

"Daddy!" Keller squealed. He ran to his father and threw his arms around him. Warren didn't hesitate for even a moment. He ignored the child completely and instead turned his attention to Albert Johnson.

"Where's my wife? Where's Beverly? Is she all right?"

"She's in the bedroom, Mr. Vance. The doctor is tending to her."

Warren shook Keller from him, nearly knocking him down in his haste to make it to the bedroom. When he came through the bedroom door, Dr. Stephens was stooped over Beverly, who was sitting on the edge of the bed. He did not have a clear vision of her, but he could see that her dress was covered with a great deal of blood. When he came nearer, he could observe the doctor as he carefully and neatly put stitches into her upper lip, where a jagged tear marred her pale skin. The cut continued without pause to her lower lip, although not as deeply as the laceration the doctor was working on. Her eye was nearly swollen shut, to the point that she could not look around to see that her husband had come into the room. It had already developed into an angry black knot of flesh. There were tears coursing down Beverly's face, leaving sooty tracks in their wake from her mascara, although she did not cry out. She remained perfectly still, as unmoving as a statue, for she had been told that the slightest movement might ruin the doctor's diligent work.

"What happened?" he burst out, horrified by what he saw. All he could think on the way over was that it might be something to do with the baby. Perhaps she had slipped on the ice and fallen. Perhaps she had taken a tumble down the front steps. Many different scenarios had run through his mind. While he was glad that the baby was in no apparent danger, the destruction to her face shocked him to the core. He felt helpless seeing her in pain as she struggled not to move during her sutures. He had seen worse while in the service, but this was Beverly; this was his wife.

Beverly could not speak as the doctor tried to finish up the stitches he was executing. It was Dr. Stephens who addressed him. "Warren, it's good you're home. It seems Beverly here has had an accident and needed some stitches to fix her up." He tried to sound as unconcerned as possible. The last thing he wanted was to get Beverly upset. If she should move her lip while he was in the midst of finishing, it might cause a permanent scar. As it was, she would likely always have a little white hairline where the laceration had been. She was a very attractive woman, and it bothered him to think of her having to suffer from a disfigured face indefinitely.

"Beverly, are you all right?" Warren gasped.

She did not move, not even a little, but she managed to get a yes out through her clenched teeth. He kneeled next to the bed, holding her hand until the doctor had finished with his chore.

"There now, all fixed up," he said, beginning to put his supplies back in his bag. "Pretty impressive, Mrs. Vance. Looks like thirteen stitches. I didn't put stitches on the cut on your lower lip. It wasn't as deep, but you'll still need to care for that too and keep it clean." The doctor was trying to sound more lighthearted than he actually was. He could see that the situation was not good and that Beverly was very nervous. "Let's get you out of this dress and clean you up, Mrs. Vance," he advised and then excused himself from the room until she was done changing.

She attempted to do it herself, but her fingers trembled so that she could not manage it. She seemed to be still recovering from shock. "Here, darling, let me do that." Warren helped her unbutton the buttons and took the dress off over her head, being careful not to touch her lip or eye. He then removed her shoes, rubbing her feet with deep pressure. She sat before him in nothing but her slip and nylons, looking as pathetic as was possible.

"You see to it that she comes in next week to get those stitches out, will you?" Dr. Stephens told Warren. "She needs plenty of rest now. She shouldn't be doing anything strenuous at this point. We don't want an early labor."

"Yes, of course."

Seeing her in such a condition was worse than anything he had ever experienced. When Keller was born, he had waited, with much apprehension, in the father's waiting room. While it had been difficult knowing what she was going through, he had not actually witnessed firsthand the mandatory discomforts she had experienced to bring Keller into the world. This was suffering beyond his ability to process. It left him feeling weak in the knees.

"Beverly, what on earth happened?" Warren interrogated, as he put his hands on her cheeks tenderly and searched her reaction. She avoided his eyes and wanted to avoid the question as well, but she knew that that was not possible. Warren would not give up without some explanation.

"It was an accident," Beverly stated defensively.

"Did you fall?" She shook her head. "Then what?" he probed with a soft, caressing voice.

She was quiet for a moment, searching for the mildest way possible to put into words what had happened. She was afraid of what would ensue if she told the truth. "It was Keller," she admitted after a long pause. "I tried to get him to put away his truck and he wouldn't. So I tried to take it away and he got upset." She saw the look of revulsion form on his face and quickly tried to appease him. "He didn't mean to hurt me. He was so frightened afterwards," she explained. "He was very sorry."

Warren's face grew hot. He was immediately furious. "What!" he roared. "Keller did this to you?"

"Warren, he didn't mean to. He doesn't know his own strength," Beverly insisted. "He didn't understand what he was doing."

He was finished talking to her. He left her with the doctor and stormed into the living room where the deputy was still standing watch over Keller. Warren was oblivious to the deputy and headed straight for his son. The boy wore puppy dog eyes, evidently aware that he had perpetrated a great wrong. "What did you do to your mother?" Warren roared. He came at Keller as if he was about to strangle him, but Deputy Johnson, attempting to diffuse the situation, interceded on Keller's behalf.

"Now, sir, you need to calm down for a minute."

"You could have killed her, you rotten little brat!" His gaze fell upon the offending truck, and with a twinge of remorse, he realized that it was the very truck that he had gotten Keller for Christmas, against Beverly's better judgment. He picked it up and drop-kicked it across the room. The awful noise scared Keller, and he began to bawl when he saw the trailer of his toy truck protruding out of the wall, like a torpedo that had only penetrated its target halfway.

"Mr. Vance, you need to try to calm down," Deputy Johnson said a little more forcefully as he put his hand on Warren's chest to try and hold him at bay.

"I want him out of here! You hear me? I want him gone!"

Beverly came running down the hall with Dr. Stephens just behind. The sight of her disfigured face brought a new rush of rage. "Go back to the bedroom, Bev," he instructed, pointing down the hall.

"Warren, he didn't mean to hurt me. He didn't," she persisted. "He just doesn't understand."

"Go back to the bedroom!" he bellowed.

Dr. Stephens tried to take her by the shoulders and guide her away from the scene, but she wouldn't have it. She stuck stubbornly to her spot. "Mrs. Vance, you ought to come lay down. You need your rest," he counseled.

"Warren, it was an accident."

"That's all he is, an accident waiting to happen. What about the baby? What if he had hit you in the stomach? He could have killed you. Just look at your face, Beverly!" There was no convincing him that Keller was innocent of any wrongdoing. If he was capable of doing this to a grown woman, what could he possibly do to an infant? He shuddered to think of it.

"It's nothing that won't mend. Really, Warren, he didn't mean to."

Warren turned to the deputy with his jaw set in determination. "I want him out of here. Take him up to Fort Wayne, I don't care, only get him out of my house."

"NO! You can't do that!" Beverly protested.

"Mrs. Vance, that boy is mentally deranged. He is capable of anything if he is capable of attacking his mother. Perhaps it's best," Dr. Stephens reasoned.

"Warren, you don't mean it . . . Please, Warren."

"You saw what he did to her. That should be enough to convince you that the right thing to do is to take him away," Warren told Deputy Johnson. Albert Johnson was about the same age as Warren, perhaps a few years older. He had a son and two daughters of his own. His heart went out to these parents. After being in the sheriff's department, he had witnessed many things that might make a man hardened. But Deputy Johnson had never grown used to viewing human suffering. He had never taken for granted the trouble and turmoil in other people's lives. It only made him sad, very, very sad. What would he do, given the same situation? How would he react if it were his own precious child?

He took the boy by the arm and led him to the door. Beverly made a move to try and stop the deputy. "No!" she was screaming. "You can't take my son!" Warren held her back, but she was not about to let it happen without a fight. She strained against her husband's arms, twisting and turning to try and get away.

Keller went peacefully until they got to the patrol car. Once he realized what the stranger intended to do, he let out a yell and began to fight. Deputy Johnson opened the door and forced the boy in. Once the door was shut behind him, Keller had no choice; he could not get out without a handle to open the door with. His yelling grew to a fevered pitch. He beat his fists against the window and rocked the car from side to side.

When Beverly finally wrestled her way loose from Warren's secure grasp, the patrol car was backing out of the driveway. Beverly flung the door open and began to chase after it.

"Keller! Keller!" she screamed in a terror.

She saw him press his little hands against the window. He was crying. "Mama. I want Mama, pwease!" he begged.

"My baby! Keller!" She was pounding on the trunk of the car, doing anything she could to draw his attention to her, to let him know that she was there.

"Beverly!" Warren yelled after her.

She ignored him. She didn't even bother to look back to see how close he was to her. She got just abreast of the car when it picked up speed and drove away. Warren was close behind, but she continued to run until the car disappeared around the corner and Warren caught up with her. He wrapped his arms around her, half picking her up, half dragging her backwards, to try and get her back to the house. She was still in nothing but her slip and nylons in the snow and freezing temperatures of February.

"Get away from me!" she screamed. "I hate you! Don't touch me!" Beverly fought against him, kicking and screaming. When that did not work, she dropped to the ground, mimicking the move that Keller always tried on her. Warren sank down with her, keeping a firm grip around her torso, just under her arms, unwilling to find out what might happen if he let go.

Dr. Stephens sprinted down the sidewalk, looking uncharacteristically frazzled. He arrived on the scene with a syringe held high in his right hand. He was nearly ready to administer it when Warren stopped him. Beverly was frantically calling after Keller, still putting up a struggle. When she saw the needle the doctor held, her panicked cries grew to a frenzied pitch.

"Dr. Stephens, she's already upset. That will only make it worse," Warren said with his voice raised so that the doctor could hear him over her shouts.

"I'm afraid she'll hurt herself," Dr. Stephens pressed. "This will put her to sleep so she can't harm herself or the baby."

"Get away from me!" she screamed. "I don't want it." As Dr. Stephens inserted the needle into her vein, she became more out of control. "Animals! I want my son! Keller! Get away from me! Get away!"

Warren held her arms down until the doctor could administer his dose. Still she would not give up, until the drug began to take effect. She gradually relaxed in Warren's arms, calling after her son, and then there was no energy left to do anything. She went limp in the snow, unable to recall why it was so cold or what she was doing outside. As frigid as it was, she also felt a warm sensation spreading through her limbs, running the route of vessels as they snaked through her frame, numbing her body and mind. Although she wished to protest, she had lost control of her mental faculties, and her body would not respond to her commands. Beverly was trying to hold her head up, but it resisted, lulling to one side and falling onto her shoulder.

Warren picked her up and carried her back to the house, laying her on the bed and covering her with a blanket. The battered eye was closed completely, discolored and bulging, while the other eye fluttered open, then dozed for a moment, only to flutter open again. In her waking moments she mumbled what seemed to be a prayer. Although her brain would not process cohesive thoughts, she instinctively thought to plead on Keller's behalf to the Maker who had formed him. "God, please," she begged. "God, please."

"Is she going to be all right?" Warren fretted.

"She should rest through the night at least. She needs to take it easy. I don't need to tell you that the last thing we want is for her to have that baby. Perhaps she'll come to her senses when she wakes up. If you have any problems, I can leave you these pills. They should help calm her." He set the pill bottle on the vanity. Before leaving, he inspected her stitches and eye, and then he was gone.

It was unnaturally quiet when he went. There was no Keller to make noise, to get into things, to throw tantrums. He was not there to climb on Warren's lap or beg for play. No sounds from the kitchen, where Beverly would normally be preparing dinner. No bubbling conversation about how her day had gone, or the latest Keller story. It was beginning to get dark, and Warren sat in the semi-gloom, alone and afraid. What had he done? Would Beverly ever forgive him?

Warren consoled himself with the thought that he had made the right decision. It was only a matter of time before Keller would have to be put away anyhow. If it hadn't been now, it surely would have been later. The larger the boy got, the more of a danger he became. It was inevitable, beyond Warren's ability to change the course of. It was his job to make the tough choices. It had fallen upon him to do the right thing. Keller would be better off in a place with children of his own kind. Better to have happened now than after the baby came. What if he had hurt the baby? Visions of Beverly's broken face floated through his mind.

Warren drifted back and forth between the bedroom and the living room to check on her frequently. He tried to speak to her several times, but she muttered incoherent nonsense, unaware of what was going on around her. She begged for something to drink at one point, but when he returned to her with a glass of water, she had fallen off to sleep again. He hoped that when she woke in the morning she would be restored to her usual self.

thirteen

Beverly hesitated when she heard the doorbell ring. She had no desire for anyone to see her in her present condition. Looking through the peep hole, she saw that it was Margaret Price come to offer a casserole dish wrapped in aluminum foil. Quietly she walked away, sitting on the couch in the semi-darkness. She had not opened the curtains that morning, so they remained drawn, blocking out any sunlight. Margaret knocked again, more insistently this time.

"Beverly, I know you are in there. Come and open the door," she persisted. When there was still no answer, she continued, "Please don't leave me standing out here like some ninny for the neighbors to poke fun at," and she knocked again.

Beverly could take it no longer. She went over to the door and opened it wide. Margaret seemed taken aback for a moment when she saw the younger woman, still dressed in her nightgown, hair uncombed, and most obvious of all, her battered face. This was a woman who always took such great pains with her appearance, always looked flawless and well groomed. She stood frozen, horrified by the stitches and swollen, bulging black eye as she held the casserole dish a little tighter in her arms. They regarded one another, each wondering what to expect.

"What did you come for, Margaret?"

"May I come in?"

"Why?"

"I heard you were not feeling well. I brought you some dinner."

"Not feeling well?" Beverly repeated sarcastically. "I don't have much of an appetite; I won't be needing your casserole."

"You need to take care of that baby, Beverly. You'll have to eat something."

"What do you care?"

Margaret could see that she was in a state and wondered how long they would have to exchange quips as she stood there on the front step in the cold. She could imagine those discreetly prying eyes behind curtained windows, watching with interest in homes all down the street. Unsure of how to proceed, she pressed her way past Beverly into the house. Beverly shut the door, following Margaret into the living room. She watched as Margaret removed her coat and gloves.

"I'm sorry, Margaret, but I'm not up for entertaining right now," she said quietly.

"I won't stay long," she advised, heading for the kitchen with her casserole. Beverly trailed after her, uncertain of what she could do to get rid of Margaret. She should never have opened the door to her. Margaret preheated the oven and then turned to the sink, full of dishes, which appeared to have been neglected for several days. She rolled up her sleeves and set to work cleaning them.

"I don't need you to do my dishes," Beverly fumed.

"I'm sure you don't, dear, but I'd like to do them for you anyhow."

"I don't want you to!"

"Sit down, Beverly. You should be resting," her voice was that of an annoyed mother, growing impatient with a child. Beverly tried to stare her down, but Margaret would not yield, so she did as she was told and sat. "Is Warren at work?"

"Yes."

"How's he holding up?"

"I don't know. He won't talk to me," she answered, keeping her eyes on Margaret's busy hands as they washed, rinsed, and then set the dish in the dish rack. She looked so forlorn that Margaret could hardly stand it; this was clearly not the Beverly she knew.

"He's hurting too."

"I don't care. I don't care what he thinks or how he feels," she vented.

"You mustn't talk that way. Warren is a good man. But we are all flawed, Beverly, every one of us."

"They took him from me, Margaret. He was crying, and he was calling for me, but they wouldn't let me go to him. They kept me from him."

"Where is he?"

"Up at the state hospital in Fort Wayne. That's where they took him," she began to sob. Margaret dried her hands on a dish towel and went to comfort her, patting her shoulder as she stood next to her. Beverly buried her face into Margaret's side, grasping the fabric of her dress as if it were a lifeline, weeping from the deepest part of herself. "What'll I do?" she wailed.

Margaret did not reply all at once. She waited until Beverly had calmed down. There was no point in trying to tell her anything in the state she was in. She simply stood there, lending her physical presence. It wasn't until she calmed down that Margaret could respond to her. "I know it doesn't seem like it will ever get better, but with time it will become less painful."

"How can it? Not without my boy, not without Keller. It can never be better."

"You don't see it now, but . . ."

"You don't know! You could never understand!"

"But I do, Beverly. I understand."

"How can you? You couldn't possible know what I am going through." She pulled away, leaning her elbows on the table and pressing her palms against her forehead. "Can you imagine what he thinks, that I've deserted him? He doesn't know anyone there; if someone were to hurt him, he can't tell anyone. He's been abandoned." The words were difficult to get out. "Please just go away and leave me alone," she said quietly as the tears rolled down her cheeks and splashed onto the laminate tabletop. She watched them pool there, waiting for Margaret to leave, but she did not.

"I understand better than you think, probably better than anyone else could."

Beverly did not react; she was not willing to be drawn in again. She was sure that this was some kind of a ploy on Margaret's part to soothe her into believing that her life would be better off without Keller. "Beverly, look at me," Margaret commanded.

Beverly slowly raised her chin, regarding Margaret, the older experienced eyes looking into the raw bloodshot troubled eyes of the younger, trying to somehow look past the bruised skin that surrounded her left eye. It brought back a flood of emotions and memories that Margaret had tried to blot out, had tried to suppress for many years now. She waited until she could control her voice before she sat down across from Beverly and took her hands in a firm clasp. And then she told Beverly her secret.

"I had two boys, Beverly. Two little babies. Charles and Arley." Beverly looked confused and skeptical all at the same time. As far as she knew, and as far as she knew that anyone else knew, Margaret had no children. She and Dale lived alone. Trying to remember back, she could not recall ever seeing pictures of children in their home; she could not think of a single time when Margaret had mentioned them.

"What?" Beverly asked incredulously.

"That's right."

"But . . ."

"Two sons that I did not raise."

"Why didn't you ever mention it before?"

Margaret tried to think of a way to tell her what she wanted to say. She sat for a moment with a troubled expression before she went on. "Charles was the older of the two. He looked like Dale when he was born—I mean *just* like Dale," she mused. "They didn't know what was wrong with him. He cried a lot. And as he got a little older we found that he was sensitive to noise and touch.

Couldn't stand to be held. Couldn't stand even the quietest of sounds." She did not look at Beverly as she made her admittance. It was more than she had ever confided in anyone but family. She was feeling very vulnerable and somewhat uncomfortable with her confession.

"They told us that he would be better off taken care of by professionals and that we couldn't take care of him properly, so we sent him down to Butlerville at the Muscatatuck State School."

Beverly cringed. She had heard of the place. Just two years ago it had acquired a new superintendent who had reported on the travesties he had witnessed when he had taken over. It was a scandal that had appeared in the papers; children not properly fed or clothed, overcrowding, not enough staff to appropriately care for the mass of mentally ill that resided there. No one generally discussed such matters, but there were whispers of what went on behind the walls of that place. Mr. Alfred Sasser Jr., the new man who ran the school, had said that he had found the conditions of the children deplorable, describing incarceration there as "the kiss of death."

While he had done much to vastly improve Muscatatuck, Beverly could not imagine ever sending a child there after what had taken place before his administration. She read pieces in the *Star* every now and again about what new improvements were being implemented and occasionally how the children went on trips or attended special functions. While it pleased her that change had taken place, she knew that she could never put Keller in such an institution. She wondered how desperate a parent had to be to do such a thing. Now, sitting across from Margaret, she beheld one such parent.

"The doctors told us they didn't know what caused Charles to have problems. So Dale and I tried again. You must understand, Beverly, that I so wanted a child. If I had only known, but you never know until it's too late. Arley was born just a few years later. We knew right away that there were problems with him. The day he was born. I never even got to hold him, and I've never seen him since." She paused when her voice began to falter.

Beverly could see she was trying very hard to control her emotions, a task that was proving difficult.

"Margaret, why didn't you tell me?"

"Dale and I moved here and started over again. We didn't want anyone to know. No one understands. No one looks at you the same. We wanted to just move on with our lives."

"Is that why you were so good to Keller?"

"I knew what you must be going through. I wanted it to be easier for you. And he was such a sweet little boy. You could see the innocence in his eyes."

"Look at me, Margaret, and tell me that you've gotten over giving up your two boys," Beverly pleaded. "Tell me it's all better for you now."

"It's not better. I haven't gotten over it, but over the years I have learned to deal with it. It has gotten easier not to think about it. That's why I say time will lessen your pain." She tried to give Beverly a reassuring smile, but it was weak and only skin deep.

"Do you regret it?"

"When I dwell on it, of course I have my doubts. I wonder what I could have done differently, but I just try not to think about it."

"How old are they?"

"Charles would have been seventeen this year, but he passed away when he was seven. Arley is close to thirteen now." She dropped Beverly's hands and got up to put the casserole dish into the oven. Then she tried to occupy herself with finishing the dishes. She had allowed herself to dwell on it for too long, bringing a flood of memories back that she would just as soon keep repressed. There was no point in wondering what might have been. It was too late for Charles, and she hadn't even known Arley.

What Beverly knew of Margaret was a woman who was kind, considerate, and above all, motherly. She didn't only take to Keller, she was good to all of the little children Beverly had seen her interact with at church. What a terrible burden she must have carried for all of those years. How devastating to live one's life as if childless, knowing all the while that your offspring were just hours away. Hours could be as deep as a great canyon and days could be as long as years, Beverly was learning.

The confession that was meant to be a comfort only brought more uneasiness and fear to her heart. Would this be her in ten or fifteen years? At least if Keller were dead, she would know where he was and not feel the anxious knot of uncertainty and dread in the pit of her stomach. There would be a finality to this suffering—death would be a place where the feeble-minded could not be abused, mistreated, taken advantage of.

For now all she could think of was Keller, alone in a strange place. Would they bathe him at seven PM? Would they feed him properly? He was so picky about what he would eat. She doubted they would care about such trivialities. But they weren't trivialities to him. It was his life, his whole existence. And what if he acted out? What would his punishment be? A shudder ran through her when she contemplated these questions. She had failed him so thoroughly, so completely, that she understood all at once that there would never be any peace for her if it remained the way it had been left.

"I suppose you cannot imagine your life without Keller. I don't blame you. But you must realize that life goes on, and this baby you are carrying needs a mother. You must be strong, Beverly. You must think of that little baby, and be strong for that."

"I don't think that I can be. I don't think there is anything left of me. I am not strong. I don't even have the desire to be anymore."

"Don't talk like that. You'll talk yourself into giving up. That won't do, Beverly."

"Is that such a bad idea?"

"Well, yes, of course it is. We don't always understand why the good Lord gives us what he does, but life goes on, and we are forced to go along with it. No matter what load we carry, life does not stop, and we must not stop either."

The sound of the front door opening in the other room brought the two women to attention. Warren was home. Beverly and Margaret exchanged glances with nervous apprehension, but for different reasons. Beverly did not want to speak to him; her feelings were raw and she still could not make sense of them enough to communicate any coherent thoughts. Margaret was worried that she might witness a scene and was concerned that she would be in the middle of a confrontation.

"Warren. He's home early," Beverly panicked.

"It will be all right," Margaret assured her. She left Beverly at the kitchen table and headed for the other room to meet Warren. She saw right away that he was on the verge of exhaustion. He had dark circles beneath his eyes, and it looked as if he hadn't slept. His expression was grim as he took off his hat and held it in his hands. Her heart went out to him. "Hello, Warren," she greeted, unable to evoke the cheerful tone she was trying for.

"Margaret," he said nodding his head to her. "Where's Bev?"

"I left her in the kitchen."

"I see," Warren replied, grimly.

"How are you holding up?" Margaret asked him with a hint of worry.

"I'm fine," he lied.

"I've brought some dinner. It's warming in the oven."

"That was good of you," he said.

"You should try and see to it that Beverly eats something. I'm terribly worried about her. She doesn't look well at all," Margaret advised.

"She won't eat," he admitted. "I spoke with the doctor, and he says that if she doesn't eat soon they might be forced to sedate her and feed her intravenously. To be frank, I don't know what to do for her, Margaret. Maybe you can speak with her."

"I did. I don't know that it'll do any good, but I did speak to her. She needs to think about that baby, but I'm afraid she's too distraught to reason with."

"So what should I do?" he asked, helplessly.

"I wish I knew the answer to that. I suppose I should go and leave the two of you to yourselves. I hate to be a nuisance."

Margaret collected her coat and gloves, adding before she left, "She needs you right now. Just try and let her know that you're there for her."

"Thank you for stopping by, Margaret." He was suddenly curiously formal and polite.

Beverly heard their whispered tones, but she could not make out what they were saying to one another. She knew when Margaret left and then the moment she was dreading came. She was alone with her husband. He came in and squatted down so that he was at her level, feeling the bile rise in his throat at the sight of her disfigured face. He was completely helpless to do anything to make it better.

"Hey, Bev, I'm home."

"I heard you come in."

"How are you doing?" His manner was nonchalant, as cool as he could muster.

"Fine," she said simply.

He noted that every word she spoke was void of emotion, hollow and empty. Unable to bring himself to begin an argument, he let it go, stood up, and went to the cupboards, pulling out silverware and dishes to set on the table for him and Beverly. "Would you like something to drink?"

"No thank you."

Warren pulled out a loaf of bread from the bread box, removed a few pieces, and buttered them. He placed them on a saucer and set them in the middle of the table before checking the turkey tetrazzini warming in the oven. When he removed it with a hot pad and placed it on the table, he did not ask if she wanted any, but took the liberty of spooning a hearty portion onto her plate. He was hoping that if he did not give her the option of turning it down she might dutifully eat it.

She watched him, with her face blank, but did not attempt to take a bite. He did not wait; he dug in, trying to remain oblivious to her careless attitude toward the dinner that sat before her. Finally he could stand it no longer. "This is really good, Bev. You ought to try it." She did not respond. "At least have a slice of bread," he coaxed, offering her the saucer with bread stacked upon it.

"I'm not very hungry," she told him.

He set the saucer down and looked at her for a good long while. Her eyes remained cautiously averted, eluding his gaze completely. It was more than Warren could handle. "Eat the food, Beverly," he prodded her angrily. There was a moment of silence before he lost control. "EAT THE FOOD!"

Still there was no reply. In one swift motion he cleared his place setting off of the table with his arm. A violent clatter ensued as the plate shattered on impact, smattering food and glass across the linoleum flooring. He bawled his fists up and groaned in rage. "What did you want me to do, Beverly? What could I have done?"

Her eyes were wide with alarm, but she responded with a firm, "You let them take our son."

"Have you looked in the mirror? Have you seen what he did to you?"

"You know he didn't mean to."

"Should I just stand by and let him hurt you? What if it had been the baby? What then, Bev? He is dangerous, even if he doesn't *mean* to be!" His declarations grew steadily louder.

"You can't really believe that," she cried.

"I do. I do believe it. He's out of control. What are we supposed to do with him? You can't just shut your eyes and pretend that you don't know."

She scowled at him but kept her mouth shut. She was not about to agree to any such thing. He could see by her obstinate expression that she was not able to see that he'd done what he did out of wanting to protect her and their unborn child. There would be no convincing her. She had always been a stubborn woman; it was part of what made her so attractive. An overwhelming sense of being alone came over him, as it dawned on Warren that not only had he lost his son, but he would lose her as well.

He sank down on his knees before her with a pleading in his eyes that shattered her cold resolve. She had never seen him cry before, and it wrung her heart anew. He laid his head in her lap, miserable and broken. "Please, Bev, don't hate me. I couldn't bare it if you hated me," he begged. She sat still in stunned silence, but his tortured expressions left her wanting to comfort him, to give him some solace. She cradled his head in her hand, stroking his hair and soothing him, allowing her tears to mingle with his.

It was a long while before he sat up and wiped his eyes. Beverly thought he looked like a little boy, with his hair disheveled and an uncertain expression in his clouded vision. He took her hands and brought them to his lips, kissing them tenderly. "I know that you are upset, darling, but please, for me, consider your health. Please eat something," he pleaded. He picked up her fork, scooping up a bite of the tetrazzini on her plate, and held it up to her lips, as a humble offering. It took a great deal of willpower for her to open her mouth and accept it, chewing slowly before forcing it down her throat. For a moment she thought she might vomit, but with determination she managed to keep it down.

Warren seemed relieved, as if a great weight had been lifted from him. The fear of having to sedate her had weighed heavily on his mind. He was afraid of what she would have done, of how she would have reacted if she had been forced into it. He knew that it could have possibly pushed her over the edge, a dark place that she might not have come back from. Testing his good fortune, he went back for another bite, which she dutifully accepted.

"I love you so much," he told her, getting emotional again. "Don't you know I would do anything for you? Anything. I just couldn't stand if I lost you. I can't lose you."

She took another mouthful from the food he offered before pushing the fork away the next time he tried to tempt her with the casserole. "I just can't eat any more. I'm afraid I won't be able to keep the rest of it down," she explained.

"Try just half of a slice of this bread," he suggested, breaking it in half with his hands. She stared at it, swallowing hard before she sunk her teeth into the buttered bread. Just one more bite and she was refusing that too.

"I'm sorry," she said. "I'm just so tired."

Warren helped her up from the table and assisted her to the bedroom, where she allowed him to lift her legs up onto the bed and cover her with the blankets. He lay down beside her, putting a protective hand over her protruding belly and pressing himself as closely to her as he could, molding himself against her silhouette. Having her so close made him feel stronger, more secure. He was finally able to rest, his cheek against her shoulder as he drifted to sleep.

fourteen

The clock next to the bed registered 7:32 AM. Warren was surprised that he had slept so soundly, but then, he hadn't slept at all the night before. The clothes that he had neglected to change out of were wrinkled and somewhat worse for wear. He rolled over to find the other side of the bed vacant. Beverly was already up. "Bev?" he called out in his morning voice. There was no response.

He got up and wandered through the house until he found his wife, properly dressed, with her coat on, sitting with her back straight and clutching her handbag on the sofa. She regarded him anxiously as he approached her and sat down next to her. Neither of them was sure what to expect from the other. The last few days had done much to make them feel like strangers, and what was once a comfortable and smooth relationship now seemed strained and unpredictable.

"What are you doing, Bev?" he asked, with a growing concern that she was planning on walking out the door and never looking back. Once he had put the question to her he wasn't sure at all if he wanted any feedback.

She looked determined as she spoke. "I'm going up to Fort

Wayne," she told him. "I'm going to go get our son back." They sat side by side in silence. She was concerned that he would try to stop her, and he was wondering what he could say to get her to come to her senses. He opened his mouth to say something, but she stopped him with a soft hand on his lips. "It's no use trying to talk me out of it. I've made up my mind, Warren."

"I have to have the car to get to work today." His reply was cold and defensive. "You won't be able to go without the car."

"I suppose I will have to take the bus then," she offered, with a tenderness that took him off guard. She was not angry, was not patronizing; on the contrary, she felt nothing but pity for Warren. She had known the man intimately for nine years. She knew that he was not capable of being malicious. Warren, in his heart, was only trying to do what was right. She did not want to hurt him any more than he was already hurting.

"You can't take the bus," he scoffed. "I can't let you do that."

"If you'll just drive me to town . . ."

"I won't let you, Beverly."

"Then I will have to walk in the cold and snow. If you won't drive me to town, I will walk to the bus depot." She was adamant about it. He realized that it would do no good to try and argue with her. He was not about to let her walk to town in the snow with the frigid winter temperatures. It did not matter how thoroughly he disagreed with her, he would have to allow her to do as she chose. He would have to drive her to town.

"Have you had breakfast?" She shook her head in the negative. "If you eat something, I'll drive you to town," he promised.

"If you don't want me to come home, I understand," she said. "But I was hoping that you would let us stay here until I can figure out what to do next." There it was. She was leaving him. He did not have the strength to respond to her. What could he say? He nodded his head, then got up to go to the kitchen.

Warren made some scrambled eggs and toast, enough for two, poured tall glasses of milk, and set out the juice cups and juice. Beverly seemed to have her appetite back, he noted with satisfaction. She ate every last morsel on her plate and drank her milk and juice as well. With her decision came peace of mind. She was frightened of what the future would hold, but she was no longer in mourning over the loss of her son. She would go and get him and all would be well again.

Although Margaret's talk yesterday had been meant to assure her that life without Keller would somehow be all right, it had done just the opposite. She had witnessed a woman who was filled with regret and longing for the two sons she had given up. Beverly had seen herself years from now, unwhole, unhappy, and heavily burdened with the knowledge that she had let Keller go. That had been the deciding factor. She would not be Margaret; she would not accept gracefully what was happening to her. She would fight it tooth and nail before she admitted defeat.

She waited as patiently as she could while Warren showered and shaved and got into a fresh suit. They were late, according to the knock on the front door. It was Barry. When Warren wasn't at his place by 8:30, he had come to the house. Warren greeted him at the door, in an aim at friendliness. "Morning," he offered. "You mind riding in the backseat? I'm taking Beverly into town."

Barry shrugged his shoulders. "I don't mind," he perjured himself. He thought that she should be the one to sit in the back. After all, she was the woman. He retreated back to the car and helped himself into the backseat. Noting, with discomfort, the side of the car that had been disfigured by Keller's destructive hands, he slid over to the opposite side. When Beverly and Warren finally emerged from the house, Barry caught sight of Beverly's face and couldn't help but stare in horrified disbelief, gaping like a grade school child with no proper manners. He couldn't pry his gaze from her, even if he wanted to. All of the neighbors were talking about what had happened at the Vance home, but it did little to prepare him for the marring of Beverly's once lovely features. He simply sat there with his mouth slightly open, eyes wide, unable to even produce a greeting.

Warren opened the car door for his wife and helped her in, then shut the door firmly after her. He climbed behind the wheel and headed toward the main downtown strip. There was no conversation to ease the disquieting situation. What was normally a short trip seemed to go on indefinitely. Barry was more than happy to climb out of the car and be off to work at the courthouse when Warren pulled up to the curb to let him off. He did not want to be in the middle of whatever was going on between the two of them. It was obvious to him from the tension he felt that there was trouble in their household.

Warren drove two blocks over and two blocks down to the bus depot, pulling up as close to the building as he could. He got out to open the door for Beverly, who struggled to get up from her position in the car; her belly made it quite a chore. He offered her his hand and she used it as leverage. Beverly paused before she headed for the door.

"Thank you," she whispered. Worried that she would begin to cry if she lingered too long, she put a hasty kiss to his lips, experiencing more than a little discomfort with her mouth still sore and tender, and then fled to the safety of the bus terminal. Warren watched her retreating form until she disappeared completely inside the station. He sat on the curb, feeling a profound sense of loss.

When he arrived at work, Miss Clark was dutifully keeping herself busy. She had noticed for the past several days, and again today, that Warren Vance was not his usual self. He had never given her any explanation for his hasty flight from the office the other day. She also found it curious that Beverly and Keller had not made there usual pilgrimage to town, although yesterday had been their scheduled day. She paused mid-task to watch him pass by her as he entered his office. The silence was unbearable as her mind raced in a hundred varying directions. After awhile, her curiosity got the better of her and she popped her head in with the pretense of asking him a question on some of his paperwork.

"Mr. Vance, did this need to be sent out today, before the weekend?" she asked, holding up the rental agreement.

"It can wait. It just needs to go out before the end of next week," he advised.

She stood, watching him with a look of concern, then took the liberty of making a full advance into his office, depositing herself across from him in the chair situated in front of his desk. "Forgive me if I am being too presumptuous, Mr. Vance, but something seems to be wrong. Is there anything I might do to help?" She looked so sympathetic, so eager to please, like a puppy nipping at its master's heels.

Warren shook his head, "No, Miss Clark. I'll be fine."

"Perhaps you would allow me to go to lunch with you. I'm very good at cheering people up. Have you ever been to that little restaurant that serves Italian? Luiciano's I think it's called. It's just a few blocks away." She laughed nervously. "I've heard they have a marvelous menu."

He was quickly beginning to feel uncomfortable. Everything that Beverly had said about this woman was flooding his mind, coming back to him in earnest. Perhaps she really was just trying to make him feel better, or perhaps she was sending him a subtle proposition. Either way, he was not about to take her up on her offer. He rifled through his files, trying to appear distracted. "I don't think that's a very good idea," he said, avoiding eye contact.

"Suit yourself," she said with a good-natured shrug. "But you can't stop me from bringing you back some dessert. That ought to bring you back to yourself." Her smile was meant to be irresistible, an alluring enticement, but Warren found it grated on him; he was not in the mood for such play. She didn't seem to take a hint very easily, continuing with her pandering rather shamelessly. Before he could say anything more discouraging, an unexpected guest interrupted them.

His father was standing in the doorway with a know-it-all sort of grin. He seemed amused, perhaps even a little smug. It ruffled Miss Clark, who was not expecting anyone. She sprung from her seat with the rental agreement in hand and hastily squeezed past him. "If you need anything else, Mr. Vance, just let me know," she said, sounding foolish and guilty all at once. She withdrew to the shelter of her desk in the lobby area, leaving Warren and Jonathan Vance to themselves.

Jonathan's eyes roamed over her body as she passed, enamored by her nearly perfect hourglass form. It did not escape Warren's attention. His father strode across the room and took the seat that Miss Clark had so recently vacated, leaning back with his hands behind his head, that same old smirk on his wicked face. "Did I break in on your conversation?" he quizzed coyly.

"Not at all, Father. We were just going over a rental agreement." He leaned forward, picking up his fountain pen to fiddle with in an attempt to appear casual. "It's good to see you," Warren lied. At this point in his miserable existence, his father was the last person he wanted to speak to. He didn't feel that he had the ability to withstand the man's patronizing today of all days.

"Well, that's good to hear, good to hear."

"Did you want to look over any of the files?" Warren asked, trying to ascertain exactly what his father's purpose in visiting was. "I can have Miss Clark pull whatever you like."

"How are you, Warren, my boy?" his father questioned, choosing to ignore Warren's offer.

"Fine, I suppose."

"You suppose?" he interrogated, with his customary all-knowing smile.

"Is there some reason that you came today, Father?"

"I got a call from Herbert Stephens last night . . . an interesting and enlightening phone call, and I thought I might swing by and make a visit to you. He tells me there have been some problems over at your place."

Warren's face burned at the mention of the doctor's name. He should have guessed that Dr. Stephens would telephone his father to make him aware of the events that had taken place with Keller. Warren did not alter his gaze; he continued to look his father in the eyes, but he did not have a response for him. As far as he could see, it was none of Jonathan Vance's business. He had never really cared before, so what did he care now?

"How's Beverly?"

"Not so good. She got hurt pretty bad. Keller hit her in the face with one of his toy trucks. Lucky he didn't kill her."

"She'll come out of it, I suppose."

Warren was disappointed by the lack of sympathy his father exhibited. If he had spoken to Dr. Stephens, perhaps the doctor hadn't told him the extent of Beverly's injuries. In which case, Warren should not be upset with him. On the other hand, Jonathan Vance was a man who made it his business to know details. Warren could picture his father probing Dr. Stephens until he had unearthed every last bit of information from him. It seemed ludicrous to think he could be so flippant.

"Why *did* you stop by, Father? I mean really?"

"No need to be impertinent, son," Jonathan scolded. "Where is young Keller?" Another question that he most likely could have answered himself.

"They took him up to Fort Wayne to the state hospital there."

"Will he stay there?"

Warren was not able to respond right away. He tossed the pen onto the desk and sighed heavily. "Beverly has gone up to get him. She left just this morning."

"Your car is parked out front."

"She took a bus."

"I see. Well, that's too bad."

"Yes." There was nothing to say but that. Warren remained still, watching his father, waiting to hear what he would do. For most certainly Jonathan would tell him. In accordance with his customary bits of wisdom that he doled out so freely, Warren was sure he would say that he was better off without her.

"You know," he said. "You got a pretty good set up here."

Warren was perplexed. "I'm sorry?"

"Got that nice little gal working here with you. Convenient."

"What are you talking about?"

"You don't have to pretend with me. I won't be voicing any objections. She has a nice tail. I was a young buck once myself. Hard to resist, I know," he chuckled to himself, as if he were recalling some fond memory of his yesterdays. "I bet she could make a man very happy."

"Who?"

"Our Miss Clark," he said, motioning with a jerk of his head toward the lobby area. "If I were a few years younger, I might have pursued her myself."

"You're mistaken. There is nothing going on with Miss Clark and me," Warren told him in surprise.

"What were the two of you talking about when I came in here? You both looked as guilty as a fox in the hen house. It's hard to mistake the evidence, son. I ought to know. They all seem worth it at the time, I can attest to it, until the next little gal comes along," he declared with a good natured wink.

"You've got the wrong idea about me, Father. I am not in a relationship with Miss Clark; I never would be. There's only ever been one girl for me, sir, and that is Beverly. I love her. I could never hurt her like that. I don't want to lose her, especially over someone as self-important and silly as Miss Clark. She's nothing but a spoiled child." His defense of himself was firm and characterized with outrage.

Warren could see his father was gearing up for a dramatic scene-stealing moment. He had the look of a man ready to deliver a great oration. He pursed his lips together, taking a deep breath before letting it all out through his clenched teeth. Warren was preparing himself for the lecture of the century, because the man could be quite long-winded, and much of the time under the mistaken assumption that his audience clung to every word that came from his mouth. With tension mounting, what happened next was a complete wild card.

"Then what are you doing here?" was all he said.

"You think I should have gone up to Fort Wayne."

"Obviously, you are made of stronger stuff than me, son. Always thought so. Your mother and I were never good for each other. We went our separate ways long ago. But I gotta tell you, Beverly's good for you. You're good for Beverly. It works. If you aren't here for another woman, then why are you here?"

"He hurt Beverly. He could have hurt the baby. He could still hurt the baby. What am I supposed to do with that? Do you think I should have acted like it never happened? I came home, and, well, you should of seen it. I won't ever forget it." He paused. "I had a choice. I tried to do what was best, that's all."

"He's your blood; you can't give up on him even if you wanted to. You will always be responsible for him, even if you try and pass the buck on to someone else. It won't change that you're his daddy. I haven't been too good at being a father, at being a husband, but I took care of you; I gave you the best I had to give. If there's one thing that I want to get you to understand, it's this: life is hard. I won't feed you bull about it. Life is misery." He pointed a finger at Warren and looked over it as if he were looking over the stock of a rifle. "But you're a man . . . one of the better of your breed. I expect more out of ya, Warren. I do."

Father and son occupied the stillness that followed, one chastised, the other glorying in the speech of his life. Warren could not remember ever having had a real conversation with his father. To say he was stunned would have been an understatement. His brain ceased working completely, just shut down. So, he said the only thing that he could think to say.

"What?"

Jonathan was pleased that he had left his son with the inability to form coherent thoughts. For once he had bested him. For many years now, he had felt inferior to Warren. He was forced to watch as Doris lavished love and attention on their son, using it all up, with nothing left for him. He had witnessed Warren in his pursuit of excellence during the course of his youth and had been jealous of the man he had become. His son had the kind of character Jonathan would have liked to possess. He laughed as he rubbed his chin and leaned in over the desk, looking Warren square in the eyes, with the greatest of conviction, and proclaimed, "I said, *go get your girl.*" Without another word, he stood up and was gone.

In the lobby, Barbara Clark had found it difficult not to hear their conversation. It *was* a small office and the door *had* been open during the entire time. She justified listening in on them by believing it would have been impossible not to hear their unguarded words. A nice sized lump had formed in her throat when the conversation had turned to her. The lump was still there when the elder Mr. Vance strode through the lobby on his way out. He paused long enough to give her a lascivious smirk and a good natured wink. "Good day, Miss Clark."

Taken aback, she still managed to try and remain professional, feigning ignorance as to what had gone on in the room next door. "Good day, Mr. Vance."

fifteen

The bus ride from Muncie to Fort Wayne was nearly unbearable. Beverly had to shift from side to side to try and appease the ache in her tailbone. The seat seemed too narrow and was growing increasingly uncomfortable, not to mention the heater blowing hot air in her face. She leaned her forehead against the cool window to try and keep herself from growing faint. They made several stops along the way, which helped a little. While other riders were getting on she could stand and stretch her legs.

By the time they had reached Fort Wayne, she had had it with the mammoth on wheels. She was not finished with that mode of transportation, however, for she still needed to reach the school. Beverly scanned the schedule to try and ascertain which bus she needed to catch to get there. She went to the window to purchase a ticket, only to be told that she would have to wait half an hour before the bus she would be taking would arrive.

There was nothing left to do but sit and wait. The benches were rudimentary wood planks with metal legs, hardly ideal for a woman who was expecting. She got up to walk often, working her legs and massaging her lower back with her hands. All the while the minutes seemed to drag on. She wondered what Keller was doing, anticipating a joyful reunion. Or perhaps he would be angry with her. Perhaps he would blame her for his recent imprisonment at the institution. Either way she was inalterable in her decided course. She was going to go and get her boy.

Another woman and her daughter were sitting patiently, waiting for what Beverly supposed was their next ride too. The mother combed the little girl's hair with her fingers, watching Beverly pacing all the while. She smiled kindly, trying to appear as if she hadn't noticed Beverly's black eye and stitched lip, as she asked, "When will the baby come?"

Beverly continued to tattoo a path on the floor. She was not in the mood for small talk, but she also was not the type to be rude. "Just a few more months. Near the end of April."

"You won't have to wait much longer then," the woman said with a consoling tone.

"I suppose not."

"I don't envy you any. It's a hard thing to carry a child," she informed Beverly. "This one here, I was in labor for sixteen hours. She was my last." The little girl was probably no more than five. She looked at her mother with her big round eyes, wondering what she was speaking of.

"That's too bad," Beverly offered. She wanted to avoid any similar revelations and so she tried to change the subject. "Where are you headed?"

"We're going to Kentucky."

"That's a long ways."

"I suppose so. Darla and I are going to visit my sister. She lives there."

"That sounds nice."

"Where are you going?"

"Oh, I'm already here. I came from Muncie to here, to Fort Wayne." The woman seemed to be waiting for Beverly to divulge her purpose in coming. Beverly did not oblige her, she let it end with that.

"What happened to your face?" the girl asked innocently.

"Darla!" the woman scolded. "I'm terribly sorry," she apologized to Beverly.

"That's quite all right," Beverly soothed, but she let the conversation die there.

After a short silence, Darla got up and wondered over near the windows, glancing outside and watching the cars go by. She would call out each color that she saw as they drove past. "Black." A brief pause. "Red. Blue. Blue."

With her nerves strained, this did little to help Beverly. She grew all the more fidgety until finally her bus pulled up. It couldn't have come at a better time. She had felt on the verge of yelling at the poor child to shut up. She wrapped her coat about herself in defense against the cold and went out to board her bus. She sat by the window once again; it seemed less claustrophobic when she could see the open space beyond the sheet of glass.

As the bus drew closer to her final stop, she grew more apprehensive. If she knew what to expect, it would be so much easier; the uncertainty made it all the more unbearable. And finally, when the driver stopped and opened the swinging doors at the front of the bus, she stood before them nearly unable to make herself move from the spot.

The driver was only willing to wait for so long. He said, in a rather cross way, "Are you getting off or ain't you?"

With that prodding, she descended the stairs. She had barely set her feet on the ground before the bus doors closed and the driver pulled away. Unable to wonder any longer, Beverly did not hesitate as she walked the remainder of the distance to where the state hospital stood. The main building faced outward toward the extended driveway, possibly meant to be welcoming to those visiting so that they might find their way to the office, which was located there. It was far from friendly, however, for it had an aura, a certain quality, that if you did not know what sort of place it was, you would still not feel beguiled by it. Behind the main edifice the other buildings were lined up to turn in toward the courtyard. The great structures were several levels high and constructed of brick, a brick that had probably once been a striking red, now faded over the decades from exposure to the elements to a dull reddish brown. Bars covered the windows, and behind those windows, faces watching with curious interest peeked out.

The land on which the state institution was situated was a vast stretch that had been acquired many years previously, all in all a total of five hundred acres. This property had been used, in part, as farmland, where many of the residents were taught to till and plant the earth. It was no longer used for that purpose. Once it had been called the Asylum for Feeble Minded Children, then Indiana School for Feeble Minded Youth, and now the Fort Wayne State School. No matter what it was called, its primary purpose had remained the same; it was a dumping ground for the mentally ill.

The closer she drew to the door, the more disquieted she felt. When she entered the office, a young, dark-haired woman in a pink dress greeted her. Beverly could see that she was shy but eager to make a new acquaintance, so she forced a pleasant face, wanting to make the girl feel comfortable. She did not seem to notice Beverly's recent injuries. This was most likely explained in part by the fact that she was used to seeing an assortment of bizarre people and situations on a daily basis.

"Hello," she said. "How can I help you?"

Beverly responded with as much affability as she could summons. "I am here to see my son, miss. What must I do?"

"Well, you'll need a pass," she informed Beverly. With that, she got up from her chair with some effort and went to get the pass. Beverly could not help but notice that the girl was physically deficient. She appeared to be paralyzed on her left side and walked by dragging the lame leg along, her foot scraping the floor. She drew a small square sheet of paper from a pile and returned to the desk triumphantly.

"How long have you worked here, if you don't mind my asking?"

She looked slightly confused. "I don't exactly work here, ma'am. They let me help out in the office, and sometimes in the store. They think I do very well."

"And you do," Beverly assured her.

"I was brought here as a baby, so I know my way around real well."

"Why were you brought here as a baby?"

"I got polio, ma'am. That's why I got a lame leg and arm." She saw the look of disbelief shroud Beverly's features and sought to console her. "Oh, but it doesn't hurt me none, and I can still do a whole lot. I can latch rugs, and they think that they're fine enough to sell there in the store."

"I'm sure they are."

"Now, what's your boy's name?"

"Keller Vance. He's only been here for a few days," she explained.

The girl appeared to know what she was doing. She rummaged through a pile of papers that seemed to be some sort of typed up list. She scanned the list with her finger until she found what she was looking for, then with her good hand took a fountain pen and filled out the square of paper she had so recently retrieved. "This here is your pass. It will allow you to go about the place freely. Here it tells you what building he's in. See? It's building number seven," she said pointing at the paper. "And then here's the room number; it's number thirty-two."

Beverly accepted it gratefully. "Thank you very much for your help. I can see why you are able to work in the office. You are very proficient." The young woman beamed with her praise.

"I'm glad to help anytime, ma'am. You just come back if you got any problems."

There was a very impersonal quality about the place, as Beverly made her way down the hallway. It was as sterile as a hospital might be, linoleum floors and tiled walls. Haunted faces filled the spaces, in doorways, along the corridors, refugees that had retreated from the real world. Some called out to her. "Hey, lady," they shouted. "Who are you?" they clamored after her. The smells were foreign and made her feel nauseated. It took a great deal of control to avoid vomiting.

There were grown women with dolls; they cradled them in

their arms, soothing them with soft tunes. A young boy followed in her shadow, unable to satisfy his inquisitive nature by merely observing from a distance. When she turned around to smile at him, he dodged away, apprehensive about actually speaking to her. Bodies rocked and writhed on the bare floor from a torture that she could not name, some reaching out their hands to her as she passed. Surreal and disturbing as it was, she did not stop to comfort them, but continued her quest for her own child, a child that she would not allow to be forgotten like these.

When she came out into the courtyard, she breathed the air deeply, dreading having to enter another one of the units. It took her a great deal of time to wander through the maze of buildings that made up the complex. It was confusing and taxing to say the least. She feared that she would search them indefinitely; perhaps unable to ever find her final destination, she would end up one of these lost souls. The thought sent a chill down her back and she pulled her coat a little tighter.

When she did locate building number seven, it was with relief that she pushed open the door, only to be assaulted by that same sickening odor. She could see, by the room number on the pass that had been given to her in the office, where Keller's room would likely be on one of the upper floors. She climbed the staircase with deliberate steps, passing the next landing and continuing on until she came to the third level. There she found room thirty-two, but when she opened the door, she found the room vacant. The only things that occupied this cubicle were beds that could have passed more readily as cots. A green wool blanket was neatly spread over the top of each; otherwise, there was no color to the drab, dispirited surroundings.

Agitated, she retraced her steps down the three flights of stairs, taking time to look down the corridors on each landing, in hopes of finding someone that could help her. When she reached the main floor again, she located a woman dressed in uniform who apparently worked at the school. Beverly didn't waste any time in approaching her with her pass in hand.

"Excuse me." The woman acted as if she hadn't heard and

continued to walk away. "Excuse me," Beverly said more insistently. She picked up her pace and drew close enough that the woman could ignore Beverly no longer.

She stopped and, with an abrupt manner, asked, "What do you need?"

"I was told I could find my son in room thirty-two. I was just up there and no one is in that room. Could there have been a mistake?"

"They aren't in their rooms right now."

"Where are they?"

She seemed bothered. "Most of them are in the dayroom."

"Where is that?"

"Down the hall and to the right." With that, she left Beverly, unwilling to spare her time for conversing any longer.

It made Beverly angry, but there wasn't a whole lot that she could do about it. She was at the mercy of anyone who was willing to help her, however grudgingly it might be. She thought it best to not push the matter but to try and locate the dayroom herself. And after passing a row of closed doors, she finally came to a stop in front of the only doors with glass panels where one could observe from the hallway what was transpiring within.

Children and adults mingled together, seeming to be unaware that they should not be peers. They toiled at aimless activities as they passed the time. Some could not suppress the physical need to be active. There were boys running around the perimeter of the room in an endless loop, as if it were a track, some of them at horseplay, wrestling like playful puppies. The more pathetic cases sat idly, watching the others, or staring off into space, apparently unaware of anything that was going on around them.

When she entered the dayroom, a few of them gravitated to her, touching the fabric of her dress or stroking the wool of her coat. They looked at her as if she were a novelty, something new and strange and different. One little girl poked a finger at Beverly's swollen belly and asked, "You got a ball in there?" But she did not have eyes for any of them. They were not her boy. They were not the reason she had come to this place. She was here for Keller. Instinctively Beverly was drawn to him, tuned to him like a radio picking up a frequency from a distant location.

He was sitting on the floor with his back against the wall, legs stretched out before him, arms slack at his sides. Stooping down to his level, with great discomfort, she attempted a smile. There was no response in his deep blue eyes, no hint of recognition, no spark of excitement at seeing his mother. Those eyes seemed bottomless, soulless. He just stared off into space, saliva forging a trail from the corner of his mouth, down his chin, its ultimate goal a wet pool on the shirt he wore. He was but a pathetic apparition of himself, hardly able to even blink his eyes.

"Keller, it's me. It's Mama," she told him, horrified and panicked.

His body was limp and easily manipulated as she moved his head into her arms, nestling close to him, cooing and soothing, just as she would have if he were a helpless babe. To see him in this condition was her worst fear manifested in the flesh. He had always been so strong, so full of energy. Having been reduced to a vegetable, there appeared to be nothing left of the boy she knew and loved. He had always been a hostage of his own little world, but his personality had shone through, despite that. Now she was not sure where he was in this desolate shell that she held to her.

"I'm here, Kel. I'm going to take you home. Mama's here." The only sign he gave that he was aware of her presence was a single tear that welled up in the corner of his eye and coursed down his full, round cheek. She brushed it away with a tender stroke of her lips. "I'm sorry, baby," she gasped. Feeling her heart wrenched beyond what she felt she could endure, she searched her mind for some resolution to the terrifying situation she found herself in. "I'm so sorry."

Beverly's gaze settled upon what she assumed was the house matron, who was observing them from across the room. Reluctant to leave Keller, even for a brief moment, she called out to her. "I need assistance. Could you please help me?" She was as powerless as a mother bird, unable to replace its fallen fledgling back to the nest.

The stout grandmotherly type woman was promptly before Beverly, towering over her with her hands clasp tightly. "How can I help you?"

"My son, he's not responding to me. He doesn't even seem to be able to move. What's the matter with him? What have you done to him?"

"He's been heavily medicated," she informed Beverly in a matter of fact tone. Beverly could sense no compassion in the woman. Many years of working here, seeing everything, exposed day after day to such conditions, had desensitized her, or perhaps coldhearted was just her nature. "He was a danger to himself and others," she went on. "We thought it best to keep him sedated."

"How did he get from his room to here?"

"Some of the orderlies carried him," she said simply. Beverly could see she was a punctual and to-the-point sort of person, someone driven by tasks on a check list. It seemed unwise to beat around the bush, so she came straight to the point.

"I need a wheelchair," she dictated to the matron, as authoritative as she could bring herself to be.

"Whatever for?"

"I'm going to take my son home, and I can't carry him by myself. Could you please see to it that I get one?"

"I'll do no such thing. You can't just make off with him. There are rules and protocol to be followed."

Beverly grew agitated, provoked in part by this stranger telling her she had no right to her own son. This woman had no vested interest in Keller, no apparent feeling or compassion; this was simply her job. Why should she care if his mother had come to collect him? Beverly was not to be denied.

"I'm here to take my son home, and I don't intend on leaving this place without him."

"As I said, you'll need to pursue it through the proper channels, if you wish to take him," the woman insisted. She appeared to be gleaning some satisfaction from her superior position.

"Who shall I speak to in order to 'pursue the proper channels'?" Beverly questioned in outrage.

"Have you spoken to the superintendent?"

"No, I have not."

"Well, you ought to."

"Would you summon him for me then?"

"You need to go to the office and request an appointment, ma'am."

"I don't want to leave my son."

"You've left him here for nearly three days. I hardly think a few minutes more would make any difference. He's perfectly safe in my care."

"I will not leave him. I'm asking for some kindness from you, something for which you do not seem capable of. Still, as an employee of the school here, you have an obligation to help its patrons. Now, if you'll please go fetch the superintendent for me, I'll take my boy off of your hands."

"As I've stated clearly and specifically, I will do no such thing. You must help yourself and go request an audience with him of your own accord. I am here to help the feeble-minded who cannot help themselves, not grown women who are prone to bouts of hysterics."

The two women were locked in a frigid stare, at an impasse, without hope for an agreeable solution. There was nothing that could adequately describe the relief that flooded Beverly when she heard a familiar voice from behind the detestable woman who was frustrating her purposes.

"What seems to be the problem?" Warren bellowed, frightening the matron nearly out of her skin.

"Warren . . ." Beverly squeaked, trying to suppress the emotion in her voice.

"I'm Keller's father," Warren explained to the house matron with a look that withered.

She seemed nervous, her eyes dodging from Warren to Beverly and back again.

"I was just telling your wife that she cannot take Keller without following the school guidelines."

"I told her I didn't want to leave him and asked if she would fetch

196

the superintendent for me, and she refused," Beverly accused.

Warren regarded the woman with solemn and unsettling eyes. "We would like to take our son home. What will it take to facilitate that?"

"The superintendent will need to be notified and paperwork signed. You can't just barge in here and expect to whisk him off," the matron scoffed.

"I think it best for you to go get the superintendent then," he commanded. When she did not oblige him right away, he added, "NOW!" She jumped and then scurried off, like a mouse avoiding a cat.

"It seems you just weren't persuasive enough," Warren observed.

Beverly began to cry, although there was a look of gladness on her face. "You came."

He nodded his head. "I came."

"I'm so glad. I didn't know what I was going to do. I asked for a wheelchair, but I don't know how I would've gotten him on the bus, or how I would have switched busses. I can't carry him. I couldn't have done it alone."

"What's the matter with Keller?"

Beverly smoothed Keller's hair, kissing him firmly on his forehead several times. "They've sedated him . . . drugged him," she lamented. "He can scarcely move."

"Keller?" he tested tenderly. "Keller, can you hear me?" An overwhelming rush of guilt overtook him, and he felt his stomach turn with dread. He could see now that sacrificing his child for the good of the family had been folly, pig-headed, and fed by fear, instead of sound thinking. He was supposed to be Keller's protector, the buffer between his son and the real world. He understood now that he had fed Keller to the wolves, disposed of him out of convenience so that life would be easier, less troublesome. The realization that life would never be a neat package dawned on him all at once. There would never be a good solution to Keller and their problems with him; it would never be an ideal situation, no matter where he was or what they did for him.

"We won't leave here without him, Bev. I swear it."

It was not long before the matron returned with Superintendent Grey in tow, her look of satisfaction most likely from the fact that she had brought in a reinforcement. He seemed like a kind enough sort, probably well educated, dignified in his glasses and suit, with hair generously oiled and combed to the side. "Miss Abner says you wished to speak to me," he addressed them, and waited expectantly for Warren to state his case. Beverly didn't have the strength to appeal to him. She was suddenly without the will to fight. She left it to her husband.

"There's been a terrible mistake. I made a mistake. My wife and I are here to take our son home. Miss Abner, here," he said, indicating with his hand to the matron, "says we need to speak to you and sign some papers in order to do that."

"Yes, well, that is generally the way that we do it."

"I see."

"But, in Keller's case, things are a bit more complicated."

Warren looked confused. "How's that?"

"He was not placed in our care by you or Mrs. Vance, sir. He was brought here through CPS. That makes it a whole new ball game."

"I don't understand."

"We must get approval through them before releasing Keller into your care."

"We're his parents. Does that count for nothing?"

"I don't mean to say that it doesn't, Mr. Vance. But Child Protective Services brought him here, and they will need to be the ones to approve of your withdrawing him."

Warren was indecisive as to what he should do. He looked down on Beverly and Keller, who were depending upon him. They needed him to be strong, to make the right move. "How long would something like that take?"

"It's hard to say," Cecil Grey told him levelly.

"We won't leave him here another single day," Beverly promised.

"I promised my wife." Warren bent down and lifted his son

into his able arms. "I can't leave without him." With his choice made, he motioned to Beverly to follow and headed resolutely for the courtyard where the automobile was parked.

The matron, Miss Abner, dodged in front of him, trying to obscure his path. It did little to dissuade him. He side-stepped her with his long confident strides and was headed down the hall before she could think twice. She trailed after him with an insistent tug on his coat. "Mr. Vance, you cannot take him out of here. You have no right," she persisted.

"He's my son. He's mine. I have every right," Warren exclaimed. Beverly was running at a trot to keep up after him. She had never been so in love with her husband as she was now. The sunlight poured over them as they burst through the front doors of the housing unit, bright and triumphant.

Superintendent Grey put out a hand to stop the matron in her attempts to keep Keller. He told her softly, "That's enough, Miss Abner. That will do. I can see that boy is wanted. We'll take care of CPS, only let them have their son back."

He had run the Fort Wayne State School for many years. In that time he had seen parents with no choice but to find a place for their child here. Others found it inconvenient to care for one of inferior qualities. More often than not, they were left here, put out of sight and out of mind, forgotten in the labyrinth of buildings and hallways and rooms. The worst thing that could happen to Keller Vance would not be to go home.

"We are severely understaffed, overcrowded, with an inadequate budget. He'll do better in a home, with a family that loves him." The two stood in the doorway and watched as Warren laid his son across the backseat of the car, then drove away, back to Muncie, where they belonged.

Epilogue

arren jumped out of the Dodge and ran around to the other side before Beverly could open the door for herself. His excitement was nearly impossible to contain. He helped her out eagerly. She smiled at him, giving him a reassuring pat before taking his arm and walking up the sidewalk to the front door. Beverly waited patiently as he opened the door for her, peeking under the blanket that swaddled their new baby. She pulled her child closer, protectively.

Stepping over the threshold into the living room, she allowed her eyes to adjust to the darker interior before she spotted Keller, dressed in his Sunday best, playing on the floor with his blocks. He looked up at his mother with a broad grin, dropping everything to focus all of his attention on her.

"Mama!" he cried, running to rap his chubby arms around her legs. It was one of the rare moments that he was actually engaged with the adults around.

"Keller, I've missed you," she laughed with delight.

The nurse followed after him, attempting to pull him away, but he would have none of it. His embrace held fast. "It looks like he won't be deterred, Mrs. Vance," she remarked.

Warren came through the door, lugging a suitcase and a flower arrangement. He set them down, with little concern for their care before he took the bundle from Beverly's arms, freeing her to deal with Keller. She took Keller by the hand and led him over to the sofa, where he huddled near her side. She looked pleased. "He knew I was gone." And it made her heart glad.

"Of course he did, darling," Warren assented.

Miss Detmer nodded her agreement. "He asked for you frequently," she attested. The young woman was a strange looking thing, thin and tall, nearly as tall as Warren, with very little curve to her form. Without the long blonde hair, which was pulled back in a severe bun, and the dress she wore, one might have been able to mistake her for a member of the opposite gender. She wore thickly cut spectacles to help with her eyesight, which did little to aid her appearance, but her voice was soft and kind, of a quality that made you instantly comfortable and willing to trust her. Warren and Beverly had known right away that she would be an ideal person to help with Keller during the two weeks that Beverly would be in the hospital. It was all in the way that Keller interacted with her and how she treated him with such patience and dignity.

"Were you a good boy for Daddy and Miss Detmer?" Keller looked up to her with sheer contentment registering in his eyes, only concerned with his mother.

From Warren's arms a fragile little howl escaped the bundle of blankets he held. Keller was surprised—and intrigued. He pointed over to his father and asked, "Oh, whas that?" Beverly motioned for Warren to bring the baby to them. With all the care of a package that is invaluable, the proud papa passed the baby back to Beverly's waiting arms, trying to anticipate how Keller would receive this new addition to their family.

"Kel, this is your new baby." She parted the cocoon of flannel, enough for Keller to glimpse the tiny little face. He was immediately in awe. He touched the top of its head, feeling the peach fuzz that would later become full fledged hair.

"Baby!" he giggled with excitement, unable to contain his joy with the new little creature being presented to him.

"Do you want to hold baby Leslie?" With her hands still firmly supporting the baby, Beverly placed her brand-new daughter into her son's arms. He clutched his sister to him. Completely and totally enraptured, he bestowed the most delicate kiss Beverly had ever seen on the little hand that was flailing about wildly, batting him with no affect on the nose.

"Would you look at that!" Warren rejoiced. There had been times when he had dreaded this meeting, with thoughts of flaming haired Nancy revived in his memory. However, in that moment it was abundantly clear that Leslie was where she belonged, in the arms of her brother, and Keller was where he belonged, in the arms of his family. It was as if the two of them already knew one another, had met sometime previous to this encounter.

It had crossed Beverly's mind many times that this child would surpass Keller in all things: attending school, quenching her thirst for knowledge with books and learning, possibly even going to college. She would grow to adulthood, seek out a mate and marry, knowing the happiness of a relationship between a grown man and woman. She would know the joys of rearing her own children, living a life as full and rich as Beverly was able to fathom in the depths of her imagination. But at one thing Keller would always be an equal, and that was in his capacity to love and be loved. There was nothing in his soul that was tarnishable by the lust for riches, power, prestige, or superiority. He was a pure being, motivated by the primary needs of hunger, thirst, and the need for love and companionship from other humans. She believed, beyond the shadow of a doubt, that Keller was an incorruptible child sent from God, destined to show others by example exactly what perfect love really was.

In that small moment, as Keller studied the miniature toes of his little sister with fascinated glee, all was right with the world. There was the briefest of euphorias that would sustain her through the hard times that would surely come, until the next shining moment would present itself. With some anguish and some struggling, Beverly had learned, over the six years that she had been entrusted with Keller's care, that there are no fairy-tale endings, just fairy-tale moments. That was her lot in life as Keller's mother, to savor the good through the bad. Without the knowledge of sorrow, one would never experience the pleasures of joy.

Author's Note

In contemplating writing this novel, I first did much research in order to paint a realistic picture of what life would have been like for Beverly, Warren, and, of course, Keller. I was able to read several out-of-print books that shed some light on what a struggle it would be to raise a child with a disability during the 1950s. One book was entitled *Retarded Children Can Be Helped*, by Maya Pines, published in 1957. Another book that I used as a resource was *Angel in Disguise*, by Dale Evans. She wrote of her experiences with her daughter Robin, who was born with Down's syndrome. Both of these pieces of literature were of great value to me.

Another source that I relied heavily upon was my dear friend Wilma Belvill, whom I had the pleasure of interviewing about her own struggles with a son who is mentally handicapped. He was born to her in the late fifties, during the time my novel took place. Her insights were more than helpful to me as I began to write my story. Therefore, not only is my book about a family and the struggles and heartache they experience as a result of a mental disability, but also a commentary on the mental health issues in our country during that time.

There was a general lack of resources, funding, and understanding when it came to the mentally handicapped, as well as the physically handicapped.

There was a great reluctance, at the time, for anyone to positively concur that a child was mentally handicapped, and there was even more confusion when it came to knowing what to do with them.

Those who had loved ones with mental disabilities were encouraged very strongly to place them in the care of the state. Because of lack of community support and the difficulties that come with caring for them, that is quite often where they ended up, in a state-run hospital. Frequently overcrowded and understaffed, these facilities were bleak and sad places. Adults were often housed with children. The very severely affected were kept with the mildly affected. There was some documentation that abuse or neglect occurred on a frequent basis.

In some situations the residents were not mentally disabled at all, as was the case of my mother's great aunt, Grace Suvain, who suffered from polio as a child and as a result was paralyzed on her right side.

There were no school programs, unless you were fortunate enough to live on the more advanced East or West Coasts. It wasn't until the mid 1960s, when President John F. Kennedy came on the scene, that much reform took place. Because of President Kennedy's efforts, public schools and other community programs became available to persons with disabilities. His crusade was driven by his own family's struggles with his sister Rosemary, who was mentally disabled.

My own personal knowledge, as a mother with two sons diagnosed as being on the autism spectrum, played a big part in chronicling the Vance's struggles. Keller is diagnosed as being mentally retarded in the book, but those of you who have lived with autism will recognize that he is most assuredly autistic. However, during the 1950s, autism was not as widely identified as it is today. Therefore, I chose to have Keller be misdiagnosed, as would likely have been the case.

Many of the experiences Beverly had with Keller were a direct result of my own personal struggles with my sons; every incident with Keller's behaviors were a reflection of something that has happened in our own lives. While some stories were changed slightly to better fit the plot, my husband and I, in a very real sense, have lived it. We are fortunate enough to live in a day and age when we have professionals and people around us who have helped and supported us through our trials.

I wanted very much to portray, as realistically as possible, what life is like with a child with a disability, the feelings of fear and loneliness, a sense of inadequacy and at times resentment. I wanted to depict the sense of loss and mourning, the worrying and stress, but also the humor and joy and pure love.

As I grow older, I am beginning to understand that life can be so contradictory and yet so marvelous all at the same time. Sometimes the bitter things in life render the sweetest tastes. While I wish that I could give my sons the normal lives I envisioned for them when they were born, I also realize that God has given me a great teaching tool. I have learned so many things that otherwise would not have factored into my life. I have also learned that as much as I would have liked to give my sons a "normal" life, autism is part of their package and I must accept it, because I accept them.

About the Author

Tracy Winegar was born and raised in Muncie, Indiana, the third of eight children. After high school graduation she moved to Provo, Utah, where she met and married her husband of ten years, Ben. Together they reside in Layton, Utah, with their four children, Brynlee, Lucas, Hayden, and Lydia.

Tracy is a strong supporter of programs for children with autism. She served on the Board of Trustees and was instrumental in helping open the first nontuition school for autistic children in Utah. Her favorite nonprofit organization is the Northern Utah Autism Program, where both of her boys attended preschool. A portion of her profit from the sales of this book will be given to this charity.

You can visit the author's website at www.tracywinegar.com.